Taming the Eagle

Jayne Castel

All characters and situations in this publication are fictitious, and any resemblance to living persons is purely coincidental.

Taming the Eagle by Jayne Castel

Copyright © 2022 by Jayne Castel. All rights reserved. No part of this publication may be reproduced, stored in a retrieval system, or transmitted in any form or by any means—electronic, mechanical, recording, or otherwise—without the prior written permission of the author.

Published by Winter Mist Press

ISBN: 978-0-473-62703-4 (paperback)

Edited by Tim Burton
Cover design by Winter Mist Press
Cover photography courtesy of www.shutterstock.com

Visit Jayne's website: www.jaynecastel.com

Her husband has exchanged her for his own freedom. Now the enemy owns her. Betrayal, belonging, and epic love in Ancient Scotland.

All Fenella has ever wanted is to choose her path in life, yet men have always determined her fate. The day Roman soldiers fight their way into her husband's crannog and demand retribution for a bloody attack, she learns how little control she really has over her destiny.

To save his own neck, her chieftain husband offers the enraged Roman general his willful wife.

Justinian Aquila governs the empire's wild northern frontier. He's dedicated his life to serving Rome, but when he takes a fiery Pict woman as his slave, his world shifts.

Fenella was made for him—and he's determined to win her heart.

Trapped inside the Roman fort of Ardoch, Fenella plans her escape. She will win her freedom, no matter the cost. Yet, even as the shadow of war falls over Caledonia once more, she fights her growing feelings for Justin.

In a world of selfish, cruel men—has she found the only good one?

Set in 2nd Century AD, during the Roman occupation of what is now Scotland, TAMING THE EAGLE is a powerful, steamy standalone romance about finding true love in the unlikeliest of places.

***

For Tim. You're one of the good ones too.

***

MAP

CALEDONIA
2ND CENTURY A.D
STRACATHRO
INVERQUHARITY
FINAVON
CARDEAN
INCHTUTHIL
ORGNA
LOCH TATHA
FENDOCH
MAEATAE
Firth of Tay
DALLINROSS
BERTHA
CALIDONES
BOCHASTLE
STRAGEATH
ARDOCH
DAMNONII
MAEATAE
DOUNE
CAMELON
CRAMOND
Firth of Forth
ANTONINE WALL
BUILT CIRCA 142 A.D
OTADINI
ESKBANK
PATHHEAD
CHANNELKIRK
DAMNONII
ST. LEONARDS
OTADINI
CASTLECRAIG
NEWSTEAD
NOVANTAE
BEATTOCK
SELGOVAE
KIRKPATRICK
VINDOLANDA
HADRIAN'S WALL
BUILT 122-128 A.D
BRIGANTES
LEGEND
ROMAN FORT
KM
50
MI
15
BRITANNIA

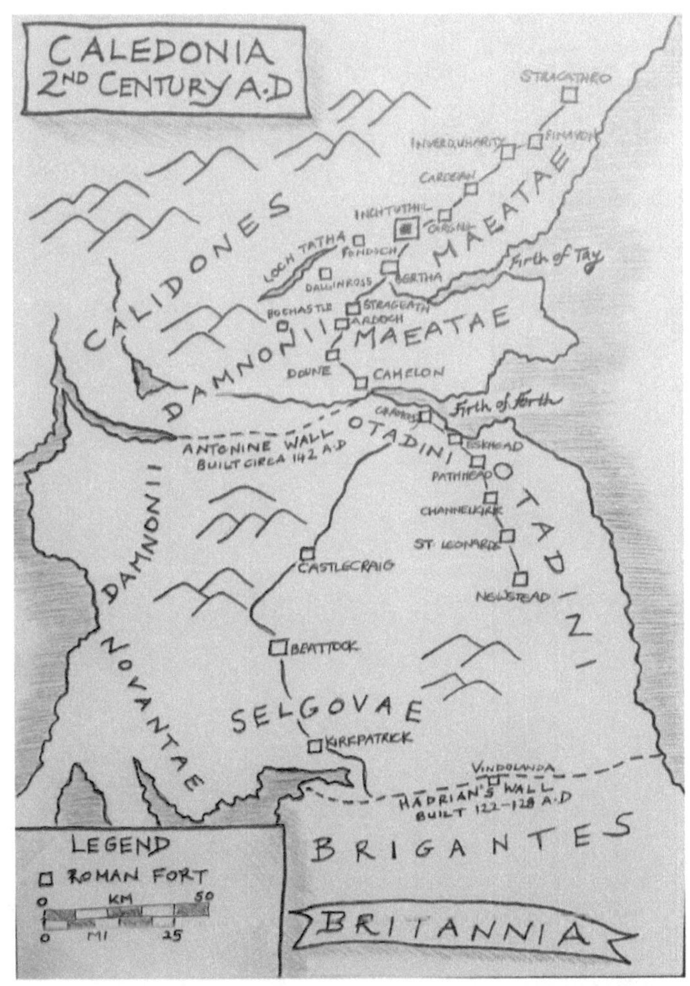

"Life without liberty is like a body without spirit."
—Kahlil Gibran

I. THE PINEWOOD

*Ten miles from the Roman fort of Ardoch,
Caledonia (Scotland)*

Autumn, 118 AD

HER FATHER'S ANNOUNCEMENT came unexpectedly, shattering the companionable silence around the hearth. "The chieftain will be arriving here this afternoon," Bricius declared. "Fenella ... I expect you to greet him."

Glancing up, from where she was slicing a small portion of blood sausage with an eating knife, Fenella frowned. "Why's that, Da?"

Bricius met her gaze across the fire as her younger sister and brothers looked up from their meals. The family of seven formed a ring around the fire pit in the center of their dimly lit roundhouse, consuming a noon meal of blood sausage, braised onions, and oatcakes. To her husband's right, his wife, Mona, looked on, her expression veiled. "Because he wishes to speak to you," her father growled.

A chill swept over Fenella. She wasn't a fool; she had seen the looks their tribe's chieftain, Toutorix 'the Wolf', had given her during the summer gathering. If Toutorix wanted to speak to her, it was because he wished to propose marriage.

The food Fenella had already consumed churned in her belly.

The Mother preserve me ... not him.

Their tribe's chieftain was her father's age. But no matter his rank, or age, she wasn't interested in becoming his wife. He was a man she'd never warmed to.

"You know that I'm going hunting today?" she replied coolly, even as her pulse quickened.

Her kin didn't know it, but this was the day she'd planned to meet her lover.

Fenella wouldn't ignore Lorcan in favor of Toutorix. She couldn't bear the thought of leaving the man she loved waiting, alone in the mossy glade by a burn where they always met. He would think something had happened to her.

Her father scowled, a deep crease forming between his dark brows. "Hunting be cursed … this is your chieftain." There was a belligerent edge to his voice now. "You will be here when he arrives."

Fenella ground her teeth. "Our supplies of fresh meat are low," she replied, stubbornness surging within her. "I must go." However, seeing the way a muscle in her father's jaw tightened and his gaze glinted in the firelight, she added, "But I will be back by mid-afternoon at the latest."

Her father leaned forward and speared the last piece of sausage with his knife. "You'd better be, girl."

Next to Fenella, her younger brother Eogan murmured an oath under his breath. He'd clearly been coveting that chunk of sausage.

They were all hungry today. The autumn chill had settled over their valley much earlier than usual, and a poor harvest meant that they were rationing their food already, even though Gateway—the festival that marked the end of autumn and the beginning of winter—was still a moon away.

Her father indeed knew that they needed more fresh meat—and Fenella was the best hunter in the family.

Despite that she always met her lover on those afternoons when she should have been hunting, she often returned home with a brace of grouse slung over her shoulder, or dragging a hind's carcass behind her.

She was lethal with her bow—a skill her family appreciated.

"Does Toutorix have wool between his ears?" Eogan muttered then. "Why would he choose such a savage as my sister for a wife?" It seemed he, too, had realized what was happening.

Bricius scowled, his big body tensing. He looked as if, had the fire pit—where a stinking brick of peat smoldered—not separated them, he'd have reached out and cuffed the eldest of his three sons.

Fenella covered her mouth with her hand, hiding a smirk.

"Our chieftain has watched Fenella for a while now," their father ground out. "And if he wishes to take her as his wife, he will."

Fenella stiffened, her brief flash of mirth fading. "Not if I have any say in the matter."

Her mother's swift intake of breath followed. Mona's eyes widened, and she cast her daughter a pained look. Her dark-blue eyes—the same shade as her eldest daughter's—held a warning.

Fenella ignored it. She'd had enough of her father's bullying. She noted then how tired her mother appeared these days. Raising five children—and losing another three—had worn her out. She was thin and pale, her dark hair limp and laced with silver.

Handing Eogan the remainder of the meal she'd been enjoying before her father's announcement had robbed her of appetite, she rose to her feet. Unlike her father and Eogan, who'd recently started to sprout like a weed, she didn't need to stoop in order to avoid hitting her head on one of the low beams overhead.

The roundhouse wasn't really big enough to accommodate all of them. The three youngest siblings slept together in one of the alcoves that lined the stacked-stone walls. Fenella and Eogan had their own alcoves, yet they were cramped.

"I'll talk to the chieftain if that's what you want," she told her father. "But I won't wed him."

"You will," her father shot back, his face twisting. "I've already agreed to it."

Fenella went still. "What?"

Bricius glared at her. "The man saved my life in battle five years ago ... and in thanks, I told him that if he ever wanted a favor, he could have it." His expression hardened further still. "He wants you."

Fenella drew in a deep breath, and then another, in an attempt to push back the red haze of rage that obscured her vision.

Her father had traded her away, as a 'favor'? She couldn't believe she was hearing this. Around the hearth, her four siblings had all stopped eating and were watching the exchange between their eldest sister and father with rapt attention.

"A handfasting between our family and Toutorix's will do us all good," her father continued, scowling deeply now. "The last two winters have been harsh ... when you wed the chieftain, we shall move to his crannog at Loch Tatha and share his riches." He paused then, his jaw bunching. "Your brothers and sisters will have full bellies for the first time in years."

Fenella stared back at him.

The Reaper take him, her father was a cunning bastard. He knew he couldn't rely on her obeying his word, but Fenella was protective over her siblings, and he was attempting to get to her that way.

Without another word, she spun on her heel and left the roundhouse, stooping through the open door and exiting into bright sunlight.

"Be back by mid-afternoon, Fen," Bricius roared after her.

Spitting a curse, she stalked to the nearby hut, where her family stored their weapons and tools, and retrieved her yew bow and quiver of hazel arrows. Then she slipped from the wooden perimeter that encircled her family's home.

Bricius and his kin resided in a steep valley, not far from a rushing river. Tall pines that climbed the valley's rocky sides loomed overhead, and wispy clouds raced across a pale sky. The roar of the wind in the trees and the gurgle of the river were familiar and reassuring sounds.

Nevertheless, they didn't soothe Fenella today. Instead, her fury burned like a stoked ember in her belly.

Her father was trying to cage her, but she wouldn't allow it.

Her heart lay with a man from a neighboring village. Her family also hailed from there, but Fenella's father had left years earlier after an altercation, and had severed all ties since. Bricius was a man who didn't like to be questioned, who demanded obedience. But she wouldn't be cowed as her mother had been.

Fenella clenched her jaw. When threatening hadn't worked, the weasel had resorted to manipulation.

Wading through the burn, she let her anger burn hot, forging an iron resolve within her.

He wouldn't succeed. Eogan was almost a man now, and the others were already big enough to help in the fields. There was a gap of four years between Fenella and her brother, as Mona had birthed two stillborn babes in that time. As such, much responsibility had fallen on Fenella's shoulders over the years. But not anymore.

Today, everything would change. It was time to strike out, to begin afresh.

"Stick your promise to the chieftain up your arse, old man," she snarled to the rushing wind. "I won't be coming back."

Fenella knew the route to the meeting place well. Roughly every seven days, over the past year, she'd walked this path through a wide vale carpeted in dark pines. It was a risky route, for it took her a little too close to the fort of Ardoch—a huge stronghold near the banks of the River Knaik. She'd never set eyes on the fort, for only a fool would wander within sight of that place; nonetheless, the only other path she knew led around the northern edge of the pinewood and would take her twice as long to reach her destination.

Dressed in hunting leathers, Fenella blended in with her surroundings. She moved swiftly, her bare feet whispering over the crunchy bed of dried pine needles.

Along the way, she silently fumed.

She'd made her decision, yet her father's behavior still rankled. She couldn't believe he'd promised her to the chieftain without consulting her.

A chill wind rushed through the pines, whipping strands of hair into Fenella's eyes. She wore her hair in a thick braid that bounced between her shoulder blades as she strode out, yet the wind tore tendrils free.

Usually, when she walked this path, Fenella's gaze swept left and right, scanning the trees for trouble. Her hunter's instincts were well-honed, her eyesight sharp, and her hearing keen. But today she had trouble concentrating; instead, she stared straight ahead, her thoughts turning inward. Her father's words rang in her ears, causing outrage to pulse within her.

And as such, she didn't hear the hoofbeats at first.

It was only when a company of men on horseback emerged from the trees to her left that she realized she wasn't alone in the pinewood.

Skidding to a halt, Fenella froze like a hind in a hunter's sight. Silver, bronze, and gold gleaming in the pale sun, crimson cloaks billowing in the wind, the Roman patrol made straight for her. Bits jangled, and leather creaked.

Fenella's heart bucked against her ribs.

The Hag curse her, she should have heard their approach.

Despite the cooling wind, sweat beaded upon her skin. All the same, she stared down the approaching soldiers, even as her palms itched to unsling her bow from across her back and notch an arrow.

Such an aggressive act could only send things in one direction though. Instinct told her to remain as she was, her hands hanging loosely at her sides, ready for action.

The horses slowed as they approached, while Fenella found her gaze drawn to the leader.

He was someone important—she could tell by the proud charcoal-colored fan upon his helmet. Cheek and nose guards shielded parts of his face, yet she marked a strong jaw, dark-tanned skin, and a pair of golden-brown eyes that reminded her of a goshawk. The man sat tall and proud in the saddle. The iron breastplate and shoulder guards—black and gold like his crested helmet—he wore made his chest and shoulders seem impossibly broad, as did his deep-purple cloak.

And despite her brave stance, fear curled up in Fenella's belly. He was the biggest man she'd ever seen, and his penetrating golden eyes made a chill slither down her spine.

For a long moment, they stared at each other, and then the soldier shocked Fenella by greeting her in her own tongue, "You stray close to Ardoch, woman." His voice was a low, deep rumble. "What is your business?"

Fenella wet her lips. She'd never thought to hear one of these Roman bastards utter a word of the Cruthini language, although some of them had lived here long enough to learn it, she supposed. Clearing her throat, she jerked her chin in the direction of the bow that hung over her shoulder. "Hunting ... there are plenty of deer in these woods."

His gaze narrowed. "The deer scare easily this close to the fort. This is no place for a woman."

Fenella's spine stiffened. Ardoch was a male domain. It was reputed that few women lived there.

"I know how to look after myself," she replied coldly.

"Do you?" His voice lowered. "And what would you do, if we tried to take you right now?" The man's mouth curved then, although there was no humor in the expression. "Would you put an arrow through each of our hearts?"

Fenella tensed, outrage shivering through her. *Arrogant goat.* He knew he had the upper hand and was playing with her.

One of the soldiers behind the man said something in their language then—a strange, clanging tongue, so different to her own. And although Fenella couldn't understand what was said, the harsh tone made her skin prickle.

Danger—her instincts screamed. And yet she didn't move. She wouldn't flee from these soldiers. She wouldn't back down.

The leader of the company replied, his voice hardening, and when his attention shifted back to Fenella, his golden gaze was narrowed. "I suggest you hunt elsewhere in future." There was no missing the warning edge to his voice. "Only a fool would travel unescorted so close to Ardoch."

Fenella sucked in a sharp breath. *A fool?*

This land, Cruithentúath, belonged to her people, not the likes of him and his foul sort. Aye, these men of the Caesars had lived amongst them for nearly sixty years now, according to her father—bringing their orderly ways and stamping their authority upon the Cruthini— but that was merely a blink of an eye in the sands of time.

Indeed, she longed to fire one of her arrows straight into his heart.

"Go now," the soldier ordered then, "before my merciful mood passes."

An insult clawed its way up her throat, fighting to be unleashed—yet good sense checked her.

This was her first day of freedom, and she wouldn't waste it. Lorcan awaited her, and if she defied this man and his rabble, she risked never seeing her lover again.

Swallowing her ire, she clenched her jaw and took a wary step back, and then another. She hadn't expected him to just let her go, but his command was clear, and she'd take her opportunity while she could. Her attention flicked then to the faces of the men who'd drawn up their horses behind him.

Some of them were looking at her with hungry expressions, their gazes predatory.

Fear spiked through Fenella, turning her bowels to water. She knew then that if their leader hadn't kept them in check, these men would have tried to rape her.

They'll have to get their hands on me first.

Fenella turned and darted away, running for the trees. Her speed increased with each stride until she was sprinting. A smile of triumph stretched across her face as she flew through the pines, as fleet as a hind.

Now, only the wind could catch her.

II. PROMISED TO THE WOLF

FENELLA TOOK A detour to her destination, traveling in a wide loop far from the path. Weaving through the trees, she cursed under her breath—cursed the men of Rome who'd taken these lands as their own. She hated that her family lived in Ardoch's shadow. The Romans' presence here had made life hard for her people.

The huge fort—which was said to house thousands of men—sucked the land of resources, and, over the years, many brave Cruthini warriors had died upon a Roman sword, while their women had been raped, murdered, or taken as slaves.

And despite that her people had made life increasingly difficult for them of late, they showed no signs of leaving.

Glancing up at the sky above, Fenella quickened her step.

"Damn those Caesars to an eternity boiling in The Hag's cauldron," she muttered. "They're a plague on us all ... *and* they've made me late."

Indeed, they had. She hoped Lorcan would wait for her.

He did, although she saw by the tense set of the warrior's shoulders as she burst into the glade, and his furrowed brow, that she'd made him worry.

As always, the mere sight of her lover made giddiness sweep over Fenella. Lorcan was tall with a shock of red-brown hair and moss-green eyes. Woad-blue tribal tattoos decorated his bare arms. He moved toward her with loose-limbed grace.

Rushing to him, Fenella threw herself into his waiting arms. They shared a lusty kiss before she drew back, breathless. "Sorry, I'm late."

Still frowning, he met her gaze. "I was about to leave ... where have you been?" Her lover had a low musical voice she could listen to all day, and a touch that made her melt like a pat of butter on a hot griddle.

"I ran into a Roman patrol on the way."

His green eyes flew wide before he cursed. "How did you manage to get away from them?"

"They let me go."

Lorcan's gaze narrowed, his expression incredulous. "Really?"

"Aye ... their leader warned me not to stray too close to Ardoch again, and then he bid me run."

Even as she recounted the incident, Fenella realized how odd it sounded. The Romans were known for showing no mercy to any stray female they happened upon. Many a lass from the nearby villages had gone missing over the years—most of them never seen again.

A shiver rippled through Fenella at the thought that might have been her fate.

Lorcan pulled her into his arms, his hold tightening upon her. "Thank The Mother, you managed to get away," he murmured.

"Aye." Fenella raised her face to his. "I ran as if a horde of demons pursued me." Her voice turned husky then. "Nothing would keep me from you, Lorcan."

He stared down at her, his gaze darkening. An instant later, his mouth slanted over hers. His kiss was possessive, hot—as it always was—and within a heartbeat, Fenella forgot all else.

Linking her arms about his neck, she pressed the length of her body against his, opening her mouth to him.

With a groan, he gathered her up against him and moved her toward the trunk of a nearby beech that towered over the glade. It was their loving place.

Sometimes he would take her upon the soft moss under it, and sometimes he would take her against the trunk.

Today, it was the latter.

Fenella's quiver and bow dropped to the ground.

Lorcan's movements were jerky, his breathing ragged, as he stripped off her hunting leathers and pushed her up against the smooth bark. Usually, he would undress too, letting her gaze feast upon the long, sleek lines of his body. But this afternoon, he did not. There was an urgency to him.

Unlacing his breeches, he freed his shaft, spread her thighs, and drove into her in swift, hard thrusts.

Fenella's surprised gasp filled the clearing. She clung to him, her legs wrapping around his hips as he plowed her. She welcomed his fierceness today, reveled in it. Lorcan was usually a leisurely, gentle lover, but sometimes she longed for him to take her roughly, wildly.

And this afternoon, he did.

Fenella wondered if today Lorcan would forget himself completely. Over the past year, he'd always taken care to withdraw at the crucial moment so he didn't spill his seed within her. The act, although practical, always left her feeling a little dissatisfied and wanting.

Just once, she wanted him to let go, to give himself to her without worrying about the consequences.

But he didn't, not even now.

With a grunt, Lorcan yanked his shaft free and let his seed gush over her belly. Feeling its warmth trickle down to the nest of hair between her thighs, Fenella leaned back against the trunk. Her limbs trembled in the aftermath of the storm that had left them both panting, their bodies slick with sweat.

Wiping off his seed from her skin with a piece of moss, Lorcan then pulled Fenella into his arms, and together they sank down upon the bank of the glittering burn that bubbled through the glade.

And as they lay there in silence, enjoying the intimacy of the moment, a shadow fell over Fenella.

With all the excitement of encountering the Roman patrol, she'd forgotten her father's announcement.

Propping herself up on an elbow, she gazed down at her lover's handsome face.

"Lorcan," she breathed. "We must talk."

His eyes opened, focusing upon her. "Aye?"

"Father wishes me to wed Toutorix."

Lorcan tilted his head, surprise rippling over his face.

"Apparently, he owes the chieftain a favor," she continued, her pulse quickening, "and promised me to him ... without talking to me first."

Lorcan's mouth compressed.

"I don't wish to wed him," she assured him. "I want to be with you."

Moments passed before her lover responded, his voice oddly calm. "You can't defy our tribe's chieftain, Fen ... surely, you realize that?"

Fenella stiffened. She hadn't expected such a response from him. She'd anticipated jealousy, or angry words, but not this—not *compliance*.

She pushed herself up into a sitting position and glared down at him. "I know your father and mine are enemies ... and so we can never ask for their permission to be together ... but it's time we thought of ourselves," she declared. "We must run away ... today ... before Toutorix forces the issue. I will not wed him."

Lorcan stared up at her, his gaze veiled.

It was as if a curtain had dropped between them. Only moments earlier, she'd felt close to him, yet with just one look, he'd distanced himself from her.

"I can't run away with you," Lorcan replied softly.

"Aye, you can. Let's go today. Leave it all behind. You're a warrior, I'm a hunter ... we'll survive."

With a sigh, Lorcan rolled into a sitting position. His gaze then swung away, focusing upon the clear water of the burn as it bubbled over the peaty earth and stones. "Let me say this another way," he murmured. "I don't *want* to run away with you."

Fenella's breathing hitched. She felt as if he'd just punched her in the belly. "What?"

Lorcan sighed once more, still refusing to meet her eye. "I'm with another, Fenella. I can't leave her."

Air rushed out of Fenella's lungs, and the world tilted.

"There's someone else?" she croaked.

"Aye, I have a wife."

A wife?

"Since when?" Fenella was stunned. In all the moons they'd been meeting, from the first day their paths had crossed out here in the woods, he'd never mentioned this detail.

Lorcan was frowning when he looked her way once more. "Since three years ago." He paused then. "We have a son, and she is expecting our second babe in the spring."

Fenella gaped at him. Shuffling back, she swallowed hard, trying to gather her wits.

"I won't leave her," he continued, his features tightening. "So don't ask me to."

Nausea rolled over Fenella. Her mind churned, frantically searching back through every meeting, looking for clues that would make sense of this sudden revelation. Yet she found none.

"But I thought you loved me?" The words came out in a hoarse whisper.

His gaze never left hers. "I do."

"And your wife?"

He shrugged. "She is a good woman, and I care deeply for her too."

Fenella dragged in a deep breath then. Underneath the shock, she could feel anger coiling. "Does she know about me?"

Horror lit his green eyes. "Of course not."

Fury ignited in her belly. "So, you planned to keep us both?"

Lorcan stared back at her, his silence damning.

Fenella rose to her feet and gathered her clothing. She then began to dress, all the while spearing Lorcan with her glare. "What about all the things we talked of?" she asked, her voice trembling. It wasn't grief that gave it a tremor, although she knew hurt would hit her like a charging boar later, but fury. "Of how we'd travel north till we found the perfect spot to build a house together ... and there we would start a family."

"It was a dream, Fen," he replied, a note of chagrin in his voice. "Nothing more."

"For you, maybe," she choked out. "But for me, it was *real*. I believed the words you spun around me. I thought we'd one day leave all of *this*" —she swept a vicious hand around her— "behind us."

He continued to watch her, something akin to pity in his eyes. "Did you really?" he asked before shaking his head. "Life isn't like that. You can't run away."

Fenella stared at him as if her lover had just sprouted a second head. Of course they could flee—people did it all the time.

It occurred to her then, like a rude slap to the face, that she didn't know Lorcan at all. The image she had of him, as a free spirit willing to do all for love, was as insubstantial as morning mist.

Now the mist was clearing, and Fenella didn't like what it revealed.

"But I love you," she murmured, as if the declaration could somehow weave magic. Although as she spoke, something splintered within her. It was as if her youth— and the hope that brightened the world even when life was difficult—had gone.

Suddenly, she felt as old as a crone.

Night was falling when Fenella approached her home once more. Often the wind died at dusk, yet this evening, it howled like a banshee. The temperature had dropped too, the cold air chafing at the exposed skin of Fenella's cheeks and arms.

However, she barely noticed.

Fenella walked through the world without connecting with it.

She'd stalked out of this valley earlier in the day, vowing never to return—yet here she was, defeated already.

For the first time in a while, she'd returned empty-handed from a hunting trip, but she didn't care. There wasn't even a grouse for her mother to roast over the fire pit. All she could think about was how Lorcan, the man she'd hoped to build a future with, had disappointed her.

Things had eventually gotten ugly. Of course, her temper had erupted, grief and rage pouring out of her like a cauldron boiling over. Lorcan had been sorry in the end, had tried to reason with her. But when he'd told her they could still meet as lovers, she'd spat at him. And when he'd remained calm, she'd eventually struck him across the face, screamed insults at him, before gathering her bow and quiver and fleeing the glade.

She'd never go back. That place was forever ruined, as was her heart.

Woodenly, she let herself in through the gate, which had been left unbarred for her, before securing it behind her. Her father had built the high wooden perimeter after they'd lost fowl to wolves a few winters back. It protected them from two-legged predators as well. This close to Ardoch, and after Bricius had fallen out with yet more of his neighbors—in a disagreement over grazing land—it was best to be prudent.

Crossing the dirt yard before her father's roundhouse, Fenella's gaze shifted to the lean-to, where the family's fen pony was stabled. There was still enough light for her to see that another pony, this one larger and as black as charcoal, had joined it.

Fenella's belly clenched.

Toutorix is still here.

Her step faltered. For a moment, she wished she could flee, could turn tail and disappear into the woods forever. Perhaps she should, even without Lorcan's companionship.

But her lover's parting words still rang in her ears. Patience exhausted, he'd snarled them. "Fate decides the course your life will take, woman—not you."

Fate. The will of the gods that watched over them all: The Mother, The Maiden, The Warrior, The Hag, and The Reaper. All of them were conspiring against her today. It was as if her hopes and desires didn't matter in the slightest.

Fenella's throat thickened, and she swallowed hard.

No, she wouldn't run, not now that Lorcan had ruined everything. Instead, she would face whatever the gods had in store for her.

Her father's roundhouse loomed before her, the conical roof outlined against the darkening sky.

Putting one foot in front of the other, Fenella walked to the dwelling, pushed open the door, and stooped to enter.

The familiar dark interior of the home she'd spent her entire eighteen winters in greeted her. The ruddy light of the fire pit caught the faces of the figures gathered around the hearth, and made their eyes gleam as they glanced her way. In one of the alcoves, Fenella spied the faces of her three youngest siblings: Ena, Maddoc, and Fife. They'd been sent to bed but weren't yet sleeping.

All of them were awaiting her return.

As was the man seated next to her father by the fire pit.

Toutorix's bald head gleamed in the glow of the embers as he watched her, his expression impassive. The fur pelt he wore around his shoulders emphasized his brawn, while around his thick neck he wore an intricately crafted golden torc. He was her father's age and yet hadn't lost any of his physical strength. Fenella might have found him handsome if his face wasn't so hard, his pale blue eyes so calculating.

Setting down her bow and quiver near the door, Fenella approached the hearth.

"Did you not catch anything?" her mother asked. Mona's face was taut this eve, her gaze veiled. Fenella wondered what she thought of all this. Did she sympathize with her daughter's situation, or did she believe she was being unnecessarily obstinate?

"No," Fenella replied, taking a seat before the hearth.

Unlike his younger siblings, Eogan was still up, and allowed to sit with his elders. Her brother cast Fenella a meaningful look, his lips parting as if he wished to comment on his sister arriving home empty-handed.

But perhaps sensing her mood, he closed his mouth and remained silent.

"It is good to see you, Fenella," Toutorix greeted her. He had a gravelly voice that matched his rugged looks. "Although I was beginning to worry you wouldn't return home tonight."

"I was delayed," she replied. "While I was out hunting, I ran into a Roman patrol."

This news caught their attention. Both her father and chieftain's bodies stiffened. Toutorix drew himself up before growling an oath. "What were they doing on my lands?"

"I was hunting a deer and ventured closer to the River Knaik than I'd realized," Fenella lied. "They gave chase, but I eventually lost them in the hills."

The chieftain stared at her, a muscle bunching in his jaw. "You shouldn't take such risks, lass," he muttered. "Those shit-eating bastards show no mercy."

"Aye, Toutorix," Fenella's father agreed. His gaze hadn't left his daughter's face, and Fenella wondered if he sensed her lie. Bricius could be unnervingly astute at times. "Fenella knows not to stray so close to Ardoch."

"It won't happen again," she assured them, her tone cool.

"Aye, you are right about that," Toutorix assured her. "For soon you will be my wife ... and I won't permit you to go out hunting alone." He cast Bricius a look of censure, wordless criticism for allowing such behavior. He then looked back to Fenella, pinning her to the spot with his ice-blue stare. "Your father has agreed ... you are to come away with me tomorrow morning, and we shall be handfasted later at Loch Tatha."

Squaring her shoulders, Fenella drew herself up. Despite the hurt, the disappointment that twisted like a nest of serpents in her belly, she wouldn't be cowed. Her future would be decided this evening, and she would do all she could to claw back control. She wouldn't be caged.

"My father promised me to you without my consent," she replied, holding the chieftain's stare. "I'm sorry, but I don't wish to wed you."

Sharply indrawn breaths followed.

Even Eogan, who usually wore a grin of amusement in all situations, looked shocked by her announcement.

No one among the *madaidhean-allaidh a tuath*—the Wolves of the North, as her tribe was known—contradicted the chieftain.

Long moments passed, broken only by the rasp of her father's angry breathing and the crackle of burning peat in the fire pit between them.

Bricius's face had gone the color of raw meat, and his gaze glinted dangerously. Fenella could tell he itched to strike her.

However, the chieftain's expression was inscrutable. He merely watched Fenella, his gaze roaming over her face as if he was looking upon her properly for the first time.

A sickly sensation washed over Fenella then, as it occurred to her that he might like women with fire. Some men did—especially if they enjoyed breaking a woman's spirit. Toutorix had buried two wives already. Perhaps he wanted his third wife to be feistier than his previous ones.

The Mother save her, she could see the iron bars of her cage slamming shut. She'd thought she'd evaded capture earlier, and had even felt a surge of vindication when she'd left Lorcan in that clearing. She wouldn't remain the lover of a man who treated her as second-best. Her father, Lorcan, and Toutorix all wanted to control her.

Ironically, that Roman today had spared her, had given Fenella her freedom, but the chieftain of the Wolves of the North would not.

As if confirming her fears, Toutorix favored her with a slow smile, revealing teeth that were surprisingly strong and white for a man of his age. The expression caused fear to arrow through Fenella's gut. Aye, her instincts hadn't lied. "What *you* wish for Fenella, daughter of Bricius, is of no consequence to me," he replied. "I take what I want … and what I want is you."

THREE YEARS LATER ...

III. IN FLAMES

*Ardunie Watchtower
Damnonii territory,
Caledonia*

Autumn, 121 AD

THE MOMENT GENERAL Justinian Valerius Aquila spied the smoke staining the afternoon sky, he knew he was too late.

As he broke free of the line of trees, his gaze alighted upon his destination: the timber watchtower of Ardunie. It was ablaze, flames licking high into the air.

Smoke caught the back of Justin's throat. Cursing, he drew his gladius. But it was a pointless gesture; whoever had done this had fled.

They hadn't arrived in time to save the men guarding this tower.

His stallion, a spirited beast of Iberian stock, tossed its head, slowing its gait as it neared the gates. His mount skidded to a halt, rearing as the fire's heat barreled into them.

The gates were open, the wooden perimeter around the signal station also burning. Peering through the smoke and flames, Justin made out the prone bodies of men scattered around the base of the tower. The charred stench of roasting flesh stung his nostrils.

Crimson settled over Justin's vision, fury pounding in his ears like the rhythmic clash of swords against shields before battle.

Behind him, a member of the cavalry unit spat out a curse. Loud muttering followed from the other soldiers he'd brought with him from Ardoch.

The guards at Ardunie had signaled that they were in trouble, and so General Aquila had rallied his men and ridden out to assist. They hadn't delayed, pushing their horses into a gallop as they covered the mile between the fort and the watchtower. Even so, they hadn't arrived soon enough.

"Futuo!" Justin snarled.

The Wolves had been bold of late—had taken to harrying the outpost forts and watchtowers in the area—yet Justin hadn't expected an attack so close to Ardoch.

This was Damnonii country, yet the local tribesmen weren't troublemakers. Their neighbors were though. On the edge of Damnonii lands resided a Picti tribe who referred to themselves as the *Madaidhean-allaidh a tuath*: the Wolves of the North.

The Wolves had been a thorn in Justin's arse for years now.

There were several Roman forts built along this spine of hills that stretched up the eastern coast of Caledonia— from Camelon in the south to Stracathro in the north— with watchtowers standing a mile apart between them; the towers were spaced close enough to alert each other of trouble.

After the disappearance of the Ninth legion, the northern forts had been abandoned, yet Ardoch still stood firm.

Justin's jaw clenched. The loss of the Ninth had caused rot to set in. The garrisons stationed on the frontier were finding it increasingly difficult to keep the territory under control. Three winters earlier, a force of over five thousand men had marched into the wild reaches of Caledonia, never to be seen again—and since then, the Picti had grown increasingly restless and aggressive.

Now only the Twentieth legion—Valeria Victrix— commanded by Legatus Justinian Valerius Aquila, remained to watch over the frontier.

The responsibility weighed heavily on Justin these days. At thirty-three, he was still a few years off retirement. These were supposed to be the golden years of his career—yet instead, he was spending them on this cold, brutal frontier. He expected his next posting to be a comfortable one, in thanks for his service in Caledonia.

"Infernus, who did this?" Marcus Camillus reined in his horse next to the legate.

Justin screwed up his face and spat on the ground. "You know who ... it's that *carnifex*, Toutorix the Wolf."

Butcher—the chieftain of the Wolves of the North was certainly that. For the past years, Justin had kept an eye on the Wolves. Their chieftain lived at Lake Taus, or Loch Tatha, as the tribesmen called it. The lake wasn't far from where craggy mountains rose to meet the sky— the highlands that made up Caledonia's wild north. Toutorix's village was a crannog, a network of densely-packed, conical-roofed lake-dwellings built upon the water.

By rights, he should have made Toutorix kneel years ago.

The last time Justin had met with Trajan, the former emperor had warned him that troublemakers should be dealt with severely. But Trajan's successor, Hadrian, had little interest in beating Caledonia into submission. Losing the Ninth had been a bitter blow, and word had reached Ardoch that the emperor planned to start work upon a great wall the following year—one that would stretch from coast to coast.

One that would keep the barbarians at bay.

But the wall wasn't yet built, and Ardoch resisted still. Justin was a seasoned veteran of both Britannia and Caledonia. He knew how easy it was to stir up rancor, and so he'd chosen to watch Toutorix the Wolf instead of moving against him.

He now bitterly regretted showing that blood-thirsty bastard any mercy.

"What now?" Marcus asked. Glancing the primus pilus's way, Justin saw his face beneath his red-crested helmet was all savage angles. It was an expression that mirrored the general's own rage. Justin's mouth twisted. Once again, Marcus knew the answer.

"Toutorix won't be attacking any more of our watchtowers," Justin growled back. "I shall personally make sure of it."

Fenella tensed, waiting for her husband to strike her again.

"Mouthy bitch." Toutorix loomed over her, fists clenched. "Speak back to me like that again, and I'll break your jaw."

Cheek burning from where he'd struck her, Fenella's chin rose in defiance. However, despair clutched at her throat. Three long, miserable years had come to this.

For a moment, husband and wife stared at each other, as the conversation around them died away. They stood near the great hearth of the chieftain's meeting roundhouse, the largest of the dwellings built in a cluster upon the loch. The roof, thatched with reed and bracken, rose above them—a wagon wheel of rafters stretching up to where a slit let out the blue fug of peat smoke. A bed of rushes lay underfoot, and drunken warriors sat around the square hearth, celebrating their successful attack with horns of mead.

Fenella didn't share their jubilation.

Instead, her heart raced and sweat bathed her skin. Careless fools, all of them—drinking and celebrating when they should be outside keeping watch.

But as her stare with Toutorix drew out, ire bubbled up, cramping her belly. Her husband was too free with his fists. How she longed to grab the poker from the fire and shove it into his belly. She fantasized about doing so sometimes when she lay in the furs at night next to her sleeping husband.

Marriage to Toutorix the Wolf had brought her nothing but misery.

"I was only pointing out that the men of Rome will know *you* torched that tower and butchered their men," she answered, stubbornness winning over good sense and fear.

Toutorix was capable of breaking her jaw and doing much worse.

Since coming to live at Loch Tatha, she'd heard whispers of what he'd done to his previous wives. The first had died after a severe beating. And although the second died in childbirth, the iron-collared slaves who served the chieftain and his household had whispered to Fenella of the numerous black eyes the woman had received, even while she'd been pregnant.

"And that being the case," Fenella pressed on, her gaze flicking to where the poker lay within arm's reach, "it would be wise to put extra men on the watch tonight."

Her husband went still.

Fenella's breathing hitched. Stillness wasn't a good sign. It usually preceded violence. Toutorix's temper was like nothing she'd ever experienced. Even her father's rages paled in comparison. When the Wolf was enraged, he was capable of anything.

"I warned you," he growled, his pale blue eyes glinting in the firelight as his right fist drew back. "A wife doesn't need a pretty face … and you won't have one when I'm finished with you."

Fenella drew taut, ready to dive for the poker.

She hadn't expected her earlier comment to enrage her husband so—but Toutorix's mood was mercurial. She didn't want to openly clash with him—but this evening, desperation and despair had driven her to it.

But if he wanted to beat her face to a pulp, he'd need to fight her first.

The wattle door to the meeting roundhouse crashed open then, bouncing off the wall, and causing all those inside to whirl toward it.

One of the chieftain's warriors lurched through the doorway. "Toutorix!" His mouth gasped like a landed trout. "We're under—"

He never finished his warning, for a spear thrust suddenly through his chest.

Fenella's heart bucked against her breastbone. She recognized the protruding iron, arrow-shaped shaft of the pike: a Roman pilum. The warrior's face went ashen, and then blood leaked from his open mouth.

An instant later, he toppled forward—only to be kicked out of the way by a helmed figure.

Toutorix's shout of rage echoed through the structure.

His warriors cast aside their horns of mead and lunged for their weapons, as did the chieftain.

But it was too late.

Roman soldiers, their plate armor glinting in the firelight, poured into the hall. Men broke upon them like waves upon the rocks, but all of them fell under the sharp jab of those vicious daggers and the short stabbing blades the enemy carried with them.

The clash was brutal but short—and it ended with Toutorix disarmed and cursing as he stood between two enemy soldiers. Blood trickled down his forehead, but the Wolf paid it no mind. Instead, he snarled like a cornered animal.

Meanwhile, Fenella backed up against the hearth.

The heavy tread of approaching soldiers filtered into the roundhouse then, and those soldiers already within parted for the newcomers.

Like everyone else, Fenella's gaze shifted to where a tall figure strode inside.

As it did so, her breathing slowed. *I know this man.*

Tanned skin, arrogantly hawkish features, and golden eyes. She recalled too the ornate helmet bearing a black fan that ran from front to back rather than side-to-side like those some of the other Roman soldiers wore, and the purple-red cloak that swept over one shoulder.

Even three years on, she recognized him: the man who'd spared her that day in the pinewood.

But that unnerving gaze ignored her, instead sweeping to the chieftain, where it rested.

"Aquila," Toutorix spat the man's name, and Fenella swallowed a gasp.

The man she'd encountered that day—the one who'd let her go rather than turning her over to his soldiers to be raped—was the infamous, and hated, general who commanded Ardoch and the other forts that ran in a spine down the eastern edge of Cruithentúath.

Her people knew him as 'an Iolaire', the Eagle.

One glimpse at those unnerving eyes, and she knew why.

Drawing a dagger at his hip, General Aquila advanced upon Toutorix. "You butchered every last man at Ardunie, Wolf," he growled in her tongue. "What did they do to provoke you?"

To her husband's credit, he didn't wilt in the face of the furious general. Instead, he eyeballed him as he approached. Toutorix's face then screwed up, and he spat on the ground between them.

"They didn't need to do anything, Roman," he snarled back. "Their presence on *my* lands is enough."

"*Your* lands." General Aquila halted, tension rippling off his big body. "Last I looked, Toutorix the Wolf wasn't High King of Caledonia. Emperor Hadrian rules here."

When Toutorix didn't respond, the general's lantern jaw tightened. His fingers flexed around the hilt of his dagger. It had a leaf-shaped blade, very different from the long, thin knives her people favored. "Tell me why I shouldn't tear out your belly right now? Tell me why I shouldn't torch your crannog and put every last one of your warriors to the sword?"

Long moments passed inside the hall. It had gone deathly silent, except for the crackling of the hearth.

Toutorix continued to stare back at General Aquila. However, Fenella noted that he'd gone pale. And despite the savage expression that twisted his face, a nerve twitched under one eye.

It hit her then that her husband feared this man.

Fenella's breathing hitched. The Wolf was afraid of no one.

But with The Reaper breathing down his neck, one skeletal hand upon his shoulder, Toutorix wasn't as confident as he'd been when his wife had dared question his foolhardy act. Aye, she hated these Roman overlords as much as he did—but a savage, unprovoked attack like the one on Ardunie was always going to end in reprisal.

That was what she'd been trying to tell him before he'd struck her.

General Aquila's attention shifted to her then, as he marked her presence for the first time. Their gazes locked. It was just for an instant, but recognition lit in his eyes.

Fenella's heart started to pound against her breastbone.

Just like her, he hadn't forgotten their meeting three years earlier.

And when she glanced back at Toutorix, she saw his gaze flick from her to Aquila. Her husband had noted the look that passed between them.

However, General Aquila's focus was now wholly upon the chieftain once more. "Whisper one last prayer to your gods, Wolf," he said as he moved forward.

"Wait!" the chieftain croaked. Toutorix's face now gleamed with sweat, and his ice-blue eyes were hunted. He was surrounded. There was no way out—although it only seemed to occur to him now that he didn't want to die upon a Roman blade. "I'll make you a bargain."

The general halted, his dark brows crashing together. "You aren't in a position to negotiate, Wolf."

Toutorix's throat bobbed. "Killing me will start a war … the other Cruthini chieftains will seek vengeance."

General Aquila's lip curled. "Really? I hear you aren't popular in the north."

Toutorix's eyes went wider still, while Fenella inhaled sharply.

Indeed, her husband had a few long-running feuds with some of the chieftains. How did the Eagle know that? Did he have spies among the Cruthini?

"Aye, there's bad blood between me and one or two of them," Toutorix admitted roughly. "However, once the others learn that you've killed me, you will have a lot of trouble on your hands. They grow restless, General Aquila. Some of them are itching to draw blades against your kind. Do want to give them an excuse to unite against you?"

Ire glinted in the general's eyes. Nonetheless, he didn't contradict him.

Fenella's gaze shifted from her husband to the Eagle. Of course, they all knew Toutorix had a point. But would it be enough to save him?

As if sensing it wasn't, Toutorix cleared his throat. "If you spare my life, I swear not to raise arms against you or your men … ever again."

The general snorted. "Why should I believe any promise you make me?"

"You can trust me." Toutorix's voice was raspy now, desperate. "I swear it."

Fenella drew in a deep breath. Her belly curdled at her husband's cowardice. She'd thought him dauntless, but now that death was looming, he was cowering before this Roman bastard. Her hands fisted at her sides. The Warrior should strike her husband down for humiliating them all like this.

Toutorix had known what he was doing when he'd led his warriors in an attack on Ardunie. And he'd had no regrets—until this moment.

"And what do you swear upon?" Aquila asked. "Your own worthless life … or gods I don't believe in?"

Toutorix drew in a deep breath, and then his gaze flicked to Fenella.

She met his eye, misgiving stealing over her when she saw how his wintry gaze glinted. Even so, the warning couldn't prepare her for the betrayal that then slipped from her husband's lips.

"Spare me … and my warriors," he croaked, "and I shall give you my wife."

IV. A SACRIFICE I MUST MAKE

SILENCE FELL ONCE more in the roundhouse.

The hiss of numerous indrawn—shocked—breaths followed.

No one within, least of all Fenella herself, could have guessed Toutorix would try to strike such a bargain. And as each moment slid into the next, she struggled to take the words in.

Surely, she'd misheard?

She stared at her husband, trying to read his expression—but Toutorix's face had shuttered.

Her stomach hardened then, hurt washing over her. First her father, and now her husband. *Is this all I am ... a sow to be traded?*

Drawing in a deep breath, Fenella took a step toward Toutorix. This had to be a mistake. Even he couldn't be so cruel.

But before she had the chance to question her husband, the general spoke. "You're offering me your wife?" There was incredulity in his voice—and something else.

Fenella swiveled, her attention moving to the Eagle.

He was watching Toutorix. The general now wore an intense, focused expression that made Fenella's heart kick like a wild pony against her breastbone.

The Mother save her, Aquila was actually considering her husband's offer.

"Toutorix!" Her voice came out strangled. "Don't do this!"

The Wolf's gaze shifted to her. He wore a pained expression now. "I'm sorry, Fenella, but Aquila leaves me with no choice."

"But we stood together on the shores of the loch and made oaths to the gods," she gasped. "Will you risk their wrath?"

"The gods will understand, for my people need me. Rest assured, your sacrifice will never be forgotten."

She stared at him, her pulse pounding in her ears now. "But I'm your *wife*! What about loyalty?"

"He clearly has none," the general cut in.

Fenella's gaze flew to the Eagle then. His eyes glinted. Did this scene amuse him?

Her gut clenched, anger quickening in her veins.

This was *his* fault. Her husband was as sharp as a whetted blade. He'd marked Aquila's interest in her and was seeking to exploit it.

Fenella glanced back at Toutorix. Aye, there was no mistaking the vindictive light in his eye. She'd been a disappointing wife, and after three years, still hadn't provided him with a son. Her womb had quickened twice, but she'd lost both babes halfway through her pregnancies.

She and Toutorix had fought like dogs ever since she'd come to live at Loch Tatha. But she'd never thought him capable of such a betrayal.

Fenella took a slow step toward the hearth. "I'll not go with you, Roman," she growled. "I'll take a knife to my own throat first."

Aquila raised an eyebrow. "I'd prefer you didn't." He then gestured to a man behind him. "Centurion ... take the woman outside so Toutorix and I can talk."

Ice washed over Fenella.

I'm not going anywhere.

And with that, she leaped for the iron poker by the fire. Her fingers clenched around it, and then she swung for Aquila. But the man was fast. He ducked before stepping under her guard. An instant later, his hard grip fastened around her wrist, stilling her.

Ripping the poker from her hands, he flung it into the fire, sending an explosion of sparks belching into the air.

"Enough of that," the general muttered. He then shoved her at the waiting centurion. "Take her out now … and keep a close eye on her," he ordered.

Tightness constricted Fenella's throat and lungs, threatening to choke her. She couldn't believe this was happening—and that her husband was permitting it.

But Toutorix remained traitorously silent.

Desperate now, Fenella writhed in the centurion's grip, gasping curses. But the man was a boulder. He merely twisted her arms behind her and marched her out of the roundhouse.

The door closed, muffling the sounds of the woman's rage.

Justin listened to her a moment, aware that Toutorix was watching him attentively, awaiting his answer. The chieftain's expression had veiled now, the glow of the fire pit reflecting off his bald head and the golden torc he wore about his neck.

Fenella.

He'd wondered at the name of the lone huntress he and his patrol had stumbled upon in that pinewood near Ardoch. He'd never forgotten her.

However, he hadn't expected to see her here, at the Wolf's side.

"Well?" Toutorix broke the silence between them. "Do you want her?"

Warmth kindled in the pit of Justin's belly. *I do.*

When he'd stridden into this roundhouse, he was focused on one thing: slitting the Wolf's throat. But from the moment he locked gazes with the chieftain's wife, everything had shifted. It was hard to concentrate with her standing next to him—that was why he'd sent her outside.

"Perhaps," he replied.

A few feet away, one of the injured Wolf warriors groaned. Toutorix ignored him. "She's fiery," the chieftain murmured. "But you like a woman with a spine, don't you?"

Justin snorted. It was a good guess, although the Wolf wouldn't know where his tastes lay.

"I can assure you, she's a fine field to plow," Toutorix continued, his mouth curving. "Hot and tight enough between her thighs to make a man lose his wits."

Frowning, Justin sheathed his pugio and folded his arms across his chest. "If you like her so much, why are you giving her up?"

Toutorix's expression sobered, and he dropped his gaze. "I don't wish to," he replied, his voice lowering. "But it's necessary."

Justin fought a lip curl. *To save your own neck.* The man was a worm.

Of course, he could have killed Toutorix and taken Fenella anyway—yet the chieftain's warning about the wrath this would incur had checked him.

Curse him, the Wolf was right.

The loss of the Ninth had stirred things up, had made the Picti bolder than before. Justin didn't have the men to withstand the might of the united northern tribes.

And Toutorix knew it.

Standing at the end of the walkway, Fenella watched General Aquila emerge from the roundhouse.

Fenella drew herself up, fists clenching at her sides.

The crisp late afternoon air caught in her lungs. Usually, she liked the scent of wood smoke this time of year, blended with the rich smell of the loch—water, mud, and reeds—but now it choked her.

Behind her, the general's army, a glittering red and silver wall, fanned out on the shore of the loch. There were so many of them—far too great a number for her husband's warriors to best.

Toutorix had indeed poked the hornet's nest when he'd razed Ardunie.

Aquila strode toward her along the walkway, four of his men following at his heel. They passed the entrances to a number of smaller walkways, all leading to the dwellings of those who resided upon the water. Fenella's kin lived in a tiny home on the western edge of the crannog, but despite that the fight in the meeting roundhouse had drawn a crowd, she couldn't see any of her family amongst those gathered.

Where are they?

Surely, neither her father nor her brother would stand by and let the Romans carry her off? Not like Toutorix had.

Too late, she recalled that the pair of them had joined a stag-hunting party three days earlier—one that would take them deep into the Cairngorms to the north—and had not yet returned. Bricius and Eogan wouldn't come to her aid.

Fenella's heart started to pound as the general drew near. "Gods, please tell me you didn't agree to this?" Her voice was high, panicked, yet she didn't care. "Tell me you didn't believe his lies?"

The Eagle halted before her. "It's done."

Fenella's mouth twisted. "Idiot," she snarled. "He's played you like a harp, hasn't he? You make a bargain with Toutorix the Wolf at your own peril. A man who treats his wife like a goat to barter at market has no honor."

The general snorted. "In that case, I've done you a favor."

"No, you haven't," Fenella shouted, fury sweeping over her in a crimson haze. "Clodhead, don't you realize he—"

"General!" The centurion still holding Fenella cut her off. "Look!"

Aquila spun around, his gaze sweeping back to the meeting roundhouse—and then to the walkways around it.

Fenella's breathing caught.

Warriors—Toutorix, among them—were descending the ladders to a landing where two large rowboats awaited. The first of the craft was already pushing away from the landing.

Toutorix stepped onto the second boat. But instead of lowering himself down into it, he turned—his ice-blue gaze spearing the Eagle. Then, raising his hand, the chieftain flipped an obscene gesture. "There will never be any peace between us, Eagle," he shouted, his voice carrying across the water. "I'll not rest until I see your kind wiped from this land." Even at this distance, Fenella could see his sneer. "Do what you want with my wife, I've been looking for an excuse to rid myself of the barren bitch anyway."

And with that, Toutorix settled himself down into the boat and shouted to his warriors. A moment later, they dug their oars in, and the craft moved away from the landing.

The general roared an order, and men rushed past him, their mailed sandals thundering on the wooden walkway. However, they were too late. By the time the first of them reached the landing, Toutorix's boat was moving out onto the loch, gaining speed as his warriors fell into a rhythm. The splash of their oars mocked those they'd left behind.

Aquila barked another command. Soldiers stepped smartly out of the ranks, raising their bows. Arrows peppered the water, clattering off the shields Toutorix's men raised. Soon they were out of range.

The general spun back to his men, his shout splintering the air once more.

Soldiers plucked flaming pitch torches from where they burned in braces at the entrance to the crannog. They then advanced down the walkway, the creak of their heavy tread rippling through the still afternoon air, their plate armor catching the lowering sun.

Moments later, shouts and screams rang out. Villagers rushed up the walkways, while others jumped into the water and swam to shore.

Fenella's breathing choked off when the thatched roofs of the dwellings nearest burst into flames. Toutorix was rowing to safety, but he'd abandoned his crannog to the enemy—as he had her.

"Please!" Fenella gasped, trying in vain to wrench herself free of the centurion's hold. She hated to plead with Aquila, but she was desperate. She couldn't bear to see the crannog-dwellers slaughtered. "These are innocent people … fishermen and farmers. Don't punish them!"

Aquila cast her an irritated look. "My men won't kill anyone," he muttered. "Unless they try to stop them." He moved away from her then, bellowing another set of orders.

A group of his men suddenly broke off from the orderly rows and began marching east, armor and weapons rattling in their haste.

Watching them go, Fenella realized they'd been sent after Toutorix.

Her mouth thinned. They wouldn't catch him. Loch Tatha was long and narrow. By the time Aquila's soldiers forded the river farther east, the Wolf and his men would have long reached the far shore.

Fenella's gaze shifted back to the crannog. Indeed, the soldiers were intent on torching the roundhouses and huts, not slaughtering the villagers. Nonetheless, the folk of Loch Tatha tried to stop them. Men rushed forward to defend their homes. Angry shouts and curses, and the clang of iron, now rang through the air.

Nausea rolled over Fenella, bile stinging the back of her throat. General Aquila might not be planning to butcher the folk of Loch Tatha, but blood would be spilled here all the same.

She whipped around to face her captor once more. "You're no better than Toutorix," she choked. "Your word means *nothing*."

"If your people wish to throw themselves upon our swords then so be it," the general replied, his voice hard. "I've shown the Wolves enough mercy."

V. OVERSTEPPING

"TOUTORIX MADE AN ass out of you."

Drawing his horse up in the shallow valley where they'd make camp for the night, Justin scowled down at the woman. Toutorix's wife had also halted. He'd bound her wrists behind her and tied a rope around her waist, leading her behind him. Like his infantry, she'd traveled on foot.

But now her gaze bored into his.

Justin clenched his jaw. There were times he wished he hadn't made the effort to learn the native tongue. This was one of them. All the way from the shore of Lake Taus, Fenella had insulted him. Toutorix hadn't been wrong—she was fiery all right. Even defeated, she stood with a defiant tilt to her chin. The walk hadn't cooled her temper, but had merely stoked it.

Inhaling deeply, to settle his own simmering anger, Justin deliberately raked his gaze over Fenella. He did so knowing it would enrage her, while at the same time giving in to the temptation to stare at the woman he now owned.

He took in her sleek body, encased in a sleeveless leather vest that revealed a deep cleavage, and her knee-length leather skirt with slits at the thighs for ease of movement. Like most Picti women, the chieftain's wife dressed in clothing that showed a lot of skin and went barefoot. Thick, silky brown hair hung in a braid over one shoulder. A swirling design of blue woad—a wolf's head—had been tattooed onto her right bicep.

"I hope I was worth it." Her voice, brittle with rage now, intruded. Justin raised his gaze back to Fenella's face to find her glaring at him. Her face was twisted in disgust. "One woman in exchange for your balls."

"That's enough," Justin growled. "One more insult, and I'll gag you."

He didn't need reminding of how easily Toutorix had deceived him back at Lake Taus. Even now, the pit of his gut burned at the memory.

He'd never forget how the Wolf had smirked as he made his escape in that boat.

Toutorix could read people. It had only taken him a few instants—when he'd seen Justin glance his wife's way in the meeting roundhouse—to understand the general wanted her.

And he'd wielded that knowledge like a weapon.

They'd left the crannog behind them a smoking ruin, but destroying it hadn't eased the fury churning within Justin.

Rage at Toutorix. At himself.

What had come over him in that roundhouse? Perhaps the pressure of leading a legion on this forgotten edge of the empire was finally getting to him. Maybe he was cracking. Some soldiers did when the strain got too much.

Still scowling, Justin shifted his attention from his captive. Whatever the reason for his impulsive behavior back at Lake Taus, he was now sorely regretting it.

You were supposed to kill Toutorix, he reminded himself. *Not take his wife and let him escape.*

Dismounting, Justin led his horse toward the nearby enclosure his men had just erected. Toutorix's wife followed in sullen silence.

Above, the last of the daylight was fading from the sky, turning it the shade of a purpled bruise, while around Justin, his men had swung into action. He'd brought three centuries—two hundred and forty men— from Ardoch, and the orders of two centurions commanding them drifted through the camp.

The third centurion led his company east, in pursuit of Toutorix.

Justin had instructed his men to track the chieftain and his warriors down and deal with them. However, Toutorix knew this land better than they did. Once he reached the far shore of the lake, he could easily lose himself in the mountains to the north. Justin's men had to catch him before he did.

As always, the marching camp rose up now in the same plan as every Roman fort—no matter how big or small. Surveyors had ridden ahead and laid out the two streets—Via Praetoria and Via Principalis—and at the intersection where the streets crossed sat the general and primus pilus's quarters. Crews of men erected neat rows of goat-skin tents, the makeshift barracks, while others got to work on a ditch and rampart on all four sides. It was a lot of work to go to for just one night, but it was their way. In the morning, everything would be removed, and even the ditch filled in. And in a few days, it would be as if they'd never camped there.

Leaving his stallion to be unsaddled and rubbed down, Justin untied Fenella and led her to his tent. He'd just shackled her to the center pole when Centurion Camillus strode inside.

Removing his crested helmet, Marcus Camillus raked a hand through his short black hair. His gaze then alighted upon the Picti woman who crouched against the tent pole, glaring at them both.

"You've got yourself a hellcat there," Marcus observed.

Justin snorted.

Marcus caught his eye then, his expression grim. "What happened back at Lake Taus?"

Justin frowned. "You know what happened, Marcus," he replied. "You were there too."

Marcus was a senior officer and commanded the first cohort of the Twentieth. He was also Justin's advisor and friend—and that was why he allowed him liberties. None of his other officers would dare speak to him like this, but at least Marcus had the wits to wait until they were alone to do so.

Even so, Justin wasn't in the mood to be questioned. His gut now ached, and his temples throbbed.

"You had the Wolf cornered, and a dagger in your hand," Marcus continued. "Why didn't you end him?"

Dragging a hand down his face, Justin muttered an oath. "I don't know."

Marcus folded his arms across his chest, a groove forming between his dark brows. He then jerked his chin in Fenella's direction. "It's her, isn't it?"

Justin scowled. He was just grateful that Marcus didn't speak the native tongue, or he'd be in no doubt of how Toutorix had played him. Even so, he didn't want to discuss Fenella. What was there to talk about? How he'd lost his wits over a woman he'd only ever met briefly once before? It didn't make any sense—even to him.

"Careful, Marcus," he growled. "You're close to overstepping."

Fenella crouched against the tent pole, watching the men talk. Her thigh muscles started to cramp, yet she didn't relax.

The general and his companion—the centurion who'd dragged her from the roundhouse—were discussing her. She was sure of it, for both of them glanced her way more than once.

Things got heated. They were speaking in their own tongue, although Fenella didn't require an interpreter to guess the soldier wanted to know why the general had let Toutorix slip through his fingers—and why he'd taken his wife.

Indeed, Fenella wondered the same thing.

Her pulse quickened, a cold sweat prickling her skin.

She'd put on a brave face since her capture, and had flung insults at her captor all the way from Loch Tatha— but on the inside, she was quaking.

She wasn't an innocent. She knew what motivated men—and there had been no mistaking the heat in Aquila's gaze when he raked it down her body earlier.

There was a reason Toutorix had been able to deceive the Eagle so easily.

He wanted her.

A few feet away, the two men finished their clipped discussion. They then departed the tent without a backward glance, leaving her alone.

Drawing in a shaky breath, Fenella let her eyes flutter shut. She then sank down onto the soft fur beneath her haunches.

How could Toutorix do this to me?

They hadn't been happily wedded, but she couldn't believe he'd traded her.

Her life for his.

Fenella swallowed hard as tears burned her eyelids. *Da will slay him for this.*

But would he? Bricius stood up to all men—except his chieftain. She'd seen her father's eyes when he interacted with Toutorix.

He feared him.

No, her father wouldn't take revenge on her behalf.

She was alone—as she'd always been.

Tears slid down Fenella's cheeks, a sob rising inside her chest. She choked it back. The Eagle would no doubt return soon, and she didn't want him to see her weep. Humiliation churned within her as it was; she wouldn't make it even worse.

Her shredded pride was all she had left.

Eyes opening, she drew in deep gulps of air until the panic subsided. However, it wasn't long before she started to shiver.

She was in shock, although the air inside the large tent had a chill to it. The brazier that sat a few feet from her wasn't yet lit. A single lantern hung from the roof, the cresset of oil burning within casting a golden light over the interior of the tent. Sheepskins lay across the ground, and stuffed cushions and colorful blankets covered a nearby sleeping pallet.

Fenella's throat closed as her gaze lingered on the pallet.

Would the Eagle release her shackles and drag her into his bed, or would he just take her here, against the pole?

At that moment, a tall, broad-shouldered figure ducked inside the space.

Aquila had removed his fancy helmet, carrying it under one arm. Without it, he seemed far less intimidating.

Fenella studied him, her mouth twisting.

Aye, she'd noted his looks—any woman would have—but that didn't matter. A beautiful exterior often hid a rotten core. General Aquila's chiseled bone structure, bronzed skin, and golden eyes made him exotic indeed. His black hair was cut close against his scalp, a harsh style that gave his attractiveness an edge.

A young, lanky soldier followed the general into the tent then. Judging from the man's plainer attire, he was of a much lower rank than the general. The soldier glanced Fenella's way, naked interest flaring in his gaze, before a terse word from the general made him hurriedly look away.

The attendant moved behind Aquila and removed his cloak and armor, hanging the items up on the iron stand behind them. The general was now clad in nothing more than a plum-colored tunic, belted at the waist, and heavy mailed sandals.

His task completed, the soldier nodded to Aquila, careful not to steal another look in Fenella's direction, before leaving the tent.

Fenella's heart started to thump against her ribs. She didn't want to be alone with the Eagle.

She'd imagined without his armor the man would appear diminished. But he didn't. The tunic merely showed off the lines of his powerful body even more clearly. Now that armor wasn't covering his limbs, she spied a number of scars—some silvered with age, others pink. The marks of a warrior.

Fenella eyed him warily. The tension was too much—she had to know what her fate was to be. However, when she spoke, her voice came out in a croak, betraying her fear. "What are you going to do with me?"

The Eagle approached her then, before hunkering down so that their gazes were level. "You're my slave now, Fenella. Wherever I go, you shall follow."

She swallowed hard. "Your *bed* slave?"

Their gazes held, and then Aquila's mouth quirked into a half-smile. "Only if you're willing?"

"Well, I'm not," Fenella shot back, her mouth twisting.

His smile faded. "Then you shall serve me in other ways."

Fenella tensed. *In other ways.* What did he mean?

Her belly started to hurt then. The Eagle's words merely highlighted her vulnerability. He could make her promises, but she trusted him no more than her husband.

She was at this man's mercy—and he knew it.

Aquila rose to his feet and took the lantern down from the roof of the tent, using the burning cresset within to light the brazier. Watching the deft movements of his hands, Fenella noted how different they were from her husband's. Toutorix had huge, coarse hands with blunt fingers, but although the general's hands were strong, he had the long elegant fingers of a craftsman.

Like Lorcan.

For the first time in a while, she thought of the man who'd once been her lover—the man she'd planned a future with. Even now, memories of Lorcan made her throat tighten and chest constrict. His lies had cut deep. There had been times, during the first months of her marriage to Toutorix, when she thought the wound would never heal. But in time, the constant ache in her chest had eased—provided she didn't think about him.

Pushing memories of her silver-tongued lover aside, Fenella tore her gaze away from Aquila's hands and the memories they dredged up. The brazier was glowing now, and soon its heat would reach her.

However, there was a chill deep within Fenella now, lodged inside her chest.

Men. How she hated them. They bullied her, lied to her, and used her.

And they'd robbed her of the thing she valued the
most.
Her freedom.

VI. THE GENERAL'S PRIZE

"ARE YOU HUNGRY?" Justin indicated to where a platter of bread, cheese, and fruit sat on a trestle table next to a ewer of wine.

His slave's midnight-blue gaze narrowed. "No."

"Something to drink then?"

She shook her head.

Shrugging, Justin moved to the table and helped himself to a small wedge of cheese and dried plums.

In truth, he didn't have much of an appetite either this evening. A boulder sat in his gut, and his temples now throbbed. His anger had eased to a simmer, yet whenever he thought of Toutorix, it flared hot once more. Justin tried *not* to think of the shit-weasel—but it was a difficult task with the man's wife sitting a few feet away.

A woman he couldn't take his eyes off. One who'd just made it clear she wouldn't let him near her.

Her reaction hadn't surprised him, although the revulsion in her eyes was a blow to his pride all the same.

She'll warm to me ... in time.

Justin lowered himself into a chair and began his light supper. However, he ate without enjoyment. Today had started badly and gone downhill from there.

Toutorix, the cunning bastard, had read him far too easily—but Justin was usually adept at hiding his emotions from others. His slave would never know just how on edge he was tonight.

Yet, as he ate, his gaze often returned to Fenella. He couldn't help it. There was something about the woman that drew his attention and made it difficult to look away.

Crouched against the tent pole, she looked uncomfortable and unhappy. But even so, his slave was lovely. The lantern light highlighted the strands of red in her brown hair and the smoothness of her pale skin.

Meeting his eye, Fenella's full mouth pursed, her jaw tightening.

"It won't be a comfortable night for you," he said, breaking the silence between them. "I'd release you from your bindings, but we both know you'd just try and escape."

"Not before I cut your throat," she growled.

Justin snorted. Earning Fenella's trust was going to be harder than he'd thought. It was just as well he was a patient man.

Washing down his last mouthful of food with a gulp of wine, Justin rose to his feet. He then unbuckled his belt and cast it aside, before removing his sandals. It was still early, but he was going to bed. Maybe sleep would ease the pounding in his skull and the knots in his gut.

"I don't understand you, Eagle." He turned to see Fenella was scowling at him. "Surely, you didn't get to your position by letting your enemies manipulate you?"

Justin's brow furrowed. He didn't need reminding of the error he'd committed today. Toutorix wouldn't fool him twice.

She was right though—his behavior was out of character. He was one of the youngest generals in the empire for a reason. Justinian Valerius Aquila was ambitious. For five years, he'd watched over this outpost, put down uprisings, and patrolled the frontier. Apart from sporadic visits to the taverna outside Ardoch, he hadn't time for women.

"I didn't," he replied gruffly, "But that was before I met you, Fenella."

Her gaze widened at this admission, but Justin let his comment lie. He might as well be honest with this woman. Even now, he was keenly aware of her, and when their gazes locked, he could almost forget what a disaster today had been.

"You don't know me," she replied, her voice roughening.

"No, I don't," he admitted, favoring her with a tired smile. "But that shall change."

Fenella's first glimpse of Ardoch was of spiked wooden palings rising against a smoke-colored sky.

Swallowing hard, she tried to ignore the frantic pounding of her heart. It was as if the Reaper stood before her with his scythe. She'd grown up within the shadow of this mighty fort—yet she'd deliberately never gotten close enough to actually see it.

How she wished she could avoid it now.

A horn announced their arrival then, the sound vibrating through the air.

Fenella's step faltered. She nearly tripped but managed to right herself. Gods, her nerves were strung tight.

Breathe, she counseled herself, dragging air deep into her lungs. *Your mind isn't sharp when you're afraid.*

Following Aquila's horse across a narrow wooden bridge, she kept her gaze upon the fort. Even from a distance, she could see Ardoch was huge—many times bigger than the largest settlement of her own people.

It rose up upon a hill, hugging the curve of the River Knaik. Like the camp of the night before, it appeared to be rectangular in shape. Dwellings fell in orderly rows to the south of the fort, around tilled fields. A sloping causeway, flanked by rows of deep ditches filled with vicious iron spikes, led up to the gates—and above the entrance reared a square wooden guard tower, where soldiers stood, their spears outlined against the sky.

Fenella craned her neck up. *Curse it, those are high walls.* Her gaze then dipped to the spike-filled ditches, and her bladder tingled. Throwing herself from the ramparts wouldn't be wise. She'd need to find another way to escape.

She sucked in another deep breath then. Aye, she *would* escape this place—the first chance she got.

She hadn't slept the night before. Instead, she'd lain upon the furs, trying to ease her chafed wrists while her mind churned. The Eagle clearly had been struck by an infatuation of sorts. He'd told her she didn't have to be his bed slave, but she didn't believe him. There was no mistaking the heat in his gaze when he looked at her. Sooner or later, he'd get frustrated and take what he wanted.

She needed to get free before he did.

Fenella walked up the causeway, her bare feet sliding on the large river stones that paved it. Before her, the entrance yawned. The heavy oak and iron gates sat open, and an iron grid with sharp metal teeth hung above them. Once this entrance was closed, there was no slipping out.

But she imagined they left the gates open during the day.

Inside the walls, noise—the roar of male voices and the rhythmic clanging of metal—assaulted Fenella. Her nostrils flared at the stench of burning peat and stale sweat.

The gateway led onto a paved street flanked by rows of low-slung, long wooden buildings. Men gathered on the edges of the street to greet Aquila and his soldiers—however, their gazes soon found Fenella. Her skin itched under their scrutiny, yet she stared back at them.

And what she saw surprised her.

She was used to seeing the enemy soldiers helmeted and wearing plate armor. She'd thought they all looked like the Eagle and the centurion he'd taken supper with the night before: tanned and dark-haired with haughty, hawkish features. But the inhabitants of this fort clearly hailed from every edge of the empire.

Her father had told her that the reach of the Caesars was wide indeed. There were men with skin even paler than her own, with ruddy cheeks and red, brown, or golden hair; and those with black hair tightly curled against their scalp, and skin the color of burnished acorn or dark walnut. Some of the soldiers were built like giants with pale eyes and pugnacious features, while others were lean and agile, with aquiline noses and obsidian eyes.

But despite their differences, all of the men watched the Eagle's prize. And as she walked by, one of them made a lewd gesture.

Sweating now, Fenella tore her attention from the ogling crowd.

Keep focused, she told herself. *Don't let them distract you.*

She needed to look out for anything that would aid her escape.

Aquila and his men traveled down the straight street to a wide space at the heart of the fort. Two buildings made of dun-colored stone with red-tiled roofs reared up before them, one slightly smaller than the other.

A row of soldiers stood at attention in front of the pillars framing the largest building's entrance. They saluted the Eagle, by slamming fisted right hands over their hearts, as he swung down from his horse. One of the soldiers—a bald, rawboned man—stepped forward from the line, his gaze sweeping to Fenella. He then frowned.

After a curt exchange, Aquila untied Fenella from his horse and handed his mount over to one of his men. He then led Fenella away to the smaller of the two buildings. The guards flanking the entrance saluted as the general walked by.

Fenella followed him inside, and the noise and stench of the fort disappeared.

It was quiet in here. The air smelled of crushed herbs, cressets burned upon the walls, and the pavers beneath her feet were cool and smooth.

A small dark-haired man clad in a knee-length tunic awaited them. His gaze swept over the general's prize, his mouth thinning.

Aquila greeted him before turning to Fenella. "This is my house steward, Caius," he said, shifting to her tongue. "He's in charge of things here."

And then, to Fenella's surprise, the Eagle stepped behind her and started untying her wrists.

"Where am I?" she asked, her pulse quickening. She'd been waiting for this moment—for when he'd finally release her bonds.

"The praetorium ... the fort commander's residence. It's my home, and yours too, now," The Eagle told her as he loosened the last of the knots. Fenella stifled a sigh of relief when he freed her wrists. The ropes had chafed at her skin, and her upper arms ached from being forced behind her all morning. She rubbed her wrists gingerly, swallowing a groan as the blood rushed back into her fingers.

She turned then, to face her captor once more.

Aquila met her gaze. "You will join my house slaves," he went on, "and take instructions from Caius. You are to share a room with another slave ... she will teach you our tongue and take you through your tasks."

Heat ignited in Fenella's belly.

I'll not learn your foul language and empty your stinking privies.

And she wouldn't warm his bed either.

She wouldn't let this man soil her—as his kind had done to this land and to so many of her people.

Aye, the walls of this fort were high, and soldiers surrounded her, but she could run like a hunted doe.

The gates were likely still open. All she had to do was get to them.

And with that, Fenella dove for the doors.

VII. NOWHERE TO RUN

SHE MOVED FAST, crashing through the doors and flying down the steps.

A shout went up behind her, but Fenella was past the stunned guards now and racing across the open area beyond.

Men thronged the square, and some of them moved to intercept her.

Head down, Fenella ducked left and right to avoid them, as if she were weaving through a stand of pines. The entrance to the street leading back to the gates drew closer, and she made for it.

Her lungs started to burn, her legs protesting—yet she pushed herself.

Speed was the only thing that would save her.

The roar of angry male voices echoed off stone, and the thunder of running feet closing in behind warned her that the Eagle would now be in pursuit.

Entering the straight street, her feet flew over the stone pavers.

She nearly collided with a cart filled with turds, towed by two men. Dodging them just in time, and ducking out of reach as one of the men lunged for her, Fenella kept her gaze focused ahead.

As she'd anticipated, the gates were still open. Daylight yawned beyond.

Freedom.

However, she was just a few yards from reaching the gates when someone barreled into her from behind.

Fenella sprawled, her knees colliding with hard stone. She bit her tongue and tasted blood. Twisting free, she scrambled to her feet—only to be shoved down once more.

Twisting around in her assailant's grip, she brought her knee sharply up, slamming it into his belly.

Aquila reared over her, his face hard, his cheekbones flushed. He grunted at the blow but didn't ease his hold on her shoulders.

"Let me go!" Fenella screeched, raking her nails down his cheek.

"There's nowhere to run, Fenella," he bit out, as she struggled under him. "Even if you made it out of the gates, we'd catch you."

"A plague on you," she snarled back. "I hope your cods rot!"

There was no getting out of his iron grip, but that didn't mean that Fenella wasn't going to fight him with everything she had.

With a curse of his own, Aquila flipped her over onto her front once more. He held her down with his knee in the small of her back, one hand keeping her wrists pinned.

Fenella bucked under him, screaming more insults, while he bound her wrists. Cheek pressed against the stones, tears of fury pouring down her face, she struggled hard.

"Enough of this, woman," Aquila snapped. "You'll only do yourself an injury."

"Kill me!" she sobbed. "My life isn't worth anything now! I'd rather be dead than a Roman slave!"

It was true. Toutorix had stripped her of all honor in the instant he'd given her to the enemy. One by one, the men in her life had betrayed her. Only humiliation and pain awaited her here.

She really would be better off dead.

Jaw clenched, Justin yanked his slave to her feet. He then turned her around and marched her back toward the center of the fort.

Of course, they'd drawn a crowd—how could they not? It wasn't every day his men saw a Picti woman racing through the fort, with their general in pursuit.

"Futuo," he muttered, marking the amusement on many of the soldiers' faces. They were enjoying this too much.

"She runs like a hare, General," an optio remarked, grinning.

"And so do I," Justin replied through gritted teeth.

In truth, he'd feared he wouldn't catch her before she reached the gates. However, fury had given him a burst of speed at the end.

His pulse pounded in his ears now, not from exertion but anger.

This woman was causing him no end of trouble. Even now, she fought his hold, her feet scrabbling on the pavers as he pushed her ahead of him.

He couldn't take her back to the praetorium, not at present. She'd only try to escape again.

She'd left him with no choice, so he took her to the pit.

It was a dark and smelly hole—a holding cell used for individuals awaiting trial or execution—at the eastern edge of the fort, behind one of the storehouses.

Fortunately, the pit was empty at present.

Aware of the curious stares he was attracting, Justin ordered one of his men to open the metal grate. He then untied Fenella's wrists and shoved her inside.

It was a drop of around six feet onto a dirt floor. His slave rolled easily to her feet, and tried to scrabble up the side, just as the metal grate came down with a resounding thud overhead.

Breathing hard, Justin stared down at her tear-streaked face.

The desperation in her eyes made his gut clench, yet he held her gaze.

"Let me out of here!" Her voice cracked, her chest heaving as she struggled with panic.

"No," Justin replied. "Not until your temper cools ... until you reflect on whether or not death really *is* better than being my slave."

Fenella's face twisted, and she spat on the ground, giving him her reply.

"Very well." Justin stepped back from the edge of the pit. His face was stinging now from where she'd clawed him. He resisted the urge to reach up and touch the wound.

Turning, his gaze swept the crowd that had gathered to gawk at the spectacle he and Fenella had put on.

Humiliation, hot and prickly, swept over Justin.

Damn Toutorix and his harpy wife to infernus—they were making him a laughing stock.

Justin strode away from the pit, cutting through the crowd, and his men fell back to let him pass. "What are you staring at?" he snarled at those closest. "Get back to your posts."

Justin hissed as Kahina dabbed some vinegar onto his cheek.

"Apologies, General," she murmured, peering close. "The grazes aren't too deep, but they will sting."

"Shall I fetch a medic from the hospital, General?" Caius asked.

Justin shifted his attention to where his house steward hovered behind his slave, before shaking his head.

"I'll be fine," he muttered. "You heard Kahina ... it isn't serious."

Caius gave a pained look at this and cleared his throat. "General," he began. "This is highly ... irregular. You can't take a woman like that as a slave ... she's a savage."

Justin snorted. Earlier, he might have disagreed with his steward. Yet now he wasn't so sure. "She'll behave once she's spent some time in the pit," he replied.

Caius made a strangled sound at that, while Kahina cast Justin a questioning look.

They were in the tablinum, the living space, of his home. Wide doors opened out into the courtyard beyond, letting in a cool breeze. This room was Justin's favorite within the praetorium. It wasn't as richly decorated as the tablinum of his father's villa north of Rome—which had frescoes covering the walls and busts of Justin's grandsire and great-grandsire—but its white-washed walls, fine oaken table, decorative urns in each corner, and two reclining couches made it a welcoming space.

Kahina had just finished tending to his scratched face, when a familiar figure strode into the room through the open doors leading out to the portico.

"It's true then?" Marcus greeted him, his gaze sweeping to Justin's scratched cheek. "Your slave tried to run off."

"She did."

"And you wrestled her to the ground, before throwing her into the pit?"

"I did."

Marcus murmured an oath under his breath, and Justin held up a hand. "Don't start, Marcus ... I don't have the patience for it." He then turned to his house steward. "That will be all, Caius. Leave us now ... Kahina, pour us some wine."

Stiff-backed, Caius departed the tablinum, while the slave went to the sideboard, where a ewer of wine and a selection of cups sat.

Marcus's gaze followed her.

Justin frowned. He'd noted the way his friend eyed Kahina whenever he paid him a visit. The behavior didn't usually bother him, although this afternoon it got on his nerves.

"Take a seat, Marcus," he snapped.

Shrugging, the primus pilus lowered himself onto the couch opposite. "So," he began, taking the cup Kahina passed him and favoring her with another smile. Kahina nodded in response, her mouth lifting at the corners, before she turned and left the room. "What are you going to do with your new slave now?"

"Nothing, for the moment. She can calm down in the pit for a day or two."

Marcus pulled a face. "And what if she doesn't?"

"She will."

In truth, Justin was beginning to sorely regret taking Toutorix's wife as his slave. But he wouldn't give up on her—not yet.

Jupiter, she had a temper, although he could hardly blame her. After all, she'd been betrayed by her husband and lost her freedom on the same afternoon.

She was proud, wild. It wasn't surprising she didn't want to be his slave.

But all the same, she fascinated him. He'd never met a woman like her.

Taking a sip of plum wine, Justin fell silent. His belly growled then, reminding him that it was a long while since his last meal. He'd eaten some salted bread and dried fruit at dawn, but nothing else. His appetite still hadn't returned, although his stomach was starting to protest.

The two men drank their wine as the aroma of the stew drifted in from the nearby kitchen. Cena, the main meal of the day, was approaching. The wine warmed Justin's empty belly, yet he couldn't relax.

Not after the humiliating scene he'd just walked away from.

His men needed a general they could respect, not one that made a fool of himself.

Caledonia was on a knife-edge these days. Ever since the Ninth had disappeared, men like Toutorix the Wolf bred dissent. The Twentieth legion was five thousand men strong, yet it often felt as if they were trying to hold back the tide.

They couldn't afford to be lenient with warmongering chieftains—but there was no denying Toutorix had bested him.

And he'd used a woman as his weapon to do so.

VIII. IN THE PIT

CROUCHED IN THE pit, Fenella cursed Aquila and all those who followed him. A few of the soldiers had stopped by during the afternoon to get a look at her. Some jeered, while others grabbed their groins and made crude gestures. But as the gloaming settled, her tormentors had eventually grown bored and let her be.

Above her, the light was fading. Soon this stinking hole would be cloaked in darkness.

Fenella screwed up her face.

Gods, did it reek. They didn't clear up after those they threw in here. Fenella had stood for a while, until her legs started to ache, before she'd tried to choose a spot that didn't have a decomposing turd in it. There she crouched, staring up at the darkening sky through the iron grate.

Bitterness filled her mouth as she waited.

If the Eagle thought this would make her submit, he was mistaken.

Her only regret was that she hadn't been fast enough to elude capture earlier.

The heavy tread of a man's footfalls approached the hole then. Tensing, Fenella glanced up, expecting to see another sneering face.

Instead, Aquila appeared.

He crouched at the edge of the grate, before pushing two items through the gaps.

"Here," he said tersely. "Grab these before they fall."

Fenella wanted to spit again. However, she knew he was handing her food and drink—and as she hadn't eaten since noon the day before, she was now light-headed and her belly ached with hunger.

Rising to her feet, she reached up, taking a bladder and a cloth-wrapped package. She then clutched the items to her breast and sank back down, resting her back against the side of the hole. She wouldn't eat or drink anything until this bastard left.

But the Eagle didn't depart—instead, he silently watched her.

He was helmetless and no longer wore his armor, clad only in a leather harness and heavy pleated leather skirt over his tunic.

"I didn't want to throw you into the pit," he said after a long pause, "but you left me with no choice."

Fenella's mouth thinned, yet she mutinously held her tongue. She just wanted him to go.

But Aquila didn't move.

"If you swear to obey me ... and not to attempt another escape, I shall let you out of here," he continued.

"I'll swear no such thing," she growled back. "I will *never* be your slave."

"You can either live in the comfort of my residence or remain in the pit," he replied, a groove appearing between his dark brows. "I should warn you though ... it gets cold in there at night."

Fenella's lip curled. She didn't care.

Aquila heaved a sigh and rose to his feet, casting one last glance down at her. "So be it," he murmured. "Perhaps you will see things differently in the morning."

"Never!"

The Eagle turned and moved away from the edge of the pit. Fenella listened to his retreating footsteps before she hastily unwrapped the package he'd passed her. It was bread and hard goat's cheese. Both were delicious—the bread salty and crunchy—and she devoured her meal. Unstoppering the bladder, she then gulped down cool ale.

Now that the edge had been taken off her hunger, and her mouth was no longer parched, resolve stiffened Fenella's spine.

Maybe Roman women weren't used to the cold, but she was. Her father had brought her up to be tough, and her time with Toutorix had made her even more resilient.

The Eagle wouldn't break her.

But by the time the dawn sky lightened, Fenella wasn't so sure of herself.

Aquila had lied—the pit wasn't cold at night. It was *freezing*.

Arms wrapped around herself, Fenella hunched in a corner of the hole, teeth chattering.

They were almost at Gateway now, the festival that marked autumn's slide into winter, and the nights had grown chill—yet this dank pit was even colder than she'd expected.

Far colder.

And as the sun rose, the chill grew unbearable.

Fenella's breath steamed before her as she climbed stiffly to her feet and started to pace the cramped space. Shivering uncontrollably, she blew on her numb hands and stamped her feet.

Gods, she wouldn't last long in here.

If it got any colder at night, she'd perish by dawn.

Above, the sky grew lighter and the rumble of men's voices punctuated the stillness. The fort was awakening.

Footsteps approached then, and wrapping her arms about herself once more, to try and control her shivering, Fenella glanced up.

Curse him, the Eagle had flown back in.

The bastard had come to gloat—or perhaps to see if the cold had killed her overnight.

It was still early; the sun had yet to crest the eastern walls of the fort. As such, Aquila's face was shadowed. Nonetheless, she knew it was him.

"Sleep well?" he greeted her.

"Go rut a dog," she replied between chattering teeth. "You filthy Roman whoreson."

He didn't respond to the insult. Instead, Aquila moved back, calling out to someone in his own tongue. A moment later, the clang of metal warned Fenella that the iron grate above her was being unlocked. It lifted then, just enough for Aquila to hand her down a large earthen cup.

Rushing forward, Fenella reached up and grasped the vessel, inhaling the aroma of meat broth. It steamed in the damp air.

Unable to help herself, she sighed as her freezing fingers wrapped around the warm cup. She took a gulp of broth. It scalded her mouth, yet she barely noticed.

"Here." Aquila passed her down another cloth-wrapped package.

Taking another, more cautious, sip of broth, Fenella reached up with her free hand and took the food.

The metal grate thudded shut.

"And what's your answer this morning?" Aquila asked, hunkering down. His gaze glinted as the first rays of morning sun bathed his proud face. "Will you behave yourself, or not?"

Fenella's fingers tightened around the package. The nutty aroma of fresh bread made her belly growl, yet she tried to ignore it.

Instead, she scowled up at the Eagle. "Let me go, Aquila." She hated to plead with him, but a night in the pit had worn her thin. "Please."

"I can't do that."

"Why not? I was a free woman. Toutorix had no right to give me to you."

The general cocked an eyebrow. "Yes, he did. You belonged to him."

Fenella's fingers clenched around her cup.

When I escape this place, I won't take another husband, she silently vowed. *Never again will I have a man determine my fate.*

"And now you belong to me," the Eagle continued. "It's best you accept that, and we can end this game."

His arrogance galled her.

"I'm not playing a game," Fenella rasped. Her voice shook, not from cold but from fury. "And you may hold me captive, but that's not the same as owning me. There are some things you can't barter, Eagle!"

Fenella passed a long, boring day in the pit.

Occasionally, someone would peer in, curious to see the general's badly behaved 'savage', but the men left her alone for the most part. The sounds of industry drifted into the hole, as well as the shouts of soldiers training. Once or twice, she caught the strains of off-tune singing.

Aquila returned at dusk with more food and another bladder of ale—and a coarse woolen blanket.

"Why give me this?" Fenella asked, even as she drew the blanket against her. The morning had started sunny, but it had clouded over at noon, the air chilling off. "Surely, the purpose of putting me in here is to make me suffer?"

Aquila flashed her a rueful smile and straightened up, nodding to the man beside him.

The grate closed with a clang.

"I want you to consider your position, Fenella," he replied, "not die of cold." He paused then, his smile fading. "It's going to be even colder tonight ... the first frost isn't far off. Without a blanket, you'll really suffer."

Fenella's belly clenched.

The Hag protect her, she didn't want another night in this hole.

Nevertheless, she drew herself up, waiting for Aquila to ask her, once again, if she was ready to behave herself.

However, to her surprise, he didn't.

"Enjoy your supper," he said, favoring her with a nod. "See you at dawn."

And then he walked off.

Scowling, Fenella waited until she was sure he wasn't coming back. Then she unwrapped the package he'd handed her, to find a large pork pie. It was freshly baked, still warm from the oven.

Hungrily, Fenella attacked it.

Frankly, the general's behavior since he'd thrown her in here confused her. He could have sent one of his men with food and drink. And he certainly didn't need to give her a blanket. She appreciated the gesture, although she couldn't help but think he was trying to manipulate her.

Finishing her meal, she took a long draft from the bladder of ale, before wrapping the blanket about her.

It wouldn't ward off all the cold, but she hoped it would keep the worst of it at bay.

A gust of wind whipped through the fort then, blowing dust into the hole and digging icy fingers into the exposed flesh on Fenella's legs.

With a muttered oath, she sank down into a corner and pulled the blanket even more tightly around her.

It was going to be another long night.

And it was.

Unlike the night before, a biting wind accompanied the cold.

Even with the blanket, it was unbearable. Fenella couldn't sleep, and nor could she sit still for any length of time. Instead, she took to pacing around the confines of her cramped hole. She stepped in a number of vile things, yet the need to keep warm made her push disgust to the back of her mind.

They were making her live in her own filth too; there was no pot for her to use. It was revolting and demeaning.

And as she walked, Fenella struggled against despair.

It was no good. This wasn't a fight she could win.

Tears of frustration burned down her chilled cheeks. She raged at fate, at the gods. Why were they so cruel? What had she ever done to offend them?

But as the night wore on, and the unrelenting chill drilled into her bones, Fenella gradually accepted her situation.

There was no point in throwing herself against the rocks, hoping they'd eventually shatter. Instead, she had to learn to scale them.

Her mind was the only weapon she had now—she had to use it.

Wits, not temper, Fen, she repeated to herself as she paced around and around. *Pretend you're beaten. Tell all the lies you have to, if it gets you out of this hole.*

Once she was in the general's household, she could begin planning a proper escape, not like her earlier opportunistic attempt that had resulted in failure. And the next time she ran, they wouldn't catch her.

But if she held onto her pride, she'd remain in this pit.

Fenella clenched her jaw, as her teeth started to chatter. *What if Aquila sees through me?*

No, he wouldn't. The man had a weakness—his attraction to her. He wanted her to submit, for it was a step closer to getting her in his bed. He was desperate for her to swear obedience.

Let him think he's beaten me, she told herself firmly, fighting against the pride that had always been her downfall. *For the moment.*

IX. SWEAR TO ME

"VERY WELL, EAGLE," Fenella greeted her captor when he appeared at dawn. "I won't try to escape again ... I promise."

Aquila frowned as he handed her food through the grate. "Your husband made a promise in one breath and then broke it the next," he replied. "How do I know you won't do the same?"

Fenella clenched her teeth. The gods curse this man. Her body ached, she couldn't feel her feet, and her eyes were gritty and sore from lack of sleep. However, she couldn't lose her temper—for she knew that wouldn't get her anywhere.

Drawing in a deep breath, she dropped her gaze. "I'm not Toutorix," she said hoarsely. "I swear I will obey you from now on."

Her throat constricted then. How those words choked her.

"Look me in the eye, Fenella." Aquila's voice hardened. "Swear to me on something that matters to you."

Clutching the package of warm bread to her breast, she raised her chin and eyeballed Aquila. "I swear," she repeated. "On The Mother, goddess of all knowledge."

Fenella whispered a silent apology to the goddess as she spoke these words. She hoped The Mother would forgive the lie.

Aquila stared down at her. His expression was wary, and for a moment, she wondered if he'd seen right through her.

Perhaps he wasn't as easy to fool as she'd thought.

Moments passed, and then he nodded.

The iron grate lifted. A moment later, strong hands hauled her out of the pit.

Fenella staggered forward, letting Aquila catch her. Fatigue and cold had rendered her limbs clumsy, and her legs nearly gave way under her. She didn't want to lean on him, but she suddenly felt as weak as a newborn foal.

"Go on," he said, not unkindly, as he propped her up. "Eat your bread."

Fenella nodded. Indeed, she was starving. With shaking hands, she unwrapped the bread, tore off a piece, and stuffed it into her mouth.

The biting wind hadn't died overnight. It howled between the storehouses and the eastern ramparts this morning. As she ate, Fenella hunched under the blanket she still wore wrapped around her shoulders.

Finishing her bread, she glanced up to see Aquila watching her. He wore an odd expression: a blend of frustration and concern. "Come." He took hold of Fenella's arm, steering her back toward the center of the fort. "Let's go inside."

Standing in the courtyard within the general's home, Fenella eyed the two individuals before her.

One was a striking woman: tall and slender with long curly black hair pulled back from fine features, peat-colored eyes, and skin the color of copper. The man standing next to her had dark-red hair and pale, lightly-freckled skin. His bright blue eyes, and the tribal tattoos on his muscular upper arms, marked him as a tribesman, most likely one of the Damnonii.

"Fenella, these are my house slaves ... Kahina and Aedan," Aquila introduced them. "As I said *before* you tried to make a break for it ... you shall take instruction from my steward, Caius, but Kahina will take you through your tasks."

The two slaves stared back at Fenella, their gazes curious. Clad in simple tunics, belted at the waist, they didn't look like the cowed, beaten slaves who served her husband—and neither wore the iron collars her own people put on their slaves.

Aquila spoke briefly in his own tongue. With a nod, Aedan walked away, returning to the pails of water he'd been filling from a well in the center of the courtyard.

Meanwhile, Kahina stayed where she was. The slave murmured something to the general, her gaze dropping respectfully.

Aquila snorted.

"What did she say?" Fenella asked. She didn't like not knowing what people were saying about her.

The Eagle glanced her way. "Kahina is happy to show you what to do ... and to teach you Latin ... but she suggests you bathe first." He paused then. "That's probably wise."

Fenella frowned. "If I stink, it's your fault," she muttered.

Aquila departed, leaving the two women alone in the courtyard. It was a wide, sheltered space, dotted with urns of cooking herbs and lined by a covered walkway. Even so, the wind still managed to find its way in.

Drawing her blanket close once more, Fenella shivered.

Kahina murmured something before beckoning for her to follow.

Jaw set, Fenella did as bid.

Feign submission, she told herself. *Try not to make enemies here on your first day.* She needed these people to trust her, to eventually grow complacent about the new addition to their household.

Only then would she be able to escape.

A few yards away, a brown and black striped cat sat upon the pavers, grooming itself. It halted its task upon spying Fenella, its topaz eyes settling upon her.

"You didn't last long in the pit, did you?" Aedan greeted Fenella in her own tongue as she walked by the well. His accent wasn't local, the cadence flatter. He wasn't one of the Damnonii as she'd thought.

"No," Fenella replied, her own response cool. "I didn't enjoy sitting in my own filth."

He huffed a laugh before his gaze raked down over her dirty clothing.

"You're not from here," she observed, fighting the urge to scowl at him.

"No, I'm Brigante."

Fenella cocked her head. The man was some way from home. His tribe dwelled in the lowlands farther south. She wondered how this warrior had ended up the property of the Eagle.

Kahina interrupted them, speaking quickly, her tone hushed yet urgent.

Aedan drawled a reply in Latin.

"What's she saying?" Fenella asked, frustrated once more that she couldn't understand.

"She's told me not to speak to you in our tongue. The general has ordered us only to communicate in Latin."

Fenella's mouth flattened. Of course he had.

Leaving Aedan to haul water, Fenella followed Kahina across the courtyard, past a profusion of honeysuckle, and into a wide covered alcove.

She then stopped short, her gaze taking in the large tiled pool before her. Steam wafted off the water, rolling toward her like morning mist from a loch.

Kahina gestured to her, making it clear she was to remove her clothes and climb into the pool.

Fenella tensed. What an odd request. What was this strange place?

Kahina spoke then and repeated the gesture, her dark gaze imploring.

"Very well," Fenella muttered. "There's no need to get worked up." She walked into the alcove and shed her blanket. Then she peeled off her soiled leather vest and skirt, letting them fall around her ankles.

Gingerly, she lowered herself into the water—and sighed.

Gods, this was an experience. She'd never bathed like this before. Fenella had grown up having hasty washes, while shivering, over a bowl of water. In the summer, she bathed in rivers and lochs, but the water was always freezing.

Murmuring in pleasure, she sank down in the warm water, letting it rise to her chin. And as she let the heat infuse her chilled and aching limbs, her eyes fluttered closed.

She hated the Caesars and everything they stood for. But she loved this pool.

She ducked under the water then, swimming like an otter from one side of the pool to the other, before floating on her back.

If she could, she'd stay in here forever.

However, it wasn't long before Kahina started gesturing again. The slave hovered at the edge of the pool, gaze anxious. She held up a large cloth and handed it to Fenella when she clambered out, dripping water onto the slippery tiles surrounding the pool.

Fenella dried herself off, and then Kahina passed her a pot of what smelled like perfumed oil, and a strange metal instrument. When Fenella merely stared at her blankly, the slave muttered something before taking the pot off her. She dipped her fingers into it and rubbed some oil onto Fenella's arm. She then picked up the instrument and scraped the oil off.

It dawned on Fenella that she was supposed to do this all over her body.

It was an odd way to clean oneself, but with a sigh, she sat down on the tiles and oiled herself. The scent of rose filled her nostrils, a welcome perfume after the stench of the pit.

While she oiled and scraped, Kahina disappeared behind the bank of honeysuckle, leaving her alone.

Fenella's pulse kicked up a notch. Two days earlier, she'd have taken the opportunity to escape. But now she resisted the urge to leap up and flee.

She'd wait until she had a plan firmly in place, for she couldn't risk the Eagle catching her again.

Fenella had just finished scraping off the last of the oil, and had to admit she liked how clean and supple her skin now felt, when Kahina returned. She'd taken

Fenella's soiled clothes away and now passed her a plain green tunic, similar to the one she wore.

With a sinking heart, Fenella took it.

Her vest and skirt might have been filthy, but she didn't want to don that slave tunic. If she did, it would be cutting the fragile thread between her old life and this one.

How could Kahina be so accepting of her situation here?

Swallowing her reaction, Fenella got dressed.

Entering his home through the atrium, Justin spied his new slave hard at work.

Slowing to a halt, his gaze settled upon Fenella, on her hands and knees as she scrubbed at the tiles of the entrance hall. A wooden pail sat at her elbow, and her brow was furrowed in concentration.

Jaw set, Fenella was scrubbing at those pavers as if they'd done her a personal injury.

Justin's mouth curved. No doubt she was imagining they were his face.

He didn't mind. He was merely relieved she'd eventually capitulated. Justin hadn't liked leaving her in the pit, especially at night, but she'd left him with little choice.

Fenella was no longer dressed in the revealing leather garments he'd captured her in, but a demure green slave tunic. However, the clothing couldn't hide her long limbs and lush curves. The slave's firm, rounded backside moved from side to side as she scrubbed, and Justin found himself staring.

He couldn't help himself.

In an instant, he imagined her naked in his bed, her pale skin gleaming in candlelight as he took her from behind. He envisaged what it would be like to unbraid that heavy plait of brown hair and tangle his hands in it, pulling her head back so that her back arched—so that delicious arse thrust up against him.

Sweat sprang up on Justin's skin, lust jolting through his groin.

Sensing someone's presence behind her, Fenella's chin kicked up. She then swiveled around, her gaze spearing his. And for a long moment, they merely stared at each other.

Justin cleared his throat, trying to ignore the ache in his balls. "Good afternoon, Fenella," he greeted her in Latin, before switching to her tongue. "You've settled in already, I see."

Her full lips thinned, and she sat back on her heels, scrubbing brush clutched in hand. The woman was bristling with resentment. She might have sworn not to escape, but she couldn't hide her displeasure all the same.

Justin wasn't gullible by nature, although after what had happened with Toutorix, his new slave likely thought so.

Fenella had been anxious to get out of the pit that morning—desperate enough to promise anything, to swear on her own life if need to be. But viewing the mutinous glint in her eye just now, Justin knew he'd need to keep a close watch on her.

X. WAITING ON THE GENERAL

"TRANSI MIHI VINUM," Fenella repeated the words. She then frowned. "Better?"

In response, Kahina nodded and passed her the ewer of wine as she'd requested. "Much."

A few yards away, Aedan snorted. "You speak Latin like a three-year-old," he said in their own tongue.

Fenella scowled. She'd been in Ardoch around ten days, long enough for her to learn a few phrases. However, she still understood little of what others said around her. Her progress was slow, and she didn't need reminding of it. "And you've got the manners of a goat," she growled back.

"Enough talk," Ava, the cook, spoke up in Latin, her tone impatient. The short, stocky woman of middling age with curly brown hair and flushed cheeks was stirring a stew that would be served for supper later, over the hearth. She then waved Fenella away, "Go!"

Grasping the ewer, Fenella made her way around the edge of the table and headed toward the door. However, once she stepped out into the portico—the covered walkway that lined the courtyard—she slowed her pace.

Many of her daily tasks in this household grated upon her, but the task she hated the most was waiting on the general. She'd rather have scrubbed pisspots.

Even so, she couldn't linger in the portico forever.

Someone would come looking for her if she didn't bring the wine.

Jaw set, she pushed her way through the door with her elbow, entering the triclinium—the space where the general took his meals. The small room had a colorful mural upon the walls, depicting a garden and flowers bathed in sunshine. Aquila and his two guests—Marcus Camillus and the camp prefect, Felix Magnus—reclined on gently sloping couches around a low table spread with roast grouse, braised onions, and bread.

Prefect Magnus was the lanky, bald soldier she'd seen greet Aquila outside the praetorium on her arrival at the fort.

As always, Caius stood in the shadows, cloth napkins draped over one forearm as he awaited instructions from the general or his guests. Spying Fenella, the steward gestured with his chin to Aquila.

She was to fill his cup first.

Moving to the legate's side, Fenella refilled his calix, a wide clay cup with a stem. And as she did so, he broke off from speaking to his companions and glanced up at her. In the light of the lantern that burned on the wall behind him, Aquila's eyes were dark gold. *Electri*—amber. She'd learned that word, for it was the name of the house cat that spent its days following Kahina around.

To her chagrin, the Eagle smiled at her.

Fenella fought the urge to scowl. She didn't want his smiles. She didn't want to pour him wine. They weren't friends. He was her master, and she hated him for it. And yet whenever they crossed paths in the past days, Aquila was amiable, charming even.

It galled her.

Swallowing her ire, she finished filling his calix before moving around the table and doing the same for his guests.

Marcus acknowledged Fenella with a nod before his gaze shifted behind her. His expression changed then, from veiled to intense.

She glanced over her shoulder to see that Kahina had entered the triclinium, carrying a tray of dried fruit and nuts. The slave had marked the centurion's stare, for she wore a flustered look.

Fenella hadn't lived here long, yet this wasn't the first time she'd seen Marcus focus on Kahina. Two days earlier, he'd smiled at the slave when she brought him some wine—and Kahina had smiled back.

Foolish girl. I wouldn't encourage him.

Turning back to her task, Fenella moved around the table to the camp prefect. Felix Magnus's bald head gleamed in the light of the lanterns. He watched Fenella with interest as she drew near and refilled his calix, before saying something to Aquila.

Fenella's skin prickled. Although she couldn't catch the words, she sensed he'd just mentioned her. The Eagle murmured a reply, and all three men laughed.

Jaw clenched, Fenella stepped back from the table and took her place next to Caius. Meanwhile, Kahina placed her tray on the table and retreated from the dining room.

Marcus watched her go.

Fenella wished she could leave as well, although as a wine-bearer, she had to wait patiently at Caius's side, in case the men wanted their cups refilled.

Glancing back at the table, her attention settled upon Aquila—which was a mistake, for he looked up, his gaze fastening upon her.

And this time, he wasn't smiling.

Justin tore his attention from Fenella and attempted to focus on the conversation he'd been having with Marcus and Felix before she'd entered the triclinium.

The woman was a distraction, and usually one he welcomed, despite her prickly temperament. However, he really had to stop staring at her like a mooncalf when his officers were around.

"Ready your men, Marcus," he said, reaching forward and helping himself to a handful of nuts. "With Toutorix still at large, we must take action."

Across the table, the primus pilus cocked an eyebrow. "We're going to hunt him?"

Justin's mouth thinned, his belly hardening. The century he'd sent after the Wolf chieftain had returned to

Ardoch three days earlier. They'd tracked Toutorix and his men from the northern shore of Lake Taus, but had eventually lost them in the mountains.

The Wolf had escaped.

Justin's mood darkened then. He wanted nothing more than to take his legion and scour the north until they flushed out his enemy. He'd strike off Toutorix's grinning head himself and mount it on a pike. Of course, his men wanted Toutorix dead too, but not as their legate did. For Justin, this was personal.

And yet common sense checked his need for vengeance. He couldn't be so reckless with his men's lives—not after what happened to the Ninth.

"We're going to re-establish our presence around Lake Taus," Justin replied, deliberately not answering Marcus's question directly. He paused then, his jaw tightening. "It's time to take back Dalginross and Bochastle. I want our outposts strong once more ... before the first of the snows. If Toutorix intends to stir up more trouble, we need to be ready for him."

Marcus nodded, his gaze gleaming in the lantern light. "Losing those forts was a real blow," he agreed. "We can't let the Picti continue to control them." Indeed, earlier in the year, they'd lost the two smaller forts that had been built to watch over the glens and straths leading into the mountainous north. "However ... we're going to need more men for the campaign," Marcus continued, swirling his calix of wine meditatively.

"There's a detachment coming from Eboracum," Justin assured him. "It should be here in a few days."

Justin had made the request as soon as he returned from Lake Taus. Eboracum had the resources, for Hadrian had moved the Sixth legion into the large fort in northern Britannia, after the decimation of the Ninth.

Marcus flashed him a smile. "I'll prepare my cohort to march then."

Across the table, the camp prefect's face had tensed. Felix shifted uncomfortably in his seat. "What if the Wolf manages to rally the northern chieftains, General?" He paused then, frowning. "Can Dalginross and Bochastle hold them at bay? The men speak of ill-omens of late ... of a change in the wind. They fear we will end up isolated and sacrificed ... like the Hispana."

An icy finger trailed down Justin's spine. Like his men, he marked omens. Nonetheless, he had to stand firm. "We won't," he countered firmly.

All the same, he'd noted the change at Ardoch over the past year. The men were quieter, and he'd caught mutterings on the walls. They were all out here on a limb, on the very edge of the empire. Trajan had sent the Ninth into the wilds, to their deaths, to bring order and secure peace. Would Hadrian use the Twentieth in the same way?

Raising the calix to his lips, Justin took a sip of wine and pondered their situation.

Men like Toutorix the Wolf could easily spell their downfall.

That was why they had to be ready for him.

Felix and Marcus departed after cena, but Justin remained within the triclinium, finishing his calix of wine. Fenella came and went, clearing up the empty plates and cups. She'd just wiped down the table, and was about to retreat to the kitchen, when Justin caught her eye.

"Fenella ... how are you settling in?" He used her tongue. Kahina had told him she was slowly learning Latin. However, it was too soon to expect her to converse with him in his language.

Fenella halted mid-turn before swiveling back to face him. Her expression was now carefully blank, even if the sharpness of her gaze gave her mood away.

"Well enough," she replied.

"Are your lodgings comfortable?"

Fenella nodded before her brow furrowed. "Why is it that you can speak my tongue?"

"Aedan taught me."

She pulled a face. "Why make the effort at all?"

Justin shrugged. "You can't rule a people if you can't communicate with them ... and I don't trust interpreters."

Fenella eyed him before she folded her arms across her front. It pulled the material of her tunic tight, revealing the fullness of her breasts. He could still see the hard outline of her nipples, and despite that he'd been talking easily with her until now, Justin's nervus—his member—sprang to attention.

Mithras spare him, this woman had a visceral effect on him, one that seemed to be growing in intensity with each passing day. His senses sharpened whenever he saw her. He looked forward to their exchanges, however brief. Unfortunately, Fenella's attitude toward him hadn't thawed. He'd hoped that once she settled into his household, she'd lower her guard. But she hadn't.

"Am I to be kept forever locked up in this house?" Fenella asked, a brittle edge to her voice.

Justin shifted upon his reclining couch, in an effort to ease his pulsing groin. "Don't you like this residence?"

Fenella's features tightened. "I'm used to having freedom of movement. Now the only contact I have with the outside is a patch of sky in the courtyard." Her throat bobbed then. "I miss seeing the world around me."

Their gazes fused, the moment stretching out.

Jupiter, he could stare into those midnight-blue eyes for eternity.

"Well then, we shall remedy that," Justin replied. "Once you've finished in the kitchen, you and I shall take a walk on the walls."

XI. UPON THE WALLS

FENELLA FOLLOWED AQUILA up the wooden steps to
the top of the walls.

Breathing in the scent of wood smoke, mingled with
the aroma of cooking meat, she drank in the sight of the
pink-streaked sky and the purple-etched mountains to
the northwest. Dusk was settling, and the air held a sting
to it. The sky was clear, promising a crisp frost the
following morning.

Fenella let out a long breath, a sudden lightness
filtering over her. She hadn't lied earlier—day after day
cooped up inside the praetorium was slowly grinding her
down. It was a relief to see the world again.

Nonetheless, there was another reason she wanted to
get out of that house.

How could she start planning her escape, if she didn't
explore the fort?

Stepping up onto the walls, Fenella was careful to
shutter her expression when the general turned to her.
Aquila had just unwittingly handed her an opportunity.
She wouldn't squander it.

"Take my arm," he ordered, holding his out to her. "I
wouldn't want you to fall off the ramparts."

Fenella stiffened. She didn't want to touch him, and
yet the Eagle could drag her down off the wall and back
to the praetorium whenever he wished. She needed to do
as she was told.

Inhaling sharply, Fenella moved closer to the general
and linked her arm through his. They'd both donned
cloaks to ward off the chill, yet he wore a short-sleeved
tunic underneath that left his arms bare. The feel of his

naked flesh against hers was a discomforting sensation. His muscles were sculpted, rock-hard, his skin warm.

Side-by-side, they began a stroll down the eastern wall. Fenella noted this was where the main entrance to the fort was located, with a high wooden guard tower looming above it. She'd been dragged into the fort through this gate. Glancing down, she counted five spike-filled ditches.

Fenella's mouth flattened. No, she wouldn't be escaping that way.

Reaching the end of the wall, they turned down the long side, which faced south over a small settlement and fields of crops. Here, she counted only two sets of ditches to traverse. Even so, she'd have to leap like a spring buck to avoid being impaled.

Curse it, why do the Caesars build such well-defended forts?

To keep her people out, of course.

Moving down the wall, they passed men on the watch. The sentries snapped to attention as the general walked by.

"Is it usually this quiet?" Fenella asked, her gaze shifting from the settlement to the roofs of the buildings within the fort itself. From this height, she spied two wide streets bisecting the fort, with the principia—the headquarters—and the praetorium at the heart of it.

Aquila glanced her way, clearly surprised by the question. Indeed, it was rare she spoke without snarling at him. "At this time of day, it is," he replied. "Although, after dark, my men grow nervous."

Fenella arched an eyebrow. "Why is that?"

Her belly tensed then. She hated speaking to this man, but she had to keep her dislike leashed for now. She wouldn't learn anything useful otherwise.

"We've been here a few years now," he answered, "but ever since Pinnata Castra fell in the north, Ardoch stands alone."

"Pinnata Castra," Fenella murmured before realization dawned. "You mean Inchtuthill?"

Aquila nodded.

"Toutorix told me there was a battle there ... three winters ago." Indeed, she recalled the gleam in her husband's eyes as he recounted the tale. The most powerful of the Cruthini chieftains had banded together with the local tribesmen, and together they'd drawn a net around the Roman army as it marched north. By the time the Caesars made their final stand at Inchtuthill, there were few of them left.

None had survived that battle.

The Eagle's expression turned grim then. "The Ninth legion passed this way ... on their journey north." His gaze shifted, looking to where the mountains reared against the darkening sky. "Five thousand men ... lost."

Fenella studied his profile, and despite that she'd wished every last Roman dead many a time, her skin prickled.

"Five thousand," she whispered. "That many?"

Aquila's attention swept back to her. "I worry sometimes ... that Valeria Victrix will suffer the same fate. The men fear it too ... and that is why the fort slumbers uneasily."

Fenella took this in, her brow furrowing.

So the Eagle wasn't made of stone, after all? The discovery should have pleased her, yet disquiet settled in the pit of her belly. She didn't want to see him as anything other than a beast.

They were halfway along the southern wall now, and she noted that there were, indeed, two more gates: one that led south into the settlement, and one that faced north. As they skirted the guard tower, a deep rumbling sound punctured the silence.

Fenella peered down at the shadowed street below. "What's that noise?"

"It's almost dark; the gates are closing."

She marked that too.

They walked on, and when they reached the eastern wall, Fenella glanced at the Eagle's proud profile once more. "I don't understand why you stay," she said, breaking the silence between them.

Aquila halted then and turned to face her. "I've been ordered to hold Ardoch, and I shall."

"But Cruithentúath isn't your home ... you owe it nothing."

The Eagle's gaze narrowed. "Caledonia belongs to Rome now."

Fenella lifted her chin, eyeballing him. "Men like Toutorix believe differently."

"You admire that bastard, do you?" Aquila's voice roughened.

"No," Fenella ground out, heat igniting in her blood. She'd been wondering how long it would take for the Eagle to vex her. "But I understand what he's fighting for."

Aquila studied her face, curiosity upon his own. "How was it that you came to be wed to the Wolf?"

Fenella frowned. "Why do you ask that?"

The Eagle's golden gaze grew limpid. "I'm intrigued by you," he said, his voice lowering. "I wish to know your story."

Fenella covered her discomfort with a scowl. She didn't want him to be intrigued by her. She didn't want him to look at her like that either.

It made her feel all hot and strange.

Her jaw tightened then.

If he made a grab for her, she'd knee him in the cods.

"My father promised me to him," she admitted finally. "The Wolf saved his life in battle once ... and in return, my father owed him a favor."

Her belly clenched as she remembered that awful day when her father had betrayed her, when Lorcan had let her down, and when the Eagle had spared her life.

It wasn't so long ago, and yet it felt like another lifetime.

"So, it wasn't your choice?" Aquila asked.

Fenella shook her head. "I hate my husband."

The general favored her with a wry look. "Since before or after he handed you over to me to save his own neck?"

Fenella gave a bitter laugh. "Before ... long before."

They continued walking, although it was Aquila who broke the silence this time. "How old are you, Fenella?"

She cast him a sidewise glance, wondering at his line of questioning. She sensed he was trying to lighten the mood, and she appreciated the gesture, for she didn't want to talk further about the men who'd betrayed her. "Twenty-one winters," she replied. "I was born at Mid-Winter ... under the eye of The Hag ... and you?"

In truth, she didn't care to learn anything about this man. However, she had to play this game if she ever wished to taste freedom again.

Wits, not temper, she reminded herself.

"I'm thirty-three and was born upon the Ides of October," Aquila replied. When this statement received a blank look, he smiled. "Around a moon before Gateway ... under the guardianship of Mars. Every year upon the day of my birth, I make a sacrifice at his altar." Aquila's mouth lifted at the corners then. "As a child, my mother used to make me wear my best clothes on that day, but she'd bake me a special cake too."

Fenella tried to imagine the Eagle as a child. Did the man actually have a mother? "And this 'Mars'? What god is he?"

"He protects the crops and livestock ... but he's also the god of war."

Fenella couldn't help but harrumph at this.

In response, Aquila flashed her a disarming smile.

They'd nearly circuited the walls now and were approaching the steps they'd climbed earlier. Fenella's walk up here was almost at an end.

Her breathing quickened. Gods, she didn't want to return to the praetorium, to the drudgery of her days.

The sun had just slipped beyond the dark swathe of pines to the west. The sight of the woodland brought back memories of Fenella's old life, before she'd resided at Loch Tatha. Back when she'd spent her days hunting and dreaming of a new life with Lorcan.

The pines also reminded her of something else.

"I never understood," she said, turning to Aquila, "why you spared me." He favored her with a questioning look, and Fenella gestured to the pinewood. "On the day we met."

Aquila reached up and scratched his jaw. Dark stubble shadowed it. The men had lit braziers upon the wall, and firelight bathed the contours of his face.

"I don't really know," he replied after a long pause, his voice lowering as his gaze met hers. "You caught me by surprise … and I acted on impulse."

Fenella's lips pursed. "Like you did at Loch Tatha?"

Aquila snorted and drew back, unlinking his arm from hers. "Indeed. It seems you wield some strange power over me, woman."

XII. IO SATURNALIA

Dalginross fort

Five weeks later ...

JUSTIN LUNGED FORWARD, jabbing his blade into the warrior's belly. He then drew a pugio and slit the man's throat, choking off his howl of agony. The warrior had tried to drive a pike into his armpit—but he'd failed. Shoving the dead man away, Justin stepped over his twitching body.

"The fort is secure," Marcus called down from the walls. "That's the last of them."

Glancing up at the primus pilus, Justin nodded. Blood dripped from Marcus's lorica—his plate armor— but Justin guessed it wasn't his own, for the man stood straight, his face still feral from the fight. "All the same, check all the buildings," he ordered. "Make sure no one's hiding."

A horn sounded then, echoing through the fort. The *cornu* gave a long, drawn-out wail. The sound was almost haunting, and it raised the hairs on the back of Justin's forearms.

Victory.

Shrugging out his shoulders, Justin surveyed the surrounding fort. Dalginross had seen better days, that was for certain, but its spiked wooden ramparts were still intact. His men would make the necessary repairs, and then he'd leave a garrison here—with twice the men as last time.

Dalginross would hold the line.

Climbing up onto the walls, stepping over the fallen as he went, Justin's mouth thinned.

The Picti had given them quite a fight.

It soured his mouth to see so many of his own soldiers among the dead, flashes of steel and crimson amongst blue-painted faces and tattooed limbs.

The men who'd made this fort their home had been unwilling to relinquish it.

However, it galled him further still that few of the Picti they'd killed bore Wolf markings upon their bodies. There hadn't been a whiff of Toutorix either.

The weasel had indeed gone into hiding.

Standing upon the guard tower, Justin let his gaze sweep over the green wooded vale below. A river, the Water of Ruchill, glittered in the wintry light. The sun was trying its best this morning, yet Justin's breath steamed in the cold air.

Mid-winter was upon them. The following day marked the beginning of Saturnalia.

The past month had been a blur.

As soon as reinforcements from Eboracum arrived, Justin had mobilized his army. It had taken them a fortnight to take back Bochastle, and scour the hills around the outpost, before turning their focus upon Dalginross.

But now it was done. The entrances to the wide glens that led into the mountains were secure once more.

A grim smile curved Justin's mouth.

He could return to Ardoch now—to Fenella.

His brow furrowed then. Not that his slave would welcome him home. He'd hoped their walk on the walls together would have gained her trust a little, but in the days before his departure, Fenella had retreated into surliness once more.

It hadn't stopped him from thinking about her ever since though—in the quiet moments, when he wasn't marching, laying siege, or fighting, she plagued him.

Their conversation on the walls had surprised him. He hadn't meant to be so open with her, although she'd revealed more about herself than she'd likely meant to. It didn't surprise him she'd been forced into marriage with Toutorix, although he noted the bitterness she still carried with her as a result.

He wanted to converse with her again, to listen to the low, musical lilt of her voice and gaze into her dark-blue eyes as she told him more about herself.

Mithras, you've got it bad.

Justin sucked in a deep breath and swiveled, his bloodied and rent purple cloak billowing behind him.

Enough of this. He was pining like a callow youth. Justin had a fort to make safe.

"Lupa!"

Halting on the steps before the general's residence, a tray of food and drink balanced on her hip, Fenella scowled.

She knew enough Latin now to understand that the soldier who'd called out from where he was going through drills on the parade ground had just called her a slut.

The man earned a barked reprimand from his centurion, but the other legionaries leered.

Fenella glared back at them. It was unfortunate that 'she-wolf' in Latin was used to insult a woman, for among her own people, it had a positive connotation—just further proof of how different the Caesars were to the Cruthini.

"May the Reaper freeze off your bollocks," she muttered, descending the steps.

Indeed, it was certainly cold enough this afternoon. The air was raw. They were in the depths of winter now; the 'Long Night' was approaching, and icicles hung from the edge of the portico that ran around the house's open courtyard.

Fortunately, she was warmly dressed. For the bitter season, she and the other slaves had donned long-

sleeved tunics, woolen leggings, and short ankle boots.
Around her shoulders, Fenella wore a goat-skin wrap,
which helped keep the chill at bay.

But despite the cold, she welcomed any chance to
leave the praetorium.

Sometimes the walls felt as if they were closing in on
her; Fenella's world had grown small indeed since she'd
come to live at Ardoch. Apart from that one walk on the
walls, she saw little beyond the interior of the general's
residence.

Aquila had been away for weeks now, and she'd
enjoyed the reprieve. She could go about her tasks
without fear of bumping into him, and she no longer had
to endure awkward conversations or lingering looks.

Instead, she could focus on plotting her escape.

Two days earlier, Ava had sent her out to collect a
sack of oats from the granary. Pulling a cart behind her,
and ignoring the hot gazes of gawking men, Fenella had
noted that both gates—the Porta Principalis Sinistra and
Porta Principalis Dextra—remained open from dawn to
dusk. The Porta Principalis Dextra—the 'right gate'—was
the busier of the two, as it opened out into the vicus, the
settlement beyond the walls. However, she'd also
counted half a dozen soldiers warding both gates, with
the same number atop the guard towers. Fenella's mood
had soured as she'd hauled the cart back to the
praetorium. How was she supposed to slip out when they
were so well guarded?

Reaching the bottom of the steps now, Fenella paused
once more. Whenever she ventured outdoors, in fact, she
always took careful note of her surroundings.
Unfortunately, she saw nothing helpful this afternoon.
There were soldiers everywhere, and towering wooden
ramparts surrounded her on all sides.

"Move on, woman," one of the guards flanking the
doors behind her spoke up. "Stop dawdling."

Casting the man a sour look, Fenella reluctantly
continued walking. She skirted the edge of the building,
to where Aedan labored at the furnace. Unlike the other
members of the household, the Brigante wasn't swathed

in furs and wool this time of year. Instead, his face gleamed with sweat, his short dark-red hair plastered against his scalp. He spent his days now hauling fuel and stoking the furnace that kept the residence warm.

Seeing her approach, Aedan straightened up, wiping his sweating brow with the back of his arm.

"At least this task keeps you warm," Fenella greeted him.

He grunted, taking the tray she passed him: a meal of bread, cheese, and dried plums, and a cup of warmed wine. He then tore into it. She watched him eat. The Brigante was as lean as a hound, and he had an appetite like one.

Fenella sidled up to the glow of the furnace, warming her numbed fingers by it. The wind today cut like a blade through her clothing. It came from the north and had a dank smell that promised snow. Straightening up, her gaze went, once more, to the high wooden ramparts that rose beyond the granaries. Helmed figures moved about the wall, their pilums bristling against a washed-out sky.

Maybe if I can steal some rope, I can creep up there at night ... and climb down from the Porta Principalis Dextra, she mused. She'd require a weapon though—for she'd have to stab a guard or two. Her brow furrowed then. She'd also need to find a way of getting out of the praetorium at night. No easy feat.

She was still studying the wall when a snort drew her attention.

Aedan watched her as he ate, his blue eyes sharp. "Planning your escape?" he asked with his mouth full.

Fenella started slightly, discomforted that he'd read her so plainly. "Don't tell me you've never tried?" she said in their own tongue. Whenever she was around Kahina or the others, she was forced to communicate in her clumsy Latin. However, they were alone now.

"Of course I did ... in the beginning," he replied, before draining the cup of wine.

Fenella raised an eyebrow. "And?"

Aedan shrugged. "It was a few days after I was taken prisoner. We'd fought the Romans and lost ... Aquila picked me out of the line of men who'd been captured. First, I tried to grab his pugio and stab him with it ... but when that went awry, I took off like a hare through his camp. They caught me before I reached the walls."

Fenella inclined her head. "How long have you been the Eagle's slave?"

"It's been over six years now," Aedan handed her back the empty platter.

"And you just accept this life ... that you'll never taste freedom again?"

The Brigante's mouth pursed. He then shrugged as if he cared not. Nonetheless, Fenella had spied the glint in his eye, the way his jaw tightened. She'd hit a raw nerve.

"So, you taught Aquila our tongue?" she asked, deciding it best to change the subject. She didn't want the Brigante to learn of her plans, for she didn't trust him.

She didn't trust anyone in the general's household.

"Aye," Aedan replied, heaving himself up off his stool and stretching out the muscles of his shoulders and back. The man worked so hard all day, she imagined he slept like the dead every night. "It didn't take him long either. He's sharp."

Fenella pulled a face. Aye, he was, although Aquila had already proved he wasn't infallible.

"Io, Saturnalia!" Justinian Aquila held up his calix.

"Io, Saturnalia!" Everyone else at the table, except Fenella, called out, raising their cups.

Brow furrowed, Fenella lifted her calix to her lips and took a sip of rich plum wine. Gods, it was delicious. However, she'd never understand these Caesars and their ways.

Aquila had returned victorious from the north. He hadn't captured Toutorix, but he'd taken back two fallen outposts. Fenella's grasp of Latin was strong enough now that she'd understood snatches of conversation between Caius and Ava. Now, a day later, the general's household sat around the scrubbed oak table in the kitchen, drinking Aquila's best wine. Before them sat a meal of suckling pig stuffed with apples and walnuts. Boughs of ivy and candles decorated the kitchen.

Aquila and Caius both wore daft-looking cone-shaped hats.

They were two days into the festival of Saturnalia. It took place at the same time as Mid-Winter Fire, when her own people would be feasting on oaten honey cakes and dancing around a bonfire.

Fenella's chest ached as she wondered if she'd ever see a Mid-Winter Fire again.

Of course you will, she told herself sternly. *You're going to get out of here ... just be patient.*

As she looked on, Aquila began carving the pork onto platters. "A fine roast, Ava," he commented.

The cook preened. "I ordered the pig from a farmer months ago ... he fattened it, especially for Saturnalia."

Passing Kahina some bread, Fenella leaned in close. "Why is Aquila sitting with us?" she whispered.

Kahina favored her with a timid smile. Despite that the two women shared their sleeping quarters and often worked together during the day, Kahina was wary of the general's new slave. Fenella could hardly blame her though, for she was usually terse and snappish with her.

"Saturnalia is a time when the roles are reversed in a household," Kahina murmured. "Masters serve their slaves. Last year, the general hosted us all in the triclinium."

Fenella glanced the Eagle's way. Even in that silly hat, he cut an imposing figure. However, it didn't seem right that he sat in the cramped kitchen with his servants and slaves. She tried to imagine Toutorix breaking bread with *his* slaves, and her mouth twisted.

"Is the wine not to your liking, Fenella?" Aquila asked.

Fenella's spine snapped straight. Curse him, the man was always watching her.

"The wine is good," she replied stiffly.

The Eagle smiled. "I'm glad to hear it."

"Pork?" Caius held out a platter, piled high with meat.

Fenella's mouth watered. Her meals usually consisted of bread, cheese, boiled eggs, and dried fruit, with vegetable stew for supper most evenings. Roast meat was a treat indeed.

Aquila's presence was putting her on edge, as had his smile—but she wasn't going to refuse this delicious feast.

Nodding, she helped herself.

XIII. OUTSIDE THE WALLS

CRUNCHING THROUGH THE snow, Fenella and Kahina made their way toward the Porta Principalis Dextra. Both women carried wicker baskets and wore heavy fur cloaks about their shoulders, their feet pushed into sturdy boots. Their breathing steamed in the gelid air.

"Ava's given me quite a list this morning," Kahina told her before ticking the items off on her fingers. "Fresh fowl … pig's liver … eggs … cabbages … and onions."

Fenella nodded, although she wasn't paying much attention.

She was too busy trying to calm her racing heart.

Finally, after nearly three moons at Ardoch, she was venturing outside the walls. There was a market in the vicus, and Kahina needed help carrying all the items the cook had requested.

She had to seize the moment. It was time to run.

Looking up at the colorless sky, Fenella frowned. It was a snow sky, warning that another blizzard wasn't far off—poor weather for travel. Even so, it couldn't be helped. Fenella knew the land around the fort well. She'd find somewhere to shelter—a safe place the Eagle and his men would never find her.

Glancing over her shoulder, she eyed the four legionaries who shadowed them.

I'll have to lose these idiots first.

The two women cut right onto Via Principalis. Rows of granaries rose up on one side of the street, opposite storehouses and lean-tos housing ovens. Through open doorways, Fenella spied cooks kneading dough, while others shoveled flat loaves into the red glowing maws of great ovens with large paddles. The nutty aroma of baking bread drifted across the street.

They were nearing the gates, when a man wearing a helmet bearing a proud red fan stepped forward to intercept them.

Marcus Camillus raised a hand in greeting. "A cold morning for an outing?"

Kahina patted her empty basket, gazing up at him through lowered lashes. "It can't be helped ... Ava's stores are getting low."

Marcus stared down at the slave, his expression softening. "You look well, Kahina."

A shy smile graced her lips. "Thank you," she murmured.

Marcus and Kahina watched each other, the moment drawing out, before one of the guards behind them cleared his throat.

Marcus snapped out of his reverie and stepped back, his attention shifting to Fenella. His gaze narrowed then, the good humor draining from his face. "The general's letting you out of the fort?"

Fenella nodded, tightening her grip on the basket. Irritation crept into her voice when she replied, "What of it?"

The centurion snorted and shifted his focus to the four men following them. "Stay close to her," he warned. "Don't let the woman distract you."

"Yes, centurion," one of the men replied. "The general has ordered us not to let her out of our sight."

Fenella ground her teeth. *Bastards.*

They could dog her heels if they wished, but they wouldn't catch her when she ran.

Marcus stepped back, flashing Kahina another smile. "Enjoy the market."

The women passed through the gate and made their way down a slippery slope, flanked by two sets of ditches and ramparts. At this angle, they were even wider than she'd thought. Fenella was athletic, but even she couldn't have jumped them.

Glancing across at her companion, she noted Kahina's pretty mouth was curved into a secret smile; she appeared lost in thought.

Fenella frowned. "Don't trust him."

Kahina's peat-dark gaze snapped up, her smile vanishing. "Excuse me?"

"The centurion ... if you let him, he'll take advantage of you."

Kahina's lips parted, her features tightening. "Marcus is a good man," she replied, her voice catching. "We've been friends for years now."

Fenella cocked an eyebrow. "That wasn't a 'friendly' look he was giving you back there," she pointed out. "Make sure he never gets you alone."

Irritation spiked through her then. What did she care if Marcus ended up using and mistreating Kahina? After today, she'd never see her again.

Ready yourself, Fen, she counseled herself as they reached the bottom of the slope. *You'll only get one chance.*

Ahead, she surveyed the neat rows of dwellings, the dark smoke from their cook fires staining the morning sky. The civilian settlement lay outside the walls of the fort, in the bend of the river. On the fringes of the vicus, the colorful awnings of market stalls stood out against the white snow. The cries of hawkers, both in Latin and in the Cruthini tongue, carried in the stillness of the icy morning.

Behind the village, Fenella spied the snow-frosted high wooden walls of another structure. It was shaped like a large roundhouse, but without a roof.

"What's that?" she asked, pointing.

"That's the arena," Kahina replied stiffly. Glancing back at her, Fenella saw that the woman's face was tense, her gaze unhappy. She'd clearly offended her. "It's where they hold games ... and fights. Sometimes they use slaves ... especially for death matches."

Fenella scowled at this revelation. "Of course they do," she muttered.

They reached the market, and Kahina made her way toward where a man was selling freshly butchered fowl. The hapless birds hung by their feet, dripping scarlet blood onto the pristine snow.

Fenella followed her. Yet, all the while, her gaze swept over the busy stalls and the shoppers. As she'd hoped, there was a decent crowd, which would make escaping easier. She noted a few Roman women among them. Most of them dressed like servants—clothed in plain tunics, heavy cloaks, and boots—like Kahina and Fenella. However, there were one or two of them who wore jewels upon their earlobes, their hair swept up in elaborate styles.

Fenella watched, fascinated as one such woman walked by, followed by two servants carrying baskets laden with food. Elegant and haughty, she wore a long tunic, with a fine woolen shawl draped over the top. This garment fell from her left shoulder and draped over her right arm. Amber gleamed from her earlobes.

"Who's that?" Fenella asked, leaning close to her companion.

"I don't know," Kahina replied, not looking Fenella's way. "Likely one of the magistrates' wives."

Fenella waited behind her companion, watching as Kahina haggled over the price of the fowl. Eventually satisfied, the slave paid for the food with small bronze coins she carried in a pouch at her waist. They ventured farther into the market then, buying the pig's liver, before heading toward the array of vegetable stalls.

Fenella's pulse quickened, and despite the cold day, she started to sweat.

She'd spied a break in the line of stalls to her right and a gap between two houses behind. This was her chance—and she'd take it.

Kahina stopped before a stall selling cabbages and greeted the vendor. Meanwhile, Fenella surreptitiously edged right. She didn't dare glance back at her escort, although she knew the men stood just a yard or two behind her. It was risky to try and distance herself, yet she wanted as big a gap as she could manage between them when she made her break.

Muscles tensing, she readied herself to throw her basket at them—a distraction that would gain her precious moments—when the resonant call of a horn shook the cold air.

Breath catching, Fenella turned toward the sound.

"The Mother," she murmured. "What's that?"

"A patrol is returning," Kahina replied, casting a quick glance over her shoulder. "They're coming our way ... look."

The horn blasted again, nearer this time, and the crowd parted, admitting a procession of legionaries, their armor gleaming despite the wintry light. Both women turned to watch their approach.

"They've got prisoners," Kahina observed.

Indeed, as the soldiers marched toward them, Fenella spied a row of men, wrists bound. They were her people—men with night-dark, oaken or russet hair; pale skin; and light eyes—proud warriors, their cheeks still streaked with blue woad.

Fenella stared at them, her planned escape suddenly forgotten. She realized then that they were heading toward the arena. Her palms gripping the now heavy basket turned slick. The Caesars were to make sport of their captives.

"Fen!"

Her name echoed across the crowd.

I know that voice.

Heart thumping against her breastbone, Fenella looked down the line of Cruthini captives—and then her gaze locked with a familiar pair of midnight-blue eyes.

A tall youth with a gash to the forehead, his long brown hair tied back at his nape, was staring at her. His hands were bound before him, and he walked with a limp.

For a long moment, they stared at each other, the rumble of the surrounding crowd and the rattle of armor disappearing.

Fenella's mouth went dry. "Eogan," she croaked. "Gods, no!"

Justin eyed the bedraggled woman standing before him. Two guards flanked Fenella. Her clothing was dirty and wet, her hair in disarray. She had a graze on one cheek, yet still managed to wear a defiant expression.

They stood in the commander's office inside the fort headquarters. He'd been writing a report for the emperor when his men knocked on the door. They'd then dragged his slave in.

With a sigh, Justin pushed himself up from behind his desk. His gaze then rested upon Fenella. "Did you try to escape?"

His slave raised her chin, her dark-blue eyes narrowing.

Justin frowned. He'd allowed her to accompany Kahina to market, and this was how she repaid him?

"She didn't try to run, General," one of the legionaries answered. "She tried to free a captive."

Justin stiffened. "What?"

"We were bringing in the Picti scouting party we caught north of here to the arena ... when one of the warriors recognized her," the soldier went on. "She then attacked a soldier escorting him and tried to take his sword."

Silence fell in the office, while Justin digested the legionary's words. He'd been in good humor today, for they'd finally managed to catch some of the elusive Wolves—men he planned to question at the arena shortly. But this news soured his mood.

Justin moved around to the front of his desk. "I will deal with this," he said quietly. "Leave us."

The two men did as bid, the heavy doors thudding shut behind them.

Justin leaned against his desk and folded his arms across his chest. His gaze raked over Fenella, and he noted she was shaking.

"Are you cold?" A brazier burned a few feet away, taking the chill off the air. Nonetheless, it wasn't warm in his office. Unlike his residence, the hypocaust system didn't heat the rooms of the principia.

She clenched her jaw, shaking her head.

"Who was he then?" Justin's belly twisted as he asked the question.

Jealousy.

It made sense she'd have a lover—for Fenella had been unhappily married to Toutorix. He should have thought of it before.

When Fenella finally answered, her voice came out in a rasp. "My brother Eogan."

The demon twisting Justin's gut relaxed its hold. *Her brother?*

"He's young," she gasped. "Barely a man. Please spare him."

Justin snorted. "Old enough to wield a blade though."

Fenella's throat bobbed. "Your men were leading him toward the arena ... I know about your *games*." She hauled in a deep breath. "You pit slaves against each other like dogs."

"So you've learned of our ways, have you?"

"It's wise to learn all you can about your enemy."

"I'm not your enemy, Fenella," he replied, his ire rising. "I thought we'd established that."

She took a step toward him, her eyes wild now. "Then prove it ... set him free."

Justin pushed himself up off the desk, looming over her. "I don't think so. He may be able to provide me with information on Toutorix. Also, you attacked one of my men ... that cannot go unpunished." He paused then, his gaze fusing with hers. "A life in the ring isn't such a bad one for a warrior. If he's unlucky enough to be selected for a death match, there are worse ways to die than with a blade in the hand. And you never know ... he might survive ... and go on to be a gladiator. Such men eventually win their freedom."

Fenella's face blanched. His words had just alarmed her further. "Please," she repeated, choking the word out. "What will it take?"

Justin frowned. "Excuse me?"

"If you free him, I will give myself to you," she blurted. Her high cheekbones flushed then. "That's what you want, isn't it?"

A brittle silence stretched between them.

Justin swallowed. Mithras, he couldn't believe she'd just offered herself to him. And curse him, he'd longed to accept. But, of course, the woman wasn't willing—just desperate.

"It is," he ground out finally, "but not like this."

XIV. ALL FOR NOTHING

THE SNOW WAS falling when Fenella finished the last
of her chores.

Putting away her pail and scrubbing brush, she
moved stiffly. Her hands were chapped, her knees sore.
As punishment for her transgression, she'd missed cena
and supper, and had spent the rest of the day scrubbing
down the atrium, tablinum, and triclinium. She wasn't
allowed to retire for the evening until she'd finished.

Heavy flurries drove into the portico as Fenella made
her way back toward her sleeping space. A thick white
crust covered the courtyard, and snow made the pavers
beneath her feet slippery. Snow had even driven into the
inset alcove she passed: a shrine to the Lares, the
household gods.

It was late. Everyone else within the general's
residence had gone to bed.

Shivering, Fenella pulled her wrap tightly against her.
Head bowed against the swirling snow, she quickened
her pace. However, heaviness dogged every step—not
just from fatigue but despair.

Today had been her chance for freedom, yet she'd lost
it. She'd spend the rest of her life scrubbing Roman
floors and pisspots—a cur to be ordered about.

Worse still, Eogan had been taken prisoner and could
die in the coming days.

She'd even humiliated herself before Aquila, but it
had been all for nothing.

The ruthless bastard wouldn't relent.

Despite the chill, heat rose to Fenella's cheeks. His
rejection still stung. She didn't understand the man. Ever

since taking her from Loch Tatha, he'd made no secret of his attraction to her. But, following her offer, his expression had turned to stone. He'd almost looked disgusted.

Fenella's face burned hotter still at the memory. *How will I ever face him again?*

Slipping into the cubiculum, the small chamber she shared with Kahina, Fenella closed the door gently behind her. It was getting late, and she didn't want to wake her companion. However, Kahina had left an oil lantern burning for her.

Moving quietly across to her sleeping pallet, Fenella's throat thickened. Her vision then misted, and she blinked rapidly. She'd shown Kahina little warmth over the past months—especially today—and yet the woman was still kind to her.

Kahina had a good heart. Unlike Fenella, she hadn't let bitterness corrode her.

The lantern's flickering flame illuminated the lime-washed walls of the room and the outline of the cat's resting form at the foot of Kahina's sleeping pallet. Although Electri had warmed to Fenella, she always slept upon Kahina's bed.

Removing her wrap and heeling off her boots, Fenella tried to quell her shivering. It was colder than the Reaper's breath outdoors tonight, and although the furnace Aedan kept stoked took the chill off the walls and floor in here, freezing air still managed to find its way in.

Sliding onto her sleeping pallet, she pulled the blankets up around her chin.

She was just about to pull the shutters down on the oil lamp when Kahina stirred and rolled toward her, her dark eyes fluttering open.

Wordlessly, she observed Fenella for a long moment. "That man today," she murmured finally, "who was he?"

Fenella huffed a sigh. "My brother." Silence fell in the cubiculum before she continued, her chest tightening. "I don't imagine Aquila's done with punishing me. Will he have me whipped?"

"I don't think so ... he's never touched me."

Fenella's mouth quirked into a tight smile. "No, but you aren't as troublesome as me."

Kahina's dark eyes twinkled. "That's true, although Aquila isn't a cruel man." Her expression shadowed then. "Not all masters are that way."

Fenella observed Kahina, frowning. She knew little about the woman who'd become her daily companion, other than she hailed from a Roman colony called Numidia—a land far to the south, which was dry and hot, and had palm trees and vast deserts. "How many masters have you had?"

"Three," Kahina replied, rolling over and staring up at the ceiling. "I was sold to a slave trader at the age of ten to pay my father's debts. My first owner was a merchant ... a huge, sweaty man with a wife and children. As soon as I began my moon bleed, he started visiting my bed. Once his wife discovered what he was up to, she flew into a rage and ordered him to sell me."

"That must have been a relief?"

"It was ... for a short while." Kahina didn't remove her gaze from the ceiling as she continued. "He sold me at a market in Siga, a busy port in the north of Numidia. My new owner was a horse trader. With him, I traveled the empire."

The words were simple, yet Fenella caught the edge to them. "He, too, came to my bed regularly. But he also beat me," Kahina continued. "Sometimes with his fists ... sometimes with a stick. And once, when I tried to defend myself, he took a whip to me."

Fenella's mouth thinned. The bastard sounded like Toutorix.

"My husband was violent too," she admitted. "He beat his first two wives ... and it was rumored that one of them died after a hiding." As always, her belly curdled when she thought about the Wolf. "But I always fought back."

Kahina took this in, her eyes widening. They were very different women, slaves from opposite edges of a vast empire. Kahina was gently-spoken and kind, while

Fenella's wild spirit raged against the confines of her narrowed world. Yet, here they were, both serving the same master.

"So how did you end up with Aquila?" Fenella asked after a pause.

Kahina's mouth quirked. "The horse trader got into a fight one eve … in a tavern in northern Gaul. Someone stabbed him in the eye. I was put to market once more, and the general bought me … and I'm glad he did. He has always let me be."

Fenella pulled a face. "You can't tell me you're happy here … so far from home?"

"I left Numidia behind many years ago. My father sold me like one of his camels. I don't miss him."

Fenella frowned. "A camel?"

"It's a beast … a bit bigger than a horse, with long legs and a fatty lump on its back. They can travel great distances in the desert." Kahina pulled a face then. "But you must be wary of them … they can be ill-tempered … and they spit."

Fenella's gaze widened as she tried to imagine such a beast. "You've seen so much of the world," she murmured. "What do you think of Cruithentúath?"

"Your land is beautiful … and wild," Kahina replied, before she hiked the blankets higher up under her chin. "Although I wish it were warmer."

With a sigh, Fenella rolled over, her gaze also fixing upon the beams that crisscrossed the ceiling. "You've been kind to me, Kahina," she said softly. Suddenly, it felt as if a boulder sat on her chest. Kindness was harder to weather than brutality, it seemed.

Fenella had never had any female friends. Growing up, she hadn't been close to her younger sisters and put-upon mother. And then when she'd become Toutorix's wife, his female kin, and even the slaves, had been wary of her. "I'm sorry about what I said today," she continued. "About Marcus."

Kahina didn't reply. Fenella glanced her way, noting the slave's guarded expression. Unsurprisingly, she didn't trust her.

Fenella favored her with an apologetic smile. "I've a poor opinion of men ... and it sometimes makes me blunt-tongued. Your friendship with Marcus is none of my business."

Silence stretched between them before Kahina heaved a deep, sad sigh. "I would like us to be more than friends ... and so would he ... but it's impossible."

Fenella's brow furrowed. "Why? Surely, Marcus could ask Aquila to free you so you could be together?"

Kahina swallowed. "Roman soldiers aren't permitted to marry while they're in service to the empire ... although the law isn't always followed, especially out here on the frontier." She paused then, looking away. "All the same, the magistrates would never allow him to wed a former slave."

"I hear your slave's brother has turned out to be quite a fighter," Marcus huffed as he parried Justin's blow. The two men fought with blunted blades in the practice ring on the edge of the parade ground.

Justin grunted, striking again. "I'm surprised he's still alive."

And he was. A month had passed since the warrior had been taken captive. They weren't out of winter yet, for spring came late this far north, yet the air wasn't quite as raw. The arena put on games every few days. They were good for the army's morale, especially after months of bitter cold.

Justin hadn't attended any of the matches, although he'd expected the young Wolf to have fallen by now. In truth, he tried not to think about Eogan. The warrior was a reminder of his slave, and how much she hated him.

Ever since he'd refused to spare her brother, Fenella had barely looked at him. Any attempts to converse with her were met with icy silence. However, he'd marked the tension on her face, the worry shadowing her eyes. She wanted to know how her brother fared, yet pride prevented her from asking.

At the time, Justin had stood by his decision, harsh as it was. He couldn't give in to his slave's demands; it would make him look weak.

The Wolves they'd taken prisoner were all dangerous men, and loyal ones too. He'd questioned them the day of their arrival, but had learned nothing about their camp, their plans, or their chieftain. It had quickly become evident that not even torture would loosen their tongues—and as such, he'd let the arena have them.

But with the passing of the weeks, Justin had started to regret taking such a hard line where Fenella's brother was concerned.

She would never warm to him now.

"He's quick ... and mean," Marcus replied, lunging forward with an attack of his own. "I saw him fight a few days ago. He was impressive." Their blades collided, a dull clang reverberating off the surrounding walls. "The Wolf Cub is fighting The Dacian this afternoon ... in a death match. Why don't you join me in the stands?"

Justin snorted. "I'm too busy." He then shoved hard, sending Marcus reeling.

However, the centurion was agile. He rolled to his feet before attacking once more. "Come on, Justin. The game promises to be a spectacle. Everyone in camp is talking about it."

Parrying Marcus's blows, Justin ducked under his guard, slamming the flat of his blade across the man's belly.

Gasping, the centurion staggered. Seizing his opportunity, Justin knocked Marcus's blade from his hand and sent it flying into the dirt. The soldiers awaiting their turn at the edge of the practice ring cheered. They always enjoyed watching the legate and the primus pilus spar.

Breathing hard, Justin eyed his friend.

Marcus cast him a rueful look and rubbed his torso. "The Dacian is a formidable fighter," he wheezed.

"I know," Justin replied. He'd heard of the former slave who'd won his freedom in Londinium. He was reputed to stand at nearly seven foot and to be built like an ox. "But can the Wolf Cub beat him?"

Marcus shrugged. "He just might."

The two men walked from the practice ring, making way for the next two soldiers. They took cloths from a waiting attendant, and wiped their sweating faces and brows, before heading toward the armory. On the parade ground, men were going through drills, and so Justin and Marcus skirted the wide space.

The thud of feet and the rattling of armor, shields, and spears drifted through the crisp morning air. The shouts of centurions mingled with the rhythmic clang of weapons being hammered into shape at a nearby forge. Carts rumbled past, filled with large sacks of wheat, barley, and oats bound for the granaries. A fort the size of Ardoch required a lot of grain, for the men lived on bread and a mash made of grain, milk, butter, and salt.

Justin surveyed the activity around him, his mouth curving. "The men seem happier of late," he noted.

Marcus cut him a look. "Taking back Dalginross and Bochastle makes them feel more secure." He then grinned. "And they're looking forward to this afternoon's game."

"This peace won't last," Justin reminded him, his mood sobering. Their outposts were still secure, and the frontier had gone very quiet of late. Yet he didn't trust the silence. "Toutorix is still at large ... and who knows what trouble he's been stirring up." His gaze fused with Marcus's then. "After the match, ready your men ... we will ride out on another patrol tomorrow."

XV. THE WOLF CUB

FENELLA WAS BEATING mats with a paddle when
Aquila strode into the courtyard. She spied him out of
the corner of her eye yet ignored the man. He'd move on
when it was clear she wouldn't acknowledge him.

But he didn't.

Instead, the Eagle stalked right up to her and halted.

"Fenella," he rumbled. "Turn around."

Clenching her jaw, she gave the mat she'd been
beating a final two thwacks—much harder than was
necessary—before eventually turning to him. A cloud of
dust swirled around them, and her nose itched, a sneeze
building.

Blinking as her eyes watered, Fenella stared at the
leather breastplate of the harness he wore over his tunic.
She refused to meet his eye.

The general coughed, stepping back to distance
himself from the dust. "Your brother is competing in a
death match this afternoon," he informed her.

Fenella's pulse started to thunder in her ears. *Eogan's
alive!* Relief weakened her limbs, although panic
followed close on its tail, cramping her belly. *A death
match?*

Her gaze snapped up then, and for the first time in a
moon's turn, she looked at Aquila fully. "Come to gloat,
have you?"

The Eagle's lantern jaw tensed. "No, I wanted to bring
you to see him ... in case he falls today."

Fenella's fingers clenched around the paddle. Gods,
how she wished to swing it at his face. "How benevolent
of you," she growled.

Aquila's dark brows drew together. "If you don't wish to speak to him, I can leave you to your chores."

Mouth twisting, Fenella threw her paddle down. It clattered across the pavers, causing Electri, who'd been sunning herself nearby, to leap to her feet and dart away. "Take me to my brother then."

Aquila eyed her, as if he was reconsidering his offer, before turning away. "Very well," he replied curtly. "Follow me."

Jaw clenched, Fenella followed him out of the praetorium and into the busy street, where four guards awaited them. Above, the watery sun was trying its best to cast some warmth over the world. As always, the fort was a flurry of activity and noise, although Fenella paid her surroundings little note.

Instead, her thoughts were on her brother.

Eogan was good in a scrap. Thank the gods, he still lived.

I have to see him.

Aquila led her through the fort and out of the Porta Principalis Dextra. Their escort tailed them, their gazes boring into Fenella's back. They would be waiting for her to bolt, but Fenella was too distracted by thoughts of Eogan to think about running this afternoon. Instead, she focused on keeping up with Aquila. He didn't speak to her on the way, and Fenella had to quicken her stride to a slow jog at times to match his long stride.

As they walked, she marked the looks they were attracting from those they passed. The men would be wondering why the general was taking his slave for a walk. Aquila ignored the stares. Instead, he strode on, leading the way through the wooden gateway and down the causeway into the vicus.

Beyond the walls, the early afternoon light gilded the skeleton trees and fallow pastures surrounding the vicus. Spring was a moon's turn away; the earth was still sleeping.

The Eagle led her across the empty market clearing and then between rows of neat wooden homes, up a straight street that led to the arena. A crowd had gathered before the entrance. Hawkers selling hot food wove through the throng. The aroma of fried garlic and the rise and fall of excited conversation drifted back toward Fenella and Aquila.

Her belly twisted. *Entertainment ... that's all it is to them.*

They approached the arena, yet instead of entering the circular structure through the wide gates, Aquila led her right, to a fenced area attached to the back. He took her through an archway into a small courtyard flanked by a low, windowless wooden building.

And there, standing in the midst of the open space, stood her brother.

Fenella scanned the courtyard for any sign of guards, but Eogan waited alone. He was barefoot and wore leather trews and vest. His hair, which had once been as long as her own, had been hacked short, and blue woad streaked his face.

Her throat tightened. He looked like he was about to go into battle.

Murmuring an oath, Fenella rushed to him, crushing him in a hug.

Eogan hugged her back, his grip as fierce as her own. "It's good to see you, Fen," he said roughly.

Fenella drew back, meeting his eye. "I wish I could do something to stop this."

Her brother's mouth twisted, his blue eyes gleaming. His gaze flicked then to the tall figure that had stopped near the entrance to the courtyard. Aquila's men had also halted, a discreet distance from their general, awaiting his order. Eogan glanced back at Fenella, his expression searching. "Why has he let you see me?"

Fenella swallowed. "I don't know."

Eogan's mouth thinned. She saw it then, the suspicion in her brother's gaze. He thought her Aquila's bed slave, and that she wielded influence over him.

But he was wrong on both counts.

Pushing aside the hurt that Eogan was so willing to think the worst of her, she stepped closer to him. "I begged him to spare you," she said, her tone urgent now, "after I saw you that day ... but he refused."

Eogan's gaze roamed over her face before it skimmed downward, taking in her slave tunic and sandaled feet. "You look ... well."

"Do I?" she rasped.

Fenella moved sideways then so that her back blocked the general's view of her brother. This was her only chance alone with him; she wouldn't waste it.

"We have to be cautious," she murmured, careful to keep her voice low, without whispering, which would only make Aquila and his men suspicious. "The Eagle speaks our tongue."

Her brother nodded, his gaze wary.

"Fenella," Aquila's voice carried over the yard. "Say your goodbyes now ... the match starts soon."

She cut the Eagle a sharp look then, resentment bubbling up. Curse him, she wished he wasn't standing nearby. She wished to speak frankly with Eogan, but she knew he would be listening.

Swallowing once more, she stepped forward and gripped her brother in another hard hug.

"I intend to escape," she hissed in his ear, "and I will ... soon."

"Good," came his whispered response. "Ready yourself, Fen ... an attack is coming at the next full moon."

Fenella stepped back, her heart galloping. "May the gods be with you, brother."

A slow smile stretched Eogan's lips in reply, and it struck her how much he'd matured of late. Her brother was a warrior now and carried himself with the same arrogance as their father did. "They always are, sister."

Marcus hadn't exaggerated. News of the fight between The Dacian and The Wolf Cub had spread throughout the fort and the vicus beyond. Spectators packed the wooden seats that made up the tiers of the circular Ardoch arena, giving the event a festive atmosphere.

Justin took his place next to Marcus in the magistrates' box in the first tier. In more heavily populated areas, four magistrates administered the civilian towns outside forts, yet Ardoch had just two. Of course, both men were present this afternoon, and their faces lit up at the sight of the legate joining them.

"Should be a good fight, General," one of them called out.

"I hope so," Justin replied.

"Great day for it," the second magistrate added, beaming.

"Indeed," Marcus agreed. "Some sun at last."

Justin had only just settled into his seat, when a food hawker entered the box and sidled up to its occupants. "A sausage, General?"

A delicious aroma wafted over Justin. He had to admit the sausages, which had been charred on sticks over a brazier, looked good, although he wasn't hungry.

"Here." Marcus pressed a coin into the man's palm and helped himself to a sausage. The magistrates also decided to indulge, digging into the purses at their belts for coin.

Meanwhile, Justin settled back in his seat, his gaze surveying the arena. It had been some time since he'd attended a game. Death matches weren't that common in this arena. They were expensive to run, for gladiators were hard to come by on the edge of the frontier, and they'd soon exhaust their supply of slaves if men died at the end of each match. However, they'd recently acquired a new cohort of slaves. One of the magistrates had sponsored this match, and owing to the interest in The Dacian and The Wolf Cub, this fight was to be to the death.

And the promise of blood had drawn men and women alike. Ardoch arena wasn't grand—not like the vast stone stadiums in other parts of the empire. Nonetheless, it was well maintained, and they'd carted in sand from the coast to cover the floor. Arena attendants were just finishing raking the sand smooth, ready for the next fight. As soon as they withdrew, trumpets blared, causing the excited chatter in the stands to settle.

Moments later, the gladiators' gate at the far end of the arena swung open. A huge man swaggered into view. This was The Dacian. Justin viewed him with interest; reports of this man's size hadn't been exaggerated. He was a giant with tanned skin and a bald head that gleamed in the sunlight. Under one arm, he carried a horsetail crested helmet, and over his shoulder hung a shield.

The crowd roared its greeting, and the gladiator strutted up to the magistrates' box across the fresh sand and saluted them. He had the weathered, scarred face of a seasoned fighter, and observing him, Justin realized why he had stopped attending fights over the past years.

Death was something he saw daily; he didn't need to pay to witness it. And unlike the whooping crowd—many of whom were calling out to the gladiator, while others threw coins and flowers his way—he didn't hunger to see blood spilled.

Instead of fighting in the arena, a talented man like The Dacian should have been a soldier, defending the walls of Ardoch.

Grinning at the adulation, The Dacian circuited the space, waving to the crowd.

Moments later, a smaller, slighter figure entered the arena.

The cheering died, replaced by heckling and catcalls.

However, The Wolf Cub ignored them.

Fenella's brother Eogan stalked across the sand, helmet under one arm and a short sword in the other. Like his opponent, he also carried a shield slung over his back. The warrior stopped before the magistrates' box, saluting them as his opponent had. His gaze, the same midnight-blue as his sister's, swept the faces of the men in the box before it alighted upon Justin.

And for an instant, their gazes fused.

A look passed between them. The Wolf Cub's expression was as hard as his gaze.

The crowd were throwing things at him now—not coins and favors but pebbles and rotten food. Yet Fenella's brother continued to ignore them.

The trumpet sounded once more, silencing the mob, and Eogan turned away, taking his place opposite The Dacian. Although tall, The Wolf Cub stood at least a foot under his opponent's height, and he lacked the man's bulk.

Both men turned and lifted their blades high, saluting those sitting in the magistrates' box one last time. They then jammed their helmets on their heads.

The fighters circled each other, blades and shields raised, while the baying of the excited crowd settled to an expectant rumble. Sunlight gleamed off The Dacian's oiled muscles, and off both men's helmets and blades.

The Dacian attacked first, moving forward with startling speed and grace for one so big. The Picti was ready for him, raising his shield to block the blow before dancing back out of range.

The crowd roared, the sound echoing high into the air.

A few yards from the magistrates' box, a finely dressed woman—a merchant's wife most likely—was on her feet shouting like a fishmonger. "Coward!" she screeched.

"They get excited about death matches, don't they?" Marcus noted from next to Justin.

Nodding, Justin kept his attention on the two gladiators, who were circling each other once more. "Just as long as they're not the ones in the ring, they do," he replied.

XVI. BECAUSE YOU ASKED ME TO

THE DACIAN ATTACKED again, his short blade thudding against The Wolf Cub's shield. However, this time, instead of dancing out of harm's way, the warrior side-stepped and followed up with a swift counter-attack.

His sword clipped The Dacian's shield arm, cutting through his leather bracer.

Dark blood dripped onto the sand, and the big man snarled a curse, backing off a few strides.

"I told you the lad was fast," Marcus murmured.

"They all are," Justin replied. "Even their women."

He thought of Fenella then, his belly tightening. He'd sent her back to the fort, flanked by all four of their escort. He'd thought the tension between them would ease, now that he'd let her see her brother. But the vicious look she'd given him, before his men led her off, warned otherwise.

"I've never understood why the Picti teach their women to fight," one of the magistrates piped up. He was licking sausage grease off his fingers as he watched The Dacian strike hard, his bellow thundering across the arena. "It's a barbaric practice."

Justin didn't reply. He was too busy watching the fight unfold. Both men were skilled fighters, and despite the size difference, evenly matched. The Dacian struck boldly, using his bulk and strength to his advantage, while The Wolf Cub darted in like a striking serpent, slipping under the bigger man's guard.

It wasn't long before both men were bleeding heavily, blood dripping onto the churned-up sand. Yet neither of them slowed, and their attention never wavered from their opponent.

Eogan's fighting style grew gradually more aggressive as the fight wore on. He parried less and went for his opponent in a series of vicious cuts that left dark scores in The Dacian's shield.

The two men's blades became a blur, the ringing sound of steel mingling with the bawling of spectators in the stands. Sweat gleamed off their faces, and the blue paint on the Picti's face and chest became smeared with blood.

There was a moment when Justin thought Eogan might win—when he used a deception tactic against his opponent. The younger man lunged forward, gladius swinging in for a strike aimed at The Dacian's head. The big warrior raised his blade to counter the blow, but instead of following through, the Picti kicked him in the groin.

His opponent bellowed and staggered backward. The crowd roared, insults raining down upon The Wolf Cub now. However, Eogan was lost in his own world. Eyes slitted, sweat pouring down his face, he lunged once more—clearly hoping to take advantage of this moment.

But The Dacian was not so easily defeated. Such a blow to the cods would have felled many men, but despite that he was doubled over, his tanned face twisted in pain, the big man managed to fend off his adversary's blows.

And then, when he'd recovered, The Dacian went in for the kill.

Like everyone in the crowd, Justin watched the gladiator with awe. There was a reason The Dacian's prowess in the ring was famed throughout Britannia and Caledonia. The man was a mountain.

Snarling, he went for The Wolf Cub, raining down heavy blows upon his shield until the wood splintered. The Picti fought back with savagery, but it wasn't enough. The two men were fighting in front of the magistrates' box now, and Justin could see that Eogan was starting to tire. There was only so much a man could withstand.

The Dacian was dauntless.

The seasoned gladiator fought like a man possessed now, his face a rictus. Finally, he got close enough to his opponent to smash him in the face with his shield, before he kicked The Wolf Cub's feet from under him.

Eogan crashed to the ground.

The Dacian threw aside his bloodied and scarred shield and knelt on his opponent's chest, raising his gladius above him, both hands on the hilt. He was readying himself to drive the blade down through the younger man's throat.

Yet, even as he stared death in the eye, the young warrior snarled up at his opponent, his gaze goading.

"Halt!"

The Dacian froze, and the crowd settled, silence falling over the arena. The onlookers' gazes flicked between the gladiator and the legate, who had risen to his feet in the magistrates' box.

"General?" The Dacian rasped.

"You fought well." Justin's voice echoed through the stands. "But the match ends here."

Gasps and mutters of outrage rippled through the arena.

"What's this," one of the magistrates sputtered. "I paid for a death match!"

"Justin," Marcus warned from next to him. "This isn't usually how it's done."

Justin ignored them both. Instead, his gaze remained upon The Dacian.

He couldn't let Eogan die. If he did, Fenella would loathe him for eternity.

And so he raised his hand and held up a closed fist with his thumb wrapped around his fingers.

The rumbles of discontent in the stands grew louder. Anger darkened the faces of many of the spectators, yet they all knew better than to speak against the legate of Valeria Vitrix.

General Aquila had spoken. Mercy had been given. The Wolf Cub's blood wouldn't stain the sand crimson this afternoon.

Fenella walked along the portico toward the tablinum. Her belly pitched as if she sat in a rowboat upon a storm-tossed loch. Dusk had settled over Ardoch, and a chill, damp wind had sprung up. Returning from the arena, she'd resumed her chores. However, her thoughts had been on her brother and the fight.

At one point, she'd heard the roar of the crowd in the arena. Heart slamming against her ribs, she'd straightened up from potting herbs.

What did that sound mean?

There was no way to know.

But now the Eagle had sent for her—and she would find out whether or not Eogan had survived the fight.

Heart in her throat, Fenella halted before the doors to the Eagle's living space. She then heaved in a deep breath, squared her shoulders, and knocked.

"Enter."

Pushing open the doors, Fenella stepped inside and closed them behind her. She halted then, spine pressed against the doors and every muscle tense, while her gaze swept straight to the man seated upon one of the two couches in the center of the space. Even in repose, dressed in a fine purple knee-length tunic trimmed with gold, a cloak of the same color draped over one shoulder, Aquila exuded coiled energy.

Aquila's amber gaze speared hers, and then he rose to his feet with the same easy grace she'd seen Electri display, and placed the calix of wine he'd been cradling upon a low table.

Anxiety now beat like a caged raven in her chest, but she forced herself to move away from the doors. Walking forward, Fenella halted a few feet from him. "Is he dead?" She blurted out the question, unable to bear not knowing any longer.

"Your brother lives," he replied, moving forward to face her.

Fenella exhaled sharply. She hadn't even realized she'd been holding her breath. "Eogan bested his opponent?" Pride constricted her chest. She should never have doubted him.

"No," Aquila replied, his gaze not leaving hers. "He fought well, but eventually the fight turned against him. The Dacian was about to finish your brother when I interceded." He paused there. "I've set him free."

For a few moments, she merely gaped at him, trying to make sense of his words.

Aquila had spared her brother? Eogan had his freedom?

"Why?" she eventually croaked, finding her tongue.

The corners of his mouth lifted. "Because you asked me to."

Fenella stilled. Suddenly, all she could hear was the pounding of her own heart. Only this time, anxiety wasn't the cause.

Feral rage washed over her—and she forgot to be wary of this man, forgot that she was his property to do with as he wished.

Snarling, she flew at him. Her fists beat against his chest. Her knee came up sharply. She'd make sure this bastard never fathered a child. However, Aquila shifted back, and her knee collided with the hard muscle of his thigh. He then caught her by the wrists.

The surprise on his face would have been almost comical, if she hadn't been so angry. As it was, she just wanted to flatten his nose.

"Why the fury?" he muttered, holding her fast as she writhed against him. "I thought you'd be relieved. Isn't this what you wanted?"

"Whoreson!" she spat. "You threw Eogan to the dogs for a month ... and you waited till the very end to save him."

He frowned down at her. "It wasn't like that ... your brother was part of a scouting party, sent to gather information on our defenses. In freeing him, I've risked much." He paused then, a muscle ticking in his jaw. "I saw you whispering with your brother earlier ... what passed between you?"

"Nothing that matters," she growled back, heat pulsing like an ember under her ribs. He'd have to roast her alive to get the truth. She wouldn't betray her people.

"Don't lie to me, Fenella." Aquila's voice hardened, his dark brows crashing together. His own temper was quickening now.

Her mouth twisted. "You like playing with other people's lives, don't you? It makes you feel powerful."

"I didn't have to save your brother," Aquila growled. "But I—"

"Did it for me?" she cut him off, seething now. "Why? You thought I'd be so grateful I'd *happily* spread my legs?" She twisted her wrists hard, but the bastard held her in an iron grip. "Why go to so much trouble, Aquila? The whole fort already thinks I'm your whore, why don't you just—"

The Eagle's mouth crashed down on hers, stopping her tirade.

The kiss was bruising and so sudden that Fenella forgot to struggle.

An instant later, he let go of her wrists and took a rapid step back. "Get out, woman," he rasped. His face was all taut angles, his eyes glittering. "Now!"

But Fenella didn't go. Instead, something snapped within her. Drawing her arm back, she struck him, hard across the cheek.

They stared at each other, and then Fenella did something that shocked herself.

She grabbed him around the neck, yanked his head down to meet her, and kissed him back.

Aquila went rigid—as surprised as she was by her move. But he recovered swiftly, hauling Fenella into his arms, his mouth slanting across hers once more. His tongue forced her lips apart and drove into her mouth. His kisses were hot and wild, and she matched him.

It was war of the sweetest kind.

He walked her backward then, slamming them both against the doors.

Fenella barely noticed. She was too busy devouring him. Justinian Aquila tasted of wine, spice, and musky maleness. His body against hers was hard, dominant, and she writhed against him, an ache blossoming between her thighs.

All thought had fled her mind now. She acted on instinct alone.

But to her surprise, Aquila drew back.

Hands on her shoulders, he pushed himself away from her.

Breathing hard, their gazes fused.

Fenella hadn't ever seen Aquila like this: his lips were swollen from the violence of their kisses, his high cheekbones flushed, and his eyes dark with hunger.

But as the moments passed, the haze of lust fogging her mind drew back. Sanity returned. Fenella sagged against the door, her legs going weak under her. *Gods, what am I doing?*

Likewise, Aquila's gaze cleared, a muscle ticking in his jaw.

Releasing her, he reached forward and fumbled for the door handle. "You need to go," he rasped, biting each word out.

This time, Fenella heeded him.

Not taking her gaze from the Eagle, she walked backward. The doors opened behind her, and she stepped out onto the portico.

Glowing lanterns bathed the colonnaded walkway in gold, and somewhere beyond the praetorium, the strains of a harp carried through the crisp evening air.

But Fenella hardly noticed. Tearing her gaze from Aquila's, she turned and fled back to her quarters.

XVII. IN THRALL

Seven miles north of Lake Taus

ICY RAIN PELTED the soldiers as they made camp for the evening. A howling wind accompanied it, causing muttered oaths and pinched faces on those struggling to erect tents. Justin walked amongst his men, watching as the marching camp rose around him. The weather had turned mid-afternoon.

Justin shouldn't have been surprised—the climate in Caledonia was notoriously fickle. Even so, he'd been enjoying the milder temperature and the sun on his face. The change in the weather reminded him how unpredictable this land could be—in all aspects.

Circuiting the rectangular camp, he viewed the wooden perimeter that had just gone up. Beyond, his men had dug ditches and lined them with vicious iron spikes. They had to be cautious in this country, for this patrol led them to the edge of the mountains. To the north, purple-grey peaks rose against the slate-colored sky: a reminder that they were skirting wild lands.

Looking to those mountains, Justin scowled. *What's Toutorix hatching in there?* The man's silence made him twitchy.

Thinking about Toutorix was a mistake; it reminded him of Fenella.

Dragging a hand down his face, he mumbled an oath. Jupiter, he'd made a mess of things with Fenella. All his adult life, he'd been in control—a man who knew what he wanted, and usually got it. But with her, he was at sea. He felt as if his wits were unraveling.

He hadn't meant to kiss her that evening. And when she'd responded in kind, his blood had caught fire. Even a week later, he could still feel the sting of her lips against his, could still taste her.

And now his belly was in knots.

She was his slave, yet he was in her thrall. Want for her was driving him slowly mad.

Why didn't you take her then?

Oh, he'd wanted to—but he'd known, even as their tongues dueled, even as his hips ground against hers, that once her ardor had cooled, Fenella would resent him even more than before.

She was right, he could have made her his whore. But instead, he wanted her as his lover. However, these days he was beginning to worry she'd hate him forever.

"The scouts have returned, General."

Justin turned to see an optio striding toward him, head bent against the wind. "Take me to them, Decimus," Justin greeted him with a tight smile.

The two men fell in step, making their way through the camp.

After visiting Dalginross and Bochastle, and ensuring that everything was in order at the outposts, Justin had led his patrol northwest to clear out the hills of warbands.

He'd brought the first cohort of the Twentieth with him—the most prestigious of the nine cohorts that made up the legion, and the one that Marcus, as primus pilus, led. The first cohort consisted of five double-strength centuries, and when they marched, they brought the legionary standard and its golden eagle with them.

They passed the eagle on their way through the camp. The men had driven it into the ground next to his tent. The great bird crouched atop the standard, its spread wings dull under the grey skies and driving rain.

Wiping the rain out of his eyes, he squinted up at the bird, the *aquila*. The men often said that it boded well that a man who bore the same name as the symbol of their legion led them. They could be a superstitious lot.

Marcus was already talking to the scouts when Justin and the optio drew near. The men were hunched under oilskins, their short hair slicked against their skulls.

"Let's hear it," Justin greeted the soldiers, not bothering with a preamble. All of them wanted to get out of the rain and wind.

"We've found their camp, General. The Wolves of the North have built a new crannog," one of the men reported. "Upon a small lake in the heart of the Cairngorms."

Justin flashed him a hard smile. "Well done. How many men does he have with him?"

"Two hundred, at least," another soldier said, blinking rain out of his eyes.

Justin considered this. Two hundred wasn't that many. Perhaps the Wolf hadn't found the allies he sought, after all.

"Since we know where Toutorix is, do you want to go after him?" Marcus asked then. Justin glanced his way to see his friend's dark gaze glinting. He wanted the Wolf dead, almost as much as his general did.

Justin considered it before shaking his head. The Cairngorms were perilous: a labyrinth of steep, pine-clad valleys and ice-cold rivers and ponds. He'd ventured into the mountains a few years previous, when pursuing a raiding party, and had been fortunate to emerge with half his men still alive.

"Toutorix will have the advantage in such terrain," he said after a pause. "And he'll see us coming." It was true. The Romans fought best in open battle, whereas the Picti preferred ambushes, using the landscape to their advantage. "It's best to wait."

His gaze swept the bedraggled line of men. They'd spent the last fortnight scouting in the mountains—dangerous work indeed, for Romans were not welcome north of here. "Anything else to report?"

"Nothing, General," the first man replied. "We spotted no warbands on our travels. The Picti are keeping to their hearths at present, it seems."

"That's good news, at least," Marcus spoke up once more. "Well done, lads."

Justin's gaze narrowed. It *was* good news. Why then did his belly harden and the hair on the back of his neck prickle?

"I heard what happened with your brother."

Fenella glanced up from where she was washing the supper dishes in a pail of water upon the kitchen table, to find Aedan in the doorway. "Aye, the whole fort will be talking about it," she replied.

Outdoors, beyond the shadow of the portico, the wind and rain pelted down. As such, the Brigante closed the door behind him.

Lips thinning, Fenella went back to her task. She'd almost finished cleaning up after supper and was keen to retire to the warmth of her cubiculum.

"You don't look happy about it." Aedan sauntered around the table before leaning up against a workbench. His sky-blue eyes settled upon her. "Why is that?"

Fenella's fingers clenched around the earthen cup she'd been washing. "I don't like being indebted to anyone, least of all the Eagle."

In truth, she didn't want to think about General Aquila at all. Her last encounter with him had left her shaken and confused. She'd been relieved when he'd departed on patrol the following day, yet each passing dawn brought his return closer.

She tried to keep busy in the interim—not difficult as Caius and Ava always had something for her to do—but memories of that savage kiss still intruded. And curse her, if heat didn't pool in her lower belly and her breathing quicken whenever thoughts of Aquila surfaced.

She hated the man, and yet she'd kissed him back with a wild need that had matched his. Disappointment had swept over her when he'd pulled back and told her to go. She'd berated herself about her 'weakness' ever since.

Aedan's mouth curved, his gaze glinting. "You're a proud Cruthini woman."

Fenella huffed a laugh as she placed the cleaned cup on the table and reached for the last dish. "Too proud, some would say."

"I've heard tales of the Madaidhean-allaidh a tuath," he replied. "Your husband strikes fear into the hearts of the fiercest warriors." He paused then. "Even the general minds him."

Fenella cocked an eyebrow. "Has Aquila talked to you of Toutorix?"

"In passing ... he's mentioned him once or twice over a game of Latrunculi. He worries the Wolf is plotting revenge."

Fenella tensed. *He is.*

She could have confided in Aedan about the coming attack, but something stilled her tongue. The Brigante had been with Aquila a few years now, and she couldn't decide where his loyalties lay. The man was difficult to read.

Even so, the days were passing.

Eogan had told her the attack would come at the next full moon. The stormy weather obscured the sky this evening, yet the night before, she'd seen the moon had reached its full quarter.

Fenella's stomach fluttered. After Eogan's capture, she hadn't been able to focus on escape. Yet now her brother was free, she needed to renew her efforts.

When her people attacked, she had to be ready to go.

Stepping outdoors, Fenella pulled her goat-skin wrap close to ward off the damp wind and made her way down the steps of the praetorium.

"Where are you off to?" One of the guards greeted her tersely.

"Ava has run out of bread," Fenella replied, patting the empty basket. "I'm to collect some loaves from the bakehouse."

The guard's dark gaze narrowed. "Alone?"

Fenella held his eye and nodded.

Even so, her heart started to race, her palms turning clammy. Aye, the cook had sent her out alone—and it was a chance she wouldn't squander. The stormy weather had lasted a few days, and Kahina had gotten drenched while at market. She'd now come down with a nasty cold, and had taken to her bed for the afternoon. As such, Fenella was doing both their chores.

"Everyone's busy," Fenella replied, forcing her tone to remain light, respectful. "Ava trusts me."

The guard snorted before sharing a look with his companion.

Fenella's breathing stilled. It had been a while since she'd caused any trouble; surely, they could give her a little freedom?

"The bakehouse is but a stone's throw from here," she murmured. "I will be back shortly."

The two legionaries exchanged glances once more, before the one she'd been speaking to shrugged and turned back to her. "Go on then," he muttered. "Don't drag your feet."

"I won't," she assured him.

Fenella then moved away from the praetorium, skirting a large puddle, before stepping out onto the wide street and turning right. And as she hurried away, a smile of victory curved her lips.

At last!

The way was wet after the heavy rains, and her boots squelched through the mud. Peering up at the sky, Fenella noted ominous purple-grey clouds hanging overhead. Spots of rain gusted in with the wind. It looked as if the bad weather wasn't ready to depart just yet.

Fenella went to the bakehouse first and loaded her basket up with round loaves. The bread was still warm from the ovens, the nutty aroma enticing.

The baker ogled her as he passed over the loaves, before murmuring something coarse.

She clenched her jaw and smiled sweetly, pretending not to understand. However, her Latin had improved considerably of late, and she wished to knee him in the balls for his insult.

Leaving the bakehouse, she crossed the street, walking purposefully. It was important not to look hesitant, or she'd arouse suspicion.

Fenella's breathing quickened. *Now for the difficult part.*

One of the granary buildings lay across from the bakehouse. The doors were open, and so she slipped inside, silently praying to the gods that she'd find it empty.

It was.

The interior of the granary was dim, making it difficult to see. Halting, Fenella blinked a few times, breathing in the musty air as she waited for her eyes to adjust. Fortunately, she knew what she'd come for here, so she wouldn't be fumbling around in the dark.

She'd spied a coil of rope a few days earlier when she'd accompanied Aedan to pick up some sacks of barley. She just hoped it was still there.

Moving right, Fenella's gaze searched the far wall. Her mouth quirked into a smile when she spied the rope.

Grabbing it, she then set her basket down—removing the loaves a moment so she could tuck the coil underneath them.

She'd just replaced the bread and was rising to her feet when a young man entered the granary.

Fenella froze.

Dressed in a white tunic edged in blue, and woolen leggings, he was one of the velites—the poorest class of soldiers. She'd seen velites whenever she ventured beyond the praetorium. Unlike the legionaries, these men didn't have plate armor or even helmets.

Unsurprisingly, the velites did most of the hard physical work within the fort.

The soldier spied Fenella instantly. "What are you doing in here?" he demanded with a scowl.

Fenella's heart bucked hard against her ribs. She needed to think fast, or she'd be found out.

Deciding that the only way through this was to be brazen, she lifted her chin high and eyeballed the soldier.

"There you are … finally!" she replied, injecting an imperious note into her voice. "General Aquila's cook urgently requires a sack of oats. I've been waiting here an age for someone to help me. She will be getting impatient."

The young man's gaze narrowed. "Get your own oats, slave," he muttered.

Fenella drew herself up even taller before patting her full basket. "I can hardly carry a sack with this, can I?"

The soldier's gaze widened at her manner, but Fenella swept past him, nose in the air. "I suggest you hurry up."

Perhaps he was too shocked at her audacity to respond, but the man actually let her go.

However, Fenella's heart galloped like a bolting pony as she walked back to the praetorium.

That was close. If the soldier had entered the granary a moment earlier, he'd have seen what she was up to. Hopefully, Ava wouldn't be suspicious when he turned up with a sack of oats. But if the cook asked, she'd just have to try and talk her way out of it.

Fenella didn't take the Via Praetoria back to the general's residence. Instead, she strode down the alley between the praetorium and workshops. The clang of iron echoed out from open doorways, and she caught the words of a bawdy song from the men working inside.

By the time she reached her destination, her pulse had settled. Even so, she was on edge.

Before going inside, she needed to hide the rope—but she couldn't do so with anyone around.

Casting a furtive glance about, Fenella exhaled sharply. The gods were favoring her, it seemed, for this alley was empty at present. Hurrying up to the furnace that warmed the praetorium, she dug into her basket and yanked the rope free. In her haste, she nearly dropped one of the loaves in the mud. Cursing her clumsiness under her breath, she rearranged the bread. Ava would box her ears if she presented her with mucky loaves.

Glancing around once more, to ensure she was indeed alone, Fenella wedged the rope at the back of a stack of peat bricks Aedan used to fuel the furnace.

It wasn't an excellent hiding spot—but it was the best she could manage at short notice. And with the attack looming, the rope didn't need to remain hidden for long.

Once the siege was well underway, she planned to climb up to the Porta Principalis Dextra and rope down the other side onto the ramp leading to the vicus.

Of course, she'd need a weapon too, and had her eye on one of Ava's wickedly sharp boning knives.

It wouldn't be easy, but with the chaos of battle, it was likely her best chance of escape.

Stepping away from the stack of peat, Fenella hugged her basket of fragrant bread close and hurried back indoors.

XVIII. YOU WERE MADE FOR ME

FENELLA SCREWED UP her face, staring down at the large—and thankfully dead—rat the cat had just dropped before her. She'd been sweeping the courtyard pavers when Electri had stalked up to her, a prize in her jaws.

The cat sat back on its haunches and gave a loud 'meow'. Electri wore an undeniably smug expression upon her face, although her amber eyes were wild, her thick tail thwacking upon the pavers. Fresh from the hunt, she had a feral look about her.

"It's official ... she loves you," Kahina croaked from behind Fenella. She was still recovering from the blocked nose and sore throat that laid her low for a few days.

After days of stormy weather, both women were catching up on their chores outdoors. Above, clouds scudded across a windswept sky, and sunshine bathed the courtyard. Time was marching on; spring would be here before they knew it.

But the attack would arrive before The Maiden brought the world to life again.

The reminder made Fenella's pulse accelerate.

She liked Kahina and didn't want any harm to come to her.

She'll be fine, she assured herself then. *Even if Toutorix breaks the fort's defenses, the praetorium will be well defended.*

Her breathing grew shallow. She hoped it wouldn't be *too* well protected, for she planned to slip out during the attack.

Pushing aside thoughts of escape, Fenella turned to where Kahina was pegging out washing on a line that had been strung up between two pillars on the northern side of the open space. "I'd prefer she showed her love in other ways."

Kahina smiled before sniffing. "You're fortunate indeed … it took her a year to bring me one of her kills."

Fenella pulled a face, swiveling back to where Electri watched her expectantly. The rodent was huge, with a plush brown coat. "I've never seen one of such size," she admitted. Her skin crawled at the sight of it; she'd never been fond of rats—a fear Eogan had exploited when they were children. He'd once left a dead rat amongst her furs in her alcove. Her yells when she'd discovered it had nearly lifted the roof.

"I have … a fort this size attracts them."

Fenella suppressed a shiver. "What am I supposed to do with it?"

"Wait until she leaves, and then grab a shovel and scoop it up."

"So, I'm just supposed to sweep around it?"

"Unless you want Electri to take offense."

Fenella snorted. Even so, she heeded Kahina. The cat had fixed her with an intense look, as if waiting to see what she'd do next.

She was about to resume her sweeping when Caius burst through the doors leading from the entranceway, crossed the portico, and stepped out into the courtyard.

Immediately, his gaze went to the dead rat, disgust rippling across his face. Recovering, he shifted his attention to the two slaves. "Finish up there, and join Ava in the kitchen," he ordered. "She will need help with cena today … the general has returned."

Fenella poured wine into Aquila's calix, careful to avoid his eye.

Cena had arrived, and, as usual, she waited on him. And despite that she wasn't looking his way, she could feel his gaze upon her, tracking her every move.

The Reaper take him, she wished he'd look elsewhere.

Tightening her grip on the handle of the ewer, Fenella moved back, next to Caius, while Kahina placed dishes of braised boar, fava beans mashed in butter, and fresh bread before him.

The general ate alone this afternoon, yet his servants and slaves waited on him in the same manner as when he had company.

In her time at Ardoch, Fenella had observed Aquila was a man of routine, of rigid discipline. He rose at the crack of dawn, took his meals at the same time every day, and although he wasn't unkind to his servants and slaves, he expected high standards in all things—not surprising since he'd dedicated his life to the military. Even so, he'd also revealed another side to himself to Fenella over the past months. Where she was concerned, the Eagle's discipline wavered.

He shouldn't stare at her so. Caius would notice.

Yet the Eagle didn't seem to care.

Gaze downcast, Fenella waited while Aquila consumed his meal. She glanced up occasionally, to see if his calix needed refilling. But he drank sparingly this afternoon.

"Is the meal to your liking, General?" Caius asked, breaking the heavy silence in the triclinium.

"Yes, thank you," Aquila replied.

"And was the patrol successful?" The house steward was in a chatty mood today. However, Aquila seemed less so.

"It was."

"Are Dalginross and Bochastle secure?"

"They are."

Discouraged by the general's terse replies, Caius lapsed into silence after that.

Finally, the meal ended. Fenella handed the ewer to the steward, in case the general requested more wine, while she started clearing the table.

Once again, she kept her gaze upon her task. All the same, it suddenly felt oppressively warm in the triclinium. She was starting to sweat.

Loading her arms up with dishes, she was about to turn when Aquila addressed her. "You are to join me in the tablinum later, Fenella ... once you've finished work for the day."

If the order was a ploy to get her to look at him, it worked.

Fenella's chin lifted, and his gaze snared hers. Her breath hitched at the impact. She swallowed hard, trying to ignore the melting sensation in the cradle of her hips.

Gods, her body responded to him as it had when he'd kissed her.

However, recalling how he'd recoiled from her, how he'd thrown her out of the tablinum that eve, she frowned. Surely, he didn't want to be alone with her again?

"Why?" Her voice was higher than she wished, yet she couldn't help it. It felt as if he were the hunter, and she his quarry.

The full moon couldn't come soon enough. She needed to flee far from this man.

She didn't want to join him in the tablinum. She wanted to finish her chores for the day and retire to her sleeping pallet.

Nonetheless, Aquila's gaze didn't waver. "It's time we talked," he replied.

Fenella sat upon the couch, as stiff as a poker. The seat was comfortable—carved out of wood with a curved back and soft cushions—yet she couldn't relax.

Not with the Eagle in the same room.

The general was facing away from her, pouring them cups of wine. She watched him, taking in his broad shoulders and long back; the black tunic he wore clung to his strong body.

Pursing her lips, Fenella looked down at where her hands were clasped upon her lap.

She was far too aware of the bastard. That kiss had unleashed something between them, something she couldn't seem to control.

Raising her gaze once more, she found Aquila before her, calix outstretched.

She took it, careful not to let their fingers touch.

Moving back, he lowered himself onto the couch opposite. This was his lounging space, where he often chatted with Marcus in the evenings. Small tables flanked the couches, and a soft sheepskin covered the cold tiles between them. The doors to the tablinium were closed as it was a chill, windy night outdoors.

"You look unhappy this eve, Fenella," Aquila observed after a pause. "Why?"

Inhaling slowly, she eyed him. "You know the reason."

His gaze grew intense. "No, I don't … tell me."

Silence fell between them, and Fenella raised the calix to her lips, taking a sip. The wine warmed her belly, emboldening her. "I don't understand you," she growled finally. "At all."

His head inclined. "We can remedy that … ask me anything you wish."

Fenella's grip tightened upon the stem of her calix. Gods, he was vexing.

"I feel toyed with," she bit out, ignoring his request. "We seem to be playing a game of cat and mouse, you and I, and I don't like it."

"Neither do I."

"Really? Then why persist?"

His gaze seared hers. "Do you not know?"

Fenella drew in a deep breath. The Mother give her patience, she hated it when he answered her with a question. "From the moment we met, you've had an obsession with me," she ground out, even as her pulse quickened. "You seem intent on bending me to your will

... yet at the same time, you want it to be my choice. What kind of man thinks this way?"

"One who has found his other half," he replied softly.

Fenella started, as if someone had just jabbed her with a pin. "What?"

"You were made for me, Fenella." His gaze never left her face. "I wish you'd let me *know* you."

Fenella stared back at him, horrified.

Aquila's mouth quirked. "I'm not like other men you've known, am I?"

Still reeling from his admission, Fenella shook her head.

"Toutorix is a brute. I can see how he'd destroy your trust."

Fenella's heart started to pound like a drum against her ribs. This conversation was getting out of control; it was making her feel light-headed. "Every man close to me has let me down," she admitted shakily. "My father, my lover ... and my husband. My father gave me to Toutorix to pay an old debt."

"The Wolf wasn't worthy of you." The words were spoken quietly, yet they fell like axe blows in the quiet of the tablinum. A moment later, Aquila continued, "You spoke of a lover?"

Fenella silently cursed herself. Emotion bubbled close to the surface tonight. She hadn't meant to be so open with the Eagle, but her mouth had run away with her. However, she'd gone this far. She might as well tell him the rest.

"His name was Lorcan," she admitted huskily. "My father was feuding with his kin, so we met in secret for a year. I was on my way to meet him that day you stopped me ... in the pinewood."

Aquila's gaze widened, understanding rippling across his face. "Ah."

"I thought we'd run away together ... start a new life, away from our families." The words stuck in her throat, but she plowed on. "But that day, I discovered he was already wedded. He never intended to make me his." Fenella dropped her gaze to the calix resting upon her lap. She swallowed hard then, for it suddenly felt as if she had a plum in her throat.

She'd said far too much.

A brittle silence settled between them before Aquila eventually broke it. "Lorcan sounds like a man of poor character."

Her mouth pursed, yet she didn't reply.

"Look at me, Fenella."

Reluctantly, she raised her gaze to meet his eye.

Aquila's features had tightened. She noted that his fingers had clenched around his calix. "If you were mine, I'd treat you like a queen."

Fenella's chest constricted, her dizziness intensifying. "Don't say things like that," she rasped.

"Why not? It's what I feel. You wanted honesty, and you have it."

Fenella's self-control snapped, and she slammed the calix down on the table next to the couch. Dark liquid sloshed over the rim, yet she paid it no mind. "I'm your slave," she ground out. "I *already* belong to you."

Rising to her feet, she realized she was shaking.

Aquila put down his wine and stood up, facing her. "Your body does," he replied, his voice lowering. "But not your heart."

Fenella's breathing choked off.

She wanted to throw his admission back at him, yet the rawness in his voice prevented her. His words wrapped themselves around her, drawing her in. And without even realizing what she was doing, she swayed toward him.

Murmuring an oath, Aquila pulled her into his arms, his mouth capturing hers.

It was inevitable really. Ever since that first kiss, the attraction between them couldn't be denied. It was like a pot of water simmering over a fire. Eventually, it would come to a boil.

A groan escaped Fenella. Reaching up, she gripped his shoulders, anchoring herself on him. He slid one hand around to the back of her neck, holding her fast in his embrace.

The last time Aquila had kissed her, it had been savage. But this embrace was sensual: a leisurely exploration, surprising in its tenderness and restraint. The kiss melted her with its gentleness.

And as she had days earlier, Fenella responded to him. Her tongue dueled with his, her teeth grazing his lips, tasting him, feasting upon him.

A moan rumbled in Aquila's throat, and he answered her passion in kind, his free hand splaying out across her back. The heat of his palm branded her, and Fenella leaned farther forward, giving herself up to his embrace.

She should stop this before she lost her wits entirely. Instead, like before, it was Aquila who ended the kiss.

Breathless, he drew back, his lips parted, gaze hooded with desire. "I pushed you away last time because I didn't want you to feel forced," he rasped. "I must know … do you want this?"

They stared at each other for a long moment, but Fenella didn't answer.

Aquila's jaw tightened, disappointment clouding his gaze. He was about to step back from her, when she caught his wrist, holding him fast. "Yes," she whispered. "I want this."

The naked hunger in his eyes was impossible to miss. Need had tightened his features. He looked like a man on a short leash, and suddenly she wanted to know what would happen if that leash snapped.

A heartbeat passed, and then his mouth was on hers once more, his tongue sweeping her lips apart.

The gods forgive her, he tasted good.

Fenella fell into him, her hands sliding up his shoulders to his neck, her fingertips tunneling through his short hair. Suddenly, she ached to touch him, to lose herself in his kisses.

She wanted to wrap herself around him, skin to skin.

XIX. WILDNESS

JUSTIN DRANK HER in, savoring the sweetness of her mouth, the feel of her soft skin under his fingertips.

He'd been playing a dangerous game tonight, asking her to join him in the tablinum. What did he think would happen when he was alone with her? Even so, he hadn't been able to stop himself.

He'd told himself he wouldn't kiss her again, wouldn't touch her, but he was weak where Fenella was concerned.

He'd meant every word too. If she'd let him, he'd make her his queen.

And now, she'd given him permission to kiss, touch, *take* her.

His blood roared, and his shaft was now painfully hard. He wanted to throw her down on the sheepskin, spread her wide, and tumble her right this instant—but he wouldn't.

He'd craved this woman for months now, and he wouldn't spoil this, wouldn't rush it.

And so he kissed her, deeply, thoroughly, his chest aching with hunger as her nimble tongue curled around his, as her teeth nipped at his lower lip. And while they kissed, his hands slid down her back to her hips.

They had a will of their own, for they soon moved to her thighs and the hem of her tunic.

A groan escaped him when his fingers slid underneath, touching smooth, soft skin. His fingers itched to explore further, to delve deeper. But he had to go slowly; he didn't want to startle her.

Fenella murmured something against his mouth. She then fumbled with the belt at her waist, unbuckling it and flinging it aside.

Encouraged, Justin grabbed the hem of her tunic and slid it up her thighs. She lifted her arms so that he could draw it up, over her head, and gave a sensual wriggle as he pulled the tunic free.

An instant later, she stood before him, gloriously naked.

Justin gently pushed her down upon the couch, his gaze feasting upon her.

Of course, he'd spent far too much time in the past months imagining Fenella in this state—and the sight was even more exciting than his sensual fantasies.

The slave tunic hung in soft folds over her body, yet he remembered what she'd looked like in the form-fitting leather vest and skirt she'd worn when he'd taken her from Lake Taus. Fenella was all lean, sleek lines—narrow-hipped with coltish limbs. And yet in contrast to her sleekness, her breasts were heavy and ripe.

Justin's gaze fastened upon them now, taking in the translucent pale skin and rose-pink nipples.

She was every erotic dream he'd had come to life in the flesh.

With a murmured oath, he sank to his knees before her and leaned down, scooping up her delicious tits in his hands and pushing them high. He then feasted upon them, suckling one nipple hard before shifting to its twin. He lathed each taut nipple with his tongue and then took it deep into his mouth, sucking hard.

And to his delight, Fenella groaned and writhed, soft mewing sounds erupting from her now. Her hands clenched his shoulders, her nails biting through the material of his tunic.

"Aquila," she moaned.

"Justin," he corrected her before gently nipping a nipple with his teeth. Fenella's sharply drawn breath caused his belly muscles to clench in excitement. Gods, he loved the sounds she made.

He wanted to hear more—much more.

Fenella reclined against the couch, bracing her arms along the back of it. Her fingers clutched the edge, digging into the wood.

Reaching up, Aquila pulled the thong off the end of her braid. He undid her hair, letting it fall in heavy, rippling waves over her shoulders. He then focused his attention once more upon her breasts.

His mouth, the way he was suckling her, made her need to grab onto something—and when his lips trailed down the valley between her breasts to her belly, her grip clenched tighter still.

An instant later, she was spread-eagled before him, completely naked while he was still fully clothed.

Aquila stared down at her, at the nest of soft brown hair between her thighs. His lips parted, his chest rising and falling swiftly. And then he lowered himself fully to the floor and leaned forward, his head nestling between her spread thighs.

Fenella's choked cry filtered across the tablinum. Fortunately, the doors were closed. Even so, anyone walking by on the portico outside would have heard her.

She had little time to dwell on this before the skillful flick of his tongue drove all thought from her mind. And when he suckled her there, as he had her nipples, another ragged cry ripped from her.

"Aquila!"

"Justin." Once again he corrected her, before his hands slid under her backside, lifting her up against him. His lips and tongue then continued their sensual assault.

The Maiden forgive her, it was too much.

Fenella bucked against him, shattering against his mouth. A delicious, throbbing pleasure rippled out from her loins, breaking over her in waves.

For a few moments, she hung there, panting, until the tide receded and she was capable of rational thought once more. And then her eyelids fluttered open, and she looked at him.

Aquila was watching her with a smoldering look that made her belly flutter.

Anticipation quickened her breathing. Of course, this was just the beginning.

Pushing herself up from where she'd slipped down on the couch, Fenella reached for Aquila.

Their mouths collided, their kisses wet and wild, while her hands clawed at his clothing. She wanted him as naked as she was.

Aquila obliged, undoing his belt and tossing it aside—as she had with her own—before pulling up his tunic and shrugging it off. Underneath, he was naked, save for a tightly fitting loincloth.

Fenella's attention slid down his heavily muscled torso to his groin, and her mouth went dry.

The loincloth fascinated her, as did the huge bulge in it. Cruthini warriors didn't wear anything under their trews. Kahina had told her that this skimpy undergarment was called a 'subligaculum'. Indeed, Kahina wore something similar—she'd even given Fenella one to wear, although she only bothered with it when her moon flow was upon her.

However, the sight of the filmy undergarment encasing Aquila's loins made her breathing quicken with excitement. Reaching out, she traced a finger over the silky material.

It left nothing to the imagination. She could feel the heat of his skin through it, and as she traced her finger up the length of him, the engorged outline of his rod became even more evident.

Murmuring encouragement, she caressed him, from root to tip, noting the damp patch that now soaked through the straining loin cloth. Her touch was clearly exciting him. Glancing up, she marked that Aquila had clenched his jaw, and he was watching her, his eyes hooded. His chest now rose and fell as if he'd been running.

Slowly, as if she were unwrapping a gift, Fenella peeled back his loin-cloth before pushing it down his thighs.

Aquila's shaft sprang free, thick and eager. Its head was slick with his need, and when she wrapped her fingers around his girth, she marveled once more at his size and the exquisite silkiness of his skin. Sliding off the couch, she lowered herself, taking the head of his rod into her mouth. The salty, musky taste of him made a groan rise in her throat, and a moment later, she was working him with her hand while her tongue explored the swollen tip.

Growling her name, Aquila tangled his hands in her hair, urging her on.

And then, suddenly, he wasn't.

Gripping her under the arms, he hauled her up so that she no longer sucked him.

Fenella gave a cry of protest—for she'd been enjoying herself, and hadn't planned to stop until he spilled his seed in her mouth—but Aquila pushed her back onto the couch.

Their gazes met, the moment raw and breathless.

Fenella's heart slammed against her ribs, sweat beading across her skin. The intensity of the moment was almost too much to bear. She wanted to look away, yet she couldn't.

Murmuring an endearment, Aquila spread her wide once more and placed his rod at her entrance.

Curled against the back of the couch, Fenella watched as he slowly worked his way into her. The sight of his thick shaft sinking into her body was the most arousing thing she'd ever witnessed; she couldn't take her gaze off it.

However, as he inched his way in, she did glance at his face, and saw he too was staring at where their bodies met.

"Gods, woman," he groaned.

Fenella whimpered. He was so big, and when he was fully seated, she felt stretched almost to the point of discomfort. But when Aquila gripped her thighs, parting them wider still, and rolled his hips, the tightness eased. Melting pleasure rippled through her loins.

Fenella's gasp echoed through the room, and her lower belly muscles clenched hard.

And when he repeated the action, she cried out. "Justin!"

"That's right," he groaned, drawing back in a slow drag, before sliding deep once more. "I like hearing my name on your lips ... say it again."

"Justin!" She writhed against him now, her thighs trembling, pleasure throbbing deep in her core.

She'd never responded to a man like this, not even Lorcan during their most passionate encounters. Justin Aquila tore the restraints away and turned her wild. She clutched at him, wanting his body against hers.

Sensing her desperation, he dragged her off the couch so that she lay under him on the soft sheepskin rug. There, he plowed her, in slow and deliberate thrusts, while she wrapped her legs around his hips, pulling him deeper with each plunge.

Aquila's mouth found hers, their tongues mating as he took her.

And with each thrust, Fenella let go a little bit more. Her fingernails dug into his back, her heels riding the hard muscles of his buttocks. She clung to him, gave all to him, lost herself in him.

Fenella closed her eyes, her head falling back as his mouth fastened on her neck. Tears of ecstasy burned behind her eyelids as she splintered against him, around him. They were both crying out now. The world spun as if she were being sucked into a whirlpool. She clung to Aquila as if her life depended upon it.

His cries were hoarse, unfettered. He thrust deeply once more and then went rigid in her arms.

Fenella opened her eyes to see Aquila throw his head back, the cords of muscle in his neck gleaming, for sweat now bathed his skin. His breathing was ragged, his big body trembling in the aftermath of their passion. His eyes were closed, pleasure still rippling over his face.

Fenella stared up at him, transfixed.

She'd never been with anyone who let go like that, who'd provoked the same wildness in her.

Sinking back into the sheepskin, she closed her eyes. Her throat constricted, her eyelids burning. A moment later, tears escaped, running down her cheeks and tickling her ears.

"Fenella." Aquila's voice was husky, raw. "What's wrong?"

"Nothing," she breathed.

"Have I hurt you?"

"No."

"But you're crying."

She opened her eyes, blinking until he came into focus. Aquila was staring down at her, his amber gaze shadowed with concern.

"I know," she whispered. "I can't help it."

XX. TAMING THE EAGLE

"WHEN DID THEY mark you?" Aquila asked, his finger tracing the outline of her wolf tattoo. They still lay upon the sheepskin, their limbs entwined, although he'd shifted his body off Fenella to avoid crushing her.

Glancing down at where he stroked her upper arm, Fenella noted, once again, the beauty of his hands—strong with long tapered fingers. Of course he had. Everything about this man was graceful, despite his strength.

Her throat tightened then. She shouldn't be lying there, enjoying the aftermath of their wild coupling. Nothing about this moment could last, yet she found herself clinging to it. Tomorrow would bring sanity; tonight, she was someone else.

"I was in my sixth winter," she murmured huskily. "My mother did it." She remembered the stinging pain of the needle, and the burning sensation that followed when Mona rubbed woad into the wounds. "My arm swelled up afterward ... and I developed a fever. They had to take me to a healer in the end."

He nodded, continuing to trace the mark. "Does it ever hurt?"

"Not now. Most of the time, I forget I even have it." It was true, such markings were commonplace amongst her people, and warriors—male and female alike—often had tattoos etched into their face, neck, and chest.

"You have skin like milk," he murmured.

"And yours is golden," she whispered back, her own fingers tracing the sculpted lines of his chest. Their gazes met then. "Like your eyes. Do many of your people have eyes that color?"

He shook his head. "It's unusual. My father has amber eyes ... I'm told I look like him."

"And are your parents still alive?" His fingertips were sending delicious shivers up and down her arm. It was difficult to concentrate.

"Yes."

There was an edge to his voice that intrigued her. "Do you not get on with them?"

Aquila pulled a face. "My father is a bully ... and my mother his hand-maiden," he replied. "Growing up, I felt suffocated by him. There was no way but his." He paused then, his gaze shadowing. "On my last trip back to Italia, we argued ... and when I left, he made it clear I wasn't welcome back."

Fenella's gaze widened, momentarily forgetting that he was still stroking her arm. "What did you argue about?"

"My career. Father was once primus pilus of the Sixth legion, but he took an injury that lamed him. Once he retired, he looked to me to bring him the glory he'd always sought. My posting to Caledonia disappointed him. He was angry I hadn't managed to get a transfer ... said I hadn't tried hard enough, and I got sick of being treated like a child."

Fenella took this in. They were different people, yet she too knew what it was like to have a harsh father.

"And do you have siblings?" she asked after a pause.

"Two elder sisters," he replied, his expression lightening once more. "And you?"

"I'm the oldest of five. I have three brothers ... and one sister."

"I would have picked you as the eldest," he replied, his hand leaving her upper arm to trace the line of her jaw. "That's why you're so strong ... you grew up taking care of others."

Fenella's mouth quirked. "And what do they say of the youngest child?"

"The baby of the family?" He smiled widely then, and Fenella inhaled sharply. Gods, his smile sucked the air from her lungs. "My sisters used to complain I was coddled ... that I got all the attention when we were growing up. They were probably right."

"Aye, that's true enough," she murmured. "Fife is the youngest of my siblings ... and Ma spoiled him shamelessly."

Aquila continued to smile down at her. The back of his knuckles now brushed across her cheek, and a familiar ache started to pulse between her thighs.

The Mother forgive her, she wanted him again.

"I've always thought youngest children are the most charming," she continued, struggling to hold onto her thoughts now. "They're used to getting what they want."

"We don't always get our way," Aquila replied, the pad of his thumb tracing her lower lip. "Once I left home, I soon learned that if I wanted something, I had to fight for it."

Seated in the courtyard, Fenella glanced up, letting the sun bathe her face. Closing her eyes, she found herself reliving the passion of the night before. Aquila had taken her once more upon the sheepskin, with a tenderness that had reduced her to tears—again.

The gods help her, she'd never wept after coupling before.

She wasn't sure what had come over her.

Moments passed, and Fenella remained there, eyes shut, while heated images flitted through her mind. She shouldn't be thinking of such things, yet she couldn't help herself.

"You're in an odd mood this morning."

Fenella's eyelids snapped open. Face warming, she lowered her chin to see Kahina viewing her.

It was mid-morning, and the two women were seated near the well shelling peas for cena. Electri was lying across Fenella's feet, asleep.

"I'm just enjoying the sun," Fenella replied lightly. She then picked up another handful of pods, dumped them onto her lap, and resumed her task. It was tedious, repetitive work, and yet Kahina had spoken true.

She'd barely said a word since they'd risen from their sleeping pallets.

A pause drew out before Kahina spoke again. "You were late to bed last night."

Fenella glanced up. "Did I wake you?"

"That doesn't matter." Kahina's frank peat-brown eyes never left Fenella's face. "Has something happened between you and the general?"

Fenella's cheeks started to glow like hot coals, and she cursed her body's betrayal. She could hardly lie now, could she?

Sighing, she reached up, dragging a hand down her face, before glancing up at the sky, silently asking The Warrior for strength. "I had a moment of ... weakness," she murmured. Her belly fluttered then, as she recalled just how *weak* she'd been.

She'd turn the color of a turnip the next time she saw Aquila. Suddenly, she wished she could dig a deep hole and bury herself in it.

Fenella swallowed hard. Soon, her people would attack Ardoch, and she would flee. This development was the last thing she needed.

She'd known for a while that Aquila wanted her, yet she hadn't realized her own latent attraction to him. She'd been too busy loathing him.

The only problem was—she didn't hate him anymore.

"I've seen the way he looks at you," Kahina said then, oblivious to the direction of her companion's thoughts. "He *devours* you with his eyes."

Fenella cleared her throat. "Aye, well ... no good was ever going to come of us spending time together." She then murmured a curse in her own tongue and viciously snapped a pea-pod in half.

"Don't look so pained, Fen." Kahina pulled her stool closer, before leaning over and placing a hand on Fenella's arm. "I'm not judging you."

"No," Fenella choked. "But I *am* judging myself."

"Why? You're not made of stone ... and Aquila is a man who'd draw any woman's eye." Kahina's grip on her arm tightened then. Fenella glanced her way to see her smiling. "I've been with the general for many years now, and I've never known him to be taken with anyone like he is with you."

Despite herself, curiosity wreathed up within Fenella. "You've met his lovers then?"

"Some ... although he's been too busy since we came to Ardoch to entertain women." Kahina's smile turned wry. "Aquila's a man used to being in control, and I've often wondered if he'd ever let a woman get to him." Her gaze twinkled then. "It seems it has taken a fearless Picti woman to tame the Eagle."

XXI. STORM BIRDS

"THE GARRISON AT Dalginross have just sent word," Marcus informed Justin when he joined him on the wall. The two men stood atop the guard tower above the Porta Praetoria, looking northwest. "Their scouts spied movement on the Strathearn, two nights ago."

Justin took this in, his brow furrowing. "They didn't approach the fort?"

Marcus shook his head. "They were traveling south ... skirting the eastern shore of Lake Earn ... a band of around a hundred warriors, taking care to travel unnoticed."

Justin's frown deepened, his mood shadowing. He'd awoken that morning in a mellow mood, his body relaxed after a night of passion with Fenella. Stepping out into a sunny morning, he'd smiled up at the cloudless sky.

It had been difficult to imagine anything could be wrong in the world today.

But Marcus's news reminded him of the reality of matters.

Toutorix was still at large.

"One hundred isn't a large band," Marcus said then, intruding on his general's thoughts.

"No, it isn't," Justin agreed. His gaze swept north, focusing on the mountains, a lilac and purple silhouette against the sky. "But there might be more. They were traveling in stealth for a reason."

Turning, Justin surveyed the fort behind him. The rumble of men's voices and the clang of iron rose up. A burst of laughter intruded then—two men standing in the parade ground were sharing a joke. Sunlight glinted off armor and shields from a line of soldiers making for the Porta Praetoria, heading out on patrol.

It was just another day at Ardoch. They'd had an easy winter, but the thawing of the earth had already seen stirrings of trouble.

"Increase our sentries around the fort … and the men at the watchtowers too," he instructed then. "We must—"

A cry above cut Justin off. Both men craned their necks up to spy an eagle gliding overhead.

The skin on Justin's forearms prickled, while the primus pilus muttered an oath under his breath. The mighty *aquila* was a symbol of Jupiter, a symbol of their legion—but it was also a 'storm bird', a herald of war.

"I haven't seen an eagle here since the day the Ninth marched from Ardoch," Marcus said, an edge to his voice now. "That's an ill omen if ever I saw one."

"The wind is changing, Marcus," Justin replied.

"Gods, this is heavy," Fenella wheezed, casting her companion a sideways glance. "How do you make it look so easy?"

Aedan snorted. The pair of them pushed barrows, stacked with urns of olive oil, cream, and milk, along the rutted street toward the praetorium. The Brigante had barely broken a sweat, while she was beginning to pant. It wasn't that surprising though; she was strong, for she labored hard from dawn till dusk, yet Aedan spent his days hauling wood and bricks of peat for the furnace and kitchen hearth.

Hitting a particularly deep rut, Fenella stumbled and nearly faceplanted onto an urn of olive oil teetering on the barrow. The pungent green oil—transported up to the frontier from lands far to the south—leaked through the wooden stopper of the urn, and she cursed.

A passing soldier barked a laugh before muttering something coarse.

Fenella snarled an insult back in her own tongue. "Pig," she muttered as she and Aedan continued on their way.

"Aye, they're a coarse lot," the Brigante agreed. "Most of them haven't had a woman in years." He paused then, as if reflecting on his own situation, which wouldn't be any different. "Your arrival here caused much excitement."

Fenella made a face. Nonetheless, she hadn't been blind to the looks she attracted whenever she ventured out of the praetorium. She was rarely unescorted, yet that didn't stop soldiers from stripping her naked with their gazes.

She was about to answer Aedan, when she spotted a column of legionaries marching up the street toward them. The two slaves wheeled their barrows to one side, to let them pass.

"It's busy in here this afternoon," she observed as the men tramped by, weapons, armor, and shields rattling. Indeed, she'd noted the increase in traffic through the fort the moment she'd stepped outdoors. Marking the grim looks on some of the soldiers' faces, her belly tightened, and unease skated down her spine.

Something was wrong.

"Aye, Aquila's got wind of movement to the north," the Brigante replied. "He's mobilizing more men."

Fenella's breathing caught.

The full moon was still five days away, yet the first signs of what Eogan had warned had appeared.

Ready yourself, Fen.

She was about to heave the barrow forward then, and cover the final stretch to the praetorium, when Aedan breathed an oath.

He was looking up, and Fenella followed his gaze.

There, perched upon the edge of the roof of the general's residence, was a coal-black raven. It stared down at them, beady eyes unblinking.

Fenella's heart started to pound. Among her people, ravens signified many things, few of them good. It was an omen of coming battle, although the bird was also a harbinger of change, upheaval, and rebirth—the old giving way to welcome the new.

Tearing her gaze from the raven, Fenella glanced Aedan's way. The Brigantes shared the same gods as her own people—he would know, as well as her, what the raven's appearance meant.

"Winter often lulls you into thinking peace has settled," Aedan said after a pause, tearing his gaze from the raven to look at her. His mouth quirked then, his blue eyes old beyond their years. "But it never does for long."

With that, he lifted his barrow and continued on his way.

Heaving a deep breath, Fenella glanced up at the raven once more.

The cursed bird still sat there, staring at her with unnerving intensity. She wished it would fly away and let her be.

Aye, she knew an attack was coming, but the lone bird reminded her of the song about ravens her mother had often sung to her as a child.

One for sorrow,
Two for joy,
Three for a girl,
Four for a boy,
Five for silver,
Six for gold,
Seven for a secret never to be told.

One for sorrow.
Fenella's breathing grew shallow. She didn't want to think about what that might mean.

For her.

For her kin.

For her people.

For the man who was now her lover.

But the gods had spoken, and soon fate would reveal itself. She could only prepare herself for what was to come.

Whispering a prayer to them, Fenella tightened her grip on the barrow handles and shoved it forward, hurrying to catch up with Aedan.

Mist wreathed through the pines like crone's hair, its milky tendrils turning the gorge ghostly.

Walking through the midst of it, Toutorix smiled. The mist was their ally, especially this close to Ardoch. Aquila's patrols were everywhere, but they had yet to venture near this hidden rocky defile, where his army camped.

Fire pits lined the length of the valley, glowing through the mist. The scent of wood smoke mingled with the resinous perfume of pine. There wasn't a breath of wind this evening—it was as if the world were holding its breath.

A great force had gathered here, waiting for the moment to strike.

Toutorix's gait slowed as he approached the center of the camp. The past five months had passed in a blur, for he'd spent them traveling from village to village in the north, prostrating himself before each Cruthini chieftain. He'd hated the task, but the fire in his belly had driven him.

He'd sworn vengeance upon General Aquila, and he would have it.

But it hadn't been easy. Some of the chieftains—those who bore longstanding grudges against the Wolf—had refused to join him. However, a surprising number had listened to his tale of Roman treachery, fury glinting in their eyes when he'd revealed how the Eagle had attacked his crannog at Loch Tatha, stolen his wife, and butchered his men.

He'd spun a tale of an unprovoked attack.

One that couldn't be ignored.

The central fire pit beckoned, and Toutorix moved toward it. The other chieftains were there, waiting for him: big men swathed in leather, fur, and plaid, their faces painted blue, their gazes gleaming in the firelight.

The Wolf's smile widened, his skin prickling. *My allies.*

"Ho, Toutorix," one of the chieftains, a raven-haired man with a heavily tattooed face, greeted him. "Is everyone accounted for then?"

"Aye, Berach," he replied, flashing him a grin. "All of us have made it south without encountering the enemy."

"That doesn't mean they haven't seen us though," another of the chieftains, a bald, bull-faced man named Declan pointed out, his heavy brow furrowing.

"We've been careful," Toutorix replied. "They might have spied shadowy figures passing through the fringes of the territory they hold"—he paused then, his gaze sweeping over the circle of chieftains— "But they'll have no idea of our might."

"And yet, the Eagle has increased his garrisons at the watchtowers and outposts," Declan growled, not yet ready to drop the subject. "His men prowl the land around Ardoch. He suspects something."

"Suspecting and knowing aren't the same thing." Toutorix's gaze narrowed. "Even so, our decision to strike tonight, instead of waiting till the full moon, was a wise one."

Ruarc, the chieftain who'd warned them all against waiting, gave a soft snort. Tall and muscular with long brown hair that glowed red in the firelight, Ruarc watched Toutorix with a veiled gaze. Meeting his eye, the Wolf was reminded that although these men had agreed to join him, to destroy Ardoch and all who lived within, it was an uneasy alliance.

They were all men used to leading, not following. The fact that Toutorix had managed to bring them together at all was a feat indeed.

But all the same, he sometimes caught Ruarc watching him, distrust in his grey eyes. After this campaign was done, he'd need to keep an eye on him.

"Our warbands waiting outside Dalginross and Bochastle will attack tonight," Ruarc confirmed after a pause.

"As will my men at the watchtowers closest to the fort," Berach assured him. "The rest of our army will hit Ardoch as planned."

Toutorix nodded, anticipation quickening in his belly. "We shall hit them on all fronts," he murmured. "Fast and hard, like an iron fist." He sucked in a deep breath then, his hands clenching as he anticipated the slaughter.

"And what of your wife, Toutorix?" Declan asked. The huge warrior was still frowning. "Are we to seek her out once we breach the defenses, and keep her safe for you?"

Toutorix schooled his features into a bland expression, meeting Declan's questioning gaze.

He didn't want Fenella back.

He'd already taken another wife, barely a moon after her departure. Talulla was plain and meek, yet her womb had already quickened with his seed, not like that barren bitch. Getting rid of Fenella had been a boon indeed; he never wanted to set eyes on her again.

"I don't want Aquila's leavings," he replied, his voice cold now. "The woman will be put to the sword, like the rest of them."

XXII. FRAGILE

FENELLA PLUCKED THE last piece of cheese off the dish and took a bite. She then paused, casting Aquila a cautious look. "I hope you didn't want that?"

Across the table, the general favored her with a half-smile. "No ... my appetite is poor this evening ... you have it."

Fenella continued to observe him, wondering at his subdued mood, while at the same time surreptitiously drinking him in.

Aquila wore a simple red tunic, belted at the waist, and his short hair was spiky and damp, revealing that he'd bathed before supper. If she leaned forward and inhaled deeply, she could smell the spicy scent of the oil he'd used after bathing. The perfume, blended with that of clean male, made her belly flutter.

The general had invited her to join him for supper. They'd shared a platter of dried fruit, various cheeses, and salty bread, washed down with bramble wine. However, they weren't in the tablinum this time, but Aquila's cubiculum: his bed-chamber.

This was the first time that Fenella had been inside this room, for Kahina cleaned and tidied this space. As such, she'd taken in her surroundings with interest when she'd followed Aquila in. It was a big chamber, even larger than the living space, and comfortably furnished. Rugs covered the paved floor, and a large wooden bed, shaped like the reclining couches in the triclinium, but three times the size, dominated one end. Colorful cushions and covers lay on the bed, while a lovely mural, of naked, cavorting women in a forest, decorated one of the walls.

Fenella had halted before the mural, fascinated by it. "Those women," she murmured. "Who are they?"

"Nymphs," Aquila had replied, "lovely maidens who guard woodlands and other realms of nature." He paused then. "My predecessor had it painted. Do you like it?"

Fenella had turned to Aquila, to see he was smiling. "Aye," she answered honestly. "Very much."

Across the table, Aquila's gaze now roamed over her face. Swallowing the last of her cheese, Fenella washed it down with a sip of wine. Her belly did a shallow dive. Gods, the man had a look that could melt iron. Warmth flowered between her thighs. Distracted, she pressed them together.

She knew a man didn't invite a woman into his sleeping space if he didn't intend to tumble her. They had already lain together—she shouldn't be on edge.

And yet she was.

She couldn't stop thinking about the raven she'd seen that afternoon—or that the full moon was fast approaching.

One for sorrow.

The bird was also a reminder that she didn't belong among these people. Whatever this was between her and Aquila, it couldn't last.

"You seem preoccupied," she observed after a pause.

He shrugged, raising his calix to his lips and draining it. "You will have noticed the change within the fort. Now the weather is warming, we must be vigilant."

Fenella tensed, her pulse quickening. "I hear your men have spied Cruthini warriors on the move," she said, forcing her tone to remain light. "Do you think Toutorix is behind it?"

Aquila held her gaze, his jaw tightening. "Most likely. You remember the last words he shouted to me at Lake Taus ... he won't rest till he's had his revenge." He paused then. "And perhaps he wants his wife back."

Fenella snorted. "Believe me, he won't."

Aquila frowned. "How can you be sure? I wouldn't let another man claim you."

Heat prickled across Fenella's chest. "You and Toutorix are different breeds of men," she murmured.

His brow smoothed, warmth igniting in his eyes. "How so?"

Fenella's spine straightened, her lips pursing. "Justinian Aquila ... I do believe you are trawling for a compliment."

He grinned, the last of his shadowed mood lifting. "What if I am?"

Shifting uncomfortably on her stool, Fenella was aware she'd started to sweat. She preferred his playful mood to brooding—and yet she didn't like the turn their conversation had taken.

"Is it that hard to think of one redeeming feature I possess?" he asked, his tone teasing now.

Fenella snorted. "Gods, the arrogance of you."

His gaze locked with hers. "Well?"

Drawing a slow breath, she considered the character of the man seated opposite. In the beginning, she'd viewed him as her captor, nothing more. She'd deliberately refused to see anything likable about him. But now, as she cast her mind back, she recalled the things he'd said and done.

He'd shown her many kindnesses over the past moons. He might have thrown her in the pit, yet he'd brought her a blanket so she wouldn't die of cold. When she'd complained of feeling trapped within the praetorium, he'd taken her up onto the walls. And despite that she'd railed at him over his treatment of Eogan, he'd still set her brother free.

"You are a man of your word," she murmured after a long pause. "A rare quality indeed."

His golden gaze darkened to amber. "You trust me then?"

Fenella cleared her throat, her discomfort intensifying. "I wouldn't go that far."

A charged silence settled between them, stretching out, before Aquila broke it. "Come here, carissima." His voice was low, gentle, yet a command all the same.

Carissima—my darling.

Fenella's palms grew damp. The Mother, he was using endearments with her now.

And the gods curse her for eternity, she obeyed, rising from her stool and going to him.

He pulled her astride him, settling her down upon his lap. And then his hand lifted, caressing her cheek as their gazes fused once more. "I wish you would trust me," he murmured.

Fenella's breathing caught in her chest before an ache rose under her breastbone. Suddenly, she wished she did. But this connection between them was as fragile as a cobweb. Soon, she would be gone from his life. "I don't give my trust easily," she whispered back.

His gaze softened, turning as warm as molten honey. "Then I will have to work harder to earn it."

Fenella couldn't help it; she leaned down, her lips slanting over his for a kiss. They'd only lain together the night before, yet she was already missing his taste. She took her fill now, and Aquila responded in kind, his hands sliding down her back to cup her backside. He pulled her against him as the kiss deepened, turning wet and wild. His arousal, hard and hot, pressed against her core.

Groaning into his mouth, Fenella ground herself against him. She slid her fingers through his still-damp hair and down the hard column of his neck, before she explored his chest. However, the tunic frustrated her.

She wanted more. She wanted him naked.

Justin held Fenella tight and rose from the stool, crossing to the bed. And all the while, he kissed her, their tongues tangling. Setting her down on the floor in front of the bed, he reluctantly dragged his mouth from hers before he started to undo his belt.

Fenella required no urging to do the same. A smile curved her full lips as she deftly untied her belt and shrugged out of her tunic, the garment pooling upon the tiles at her feet.

His gaze took her in greedily, as if he hadn't already seen her naked.

They sprawled upon the bed together, scattering cushions as their hands and mouths sought each other once more. Limbs tangled, they rolled over and over, while Justin feasted on her lush breasts and trailed his tongue and lips over her sweet skin. Fenella sighed and groaned under his touch, her body quivering in anticipation when he rolled her over onto all fours and slid into her from behind.

The deep, needy moan that escaped her, as he slid in to the hilt, nearly made him lose control then and there, as did the tremors that shivered through her lithe body. He loved how responsive she was to him.

Justin took her slowly at first in languorous, deep thrusts, while his hand explored the smoothness of her buttocks and the long sweep of her back.

Fenella was lost now, her hair spread out across the pillow, sweat gleaming upon her pale skin. And when she twisted, turning her face so she could glance back over her shoulder at him, the want in her eyes, her shallow, ragged breathing, undid him.

Leaning over her, Justin stroked the wetness between her trembling thighs with one hand, while he braced them both against the bed with the other.

And as she bucked and cried out beneath him, he let himself go. He took her hard, the slap of their skin filling the chamber.

Soon Justin was holding Fenella up as she unraveled under him. Heat gathered at the base of his spine, his vision darkening. And when the fluttering muscles of her core rippled down the length of his rod, he spent himself deep within her.

Panting, Justin braced himself above Fenella, even as he remained buried inside her. He placed both hands upon the bed now, for fear of crushing her under his weight. His eyes fluttered shut, heat still pulsing through him. That climax had set every nerve in his body alight, and his limbs shook in the aftermath.

Gently, he withdrew from Fenella, smiling at her groan of disappointment. He understood how she felt—he wanted to remain buried inside her forever. However, if he remained in this position for much longer, he risked collapsing on top of her.

Justin lowered himself onto the bed, pulling Fenella close to spoon against him. He then pushed aside the curtain of her hair and kissed her neck. His lover sighed her pleasure, wriggling back against him.

A wave of tenderness swept over Justin—the sensation so intense that the back of his eyelids prickled.

Mithras, he was in deep now.

He'd never thought to meet a woman like Fenella in his lifetime, least of all on this northern frontier. She roused feelings in him that nearly overwhelmed him at times, and yet he wouldn't shy from them.

Instead, he found himself imagining what his future would look like with this woman part of it.

XXIII. STEALTH

A LOUD KNOCK at the door roused Fenella from a deep sleep.

After their first passionate coupling, Justin had taken her twice more before they'd collapsed onto the bed, exhaustion claiming them both. Limbs entwined, they'd fallen asleep.

Fenella was usually a restless sleeper, yet not tonight. Curled against her lover, her head resting upon his chest, she slumbered peacefully.

Until the knock at the door shattered her peace.

Justin came awake more swiftly than she did, untangling himself from her, and rolling off the bed. Blinking owl-like in the glow of a nearby lantern, Fenella found herself admiring the strong, sculpted planes of his body. She'd explored every inch of him tonight, tasted the salt of his skin, felt the thunder of his heart against her cheek.

The knock sounded again, impatient this time.

"Coming," Justin called out.

Justin. She couldn't think of him as Aquila anymore, not after all they'd done and shared.

Scooping up his tunic from the floor, he yanked it over his head. Meanwhile, Fenella pulled the covers up to conceal her nakedness. He was just making his way toward the door, when the knock sounded a third time, urgent now.

Justin growled a curse under his breath and yanked open the door. "Optio Gavia," he barked at the man standing in the doorway. "What is it?"

"Sorry to bother you at this hour, General." The helmed soldier slammed his fisted right hand over his heart in greeting. Fenella noted that the man didn't glance over at the bed; instead, he kept his gaze firmly upon the legate. "But the fort's under attack."

Fenella's breathing hitched, coldness seeping over her.

It's too early. The full moon was still a few days off.

The deep, resonant boom of a horn ripped through the air then, shattering the night's calm, and Justin swore once more.

Fenella's heart bucked against her ribs. Toutorix had clearly decided to strike early.

"I'll be right there," Justin told the optio, stepping back. "In the meantime, alert the rest of my officers."

The optio nodded, turned, and marched off, his heavy sandals slapping on the pavers.

Fenella watched Justin dress. He moved deftly, his jaw clenched and gaze narrowed.

Nervousness coiled in her belly. Already the memory of him as her tender, passionate lover was fading.

General Aquila now stood before her.

Over his tunic, Justin fitted a leather harness and a pleated leather skirt. He then glanced Fenella's way. They hadn't spoken since the optio had delivered the news, although their gazes fused.

"Can you help me?" he asked, gesturing to where his armor hung upon a stand near the bed. It was a request, not an order. He wasn't speaking to her as her master but as a lover. "Usually Aedan does this, but there's no time to fetch him."

Nodding, Fenella climbed naked out of bed and retrieved the lorica, strapping it onto his shoulders, back, and chest. Kneeling at his feet, she then fastened greaves about his legs before helping him strap on the bracers about his forearms.

And all the while, they didn't speak.

There was little to be said.

Ardoch was under attack, and he needed to be out there, leading his men.

Fenella's belly cramped then.

Against my people.

She had to gather her wits and ready herself to go.

Nausea rolled over her. It was too soon—she wasn't ready. She wasn't just unprepared in a practical sense, but also emotionally. Her encounters with Justin had distracted her, disarmed her. Spending the night in his arms had roused conflicting thoughts—ones she now desperately pushed aside.

Nonetheless, she had no choice, for the attack was upon them.

She finished helping Justin dress and stepped back, watching as he strapped his gladius around his hips. Justin then glanced up, and their gazes held for a heartbeat.

"Stay inside the praetorium, Fenella," he commanded, moving close to her and brushing his knuckles across her cheek. "No matter what happens ... don't venture outside." He kissed her then—a brief, bruising embrace—before he turned, his purple cloak billowing behind him. Grabbing his plumed helmet, he stalked from the room.

The thunder of soldiers' feet, as they rushed up the steps and ladders onto the wall, rumbled across the fort. The sour tang of fear filled the air, yet the men's training prevented any of them from giving in to panic. Instead, they formed orderly ranks, waiting for their general's command.

"They've got us surrounded," Marcus informed Justin when he joined him upon the northern guard tower that spanned the Porta Praetoria.

"Futuo," Justin muttered. Had his sentries all been asleep tonight? "How did they manage to get so close without anyone raising the alarm?"

"Stealth. They took down our two nearest watchtowers before the men could alert us," Marcus replied, his tone grim. "They also killed most of our men there … before two of our sentries made it back to warn us."

Justin's mouth thinned. Raising a shield an optio had just passed him, he moved close to the spiked palings, his gaze sweeping the darkness below. Fires burned upon the walls of Ardoch, casting a glow over the series of ditches and ramparts below the walls.

A waxing gibbous moon sailed high in the clear skies overhead. And now that Justin's eyes had adjusted to the darkness, he spied the outlines of men below: eyes, bare limbs, and unsheathed blades gleaming in the moonlight. Many of them carried flaming torches, which made it look as if fireflies swarmed around the base of the fort.

Justin swore again. "Curse that storm bird," he growled.

After spying the eagle, he'd taken precautions. He'd increased the watch upon the walls and doubled the men at the nearest watchtowers. Yet it hadn't been enough— and the sheer size of the army encircling Ardoch now was daunting.

"Toutorix has been busy," Marcus muttered next to him. "Somehow, the cunning bastard has united the northern tribes."

Justin scowled. Indeed, the Wolf managed to achieve what few of the Picti chieftains had. They'd underestimated him.

Peering closer, he noted one or two robed figures capering back and forth amongst the front ranks. These individuals had wild hair and long beards. Brandishing staffs aloft, they called out to the warriors, their shrill voices rising above the rumble of the gathered army.

Justin's lip curled. *Druids.*

Like most Roman soldiers, he distrusted these sorcerers. Druids wielded much power over the chieftains of this land and could whip them up into a frenzy. They were dangerous men indeed.

Justin continued to survey the sea of blue-painted bodies. They appeared to surround the fort on all sides, seeking its weakest point.

Cries to the southwest, followed by the faint clang of steel and iron, drew his attention then.

The vicus.

The settlement outside the walls had guards defending it, but no high walls.

Justin whirled to where the camp prefect, Felix Antonius Magnus, had stepped up next to him. "Did we warn the magistrates in time?"

"Barely," Felix replied, his leathery face set in hard lines. "We managed to get some of the residents inside the fort before the Picti reached them." His mouth thinned. "The rest are now fending for themselves."

Justin's jaw clenched at this news. However, there was little he could do for the hapless souls facing the attackers outside the walls. "Have we got reinforcements at the other gates?"

The Porta Principalis Sinistra and Porta Principalis Dextra were both smaller than this one, with steeper yet less perilous access.

"Yes, General," Felix replied. "Your men are ready."

No sooner had the camp prefect spoken when the twang of bowstrings releasing cut through the night. An instant later, flaming arrows hurtled toward them.

"Shields up!" Justin bellowed, raising his own just in time. As one, the ranks of legionaries obeyed, and a wall of shields lifted.

An instant later, arrows clattered against wood and metal, the odor of burning pitch filling the air.

"Parati!" Justin shouted.

Get ready!

A second volley of arrows loosed, peppering the wall.

Pained grunts and cries followed, as one or two found their mark, despite the tightly-packed shield wall his men created.

Rising to his feet, Justin drew in a deep breath, before shouting, "Arm the catapults!"

This fort had a few of these large wooden and iron contraptions, installed above each of the gates and along the walls. Shouts followed, as men hauled boulders into the payload of the catapult above the Porta Praetoria and awaited his order.

"Loose!"

Rocks flew from the walls, smashing through the boiling tide of warriors.

Screams drifted up from below, yet the reprieve was brief. Another volley of arrows rained down upon them as the Wolves and their allies inched forward. A few of the bravest warriors raced up the causeway between the sloping ramparts and ditches. Some were cut down, while others managed to put up ladders.

The men defending the walls killed many of them with rocks and arrows before they managed to climb the first few rungs. But as Justin looked on, he saw the attackers had brought long planks of wood with them, which they hurled across the ditches. Vicious iron spikes lay within those trenches, ensuring a painful death for any who tried to climb the walls that way, although the wooden planks soon created a number of rickety bridges.

"Archers ready!" Marcus bellowed, his red cloak billowing behind him as he slid down the ladder from the guard tower to the wall.

Men wielding crossbows stepped up to the edge of the palisade, braving the hail of arrows from the attackers, to fire bolts of their own.

"Loose!"

Heavy crossbow bolts rained down on the warriors now clambering across the ditches, sending some of them flailing down upon the spikes.

But they kept coming, warrior after warrior.

Justin watched the advance, a chill sweeping over him.

He'd once called Toutorix a '*carnifex*'—a butcher—after the slaughter at Ardunie, but it seemed the chieftain of the Wolves of the North was just as happy to send his own people to die.

The Wolf would breach their defenses tonight, even if he had to use every warrior he had to do so.

He wanted blood.

He wanted Justin Aquila's head on a pike.

Another ladder went up, and then another, and soon the walls were crawling with Picti. The defenders sent many down to their deaths, but many more kept climbing—and it wasn't long before the first of them breached the top of the wall.

The garrison, still holding position, were ready for them when they did.

Justin moved from the top of the guard tower and descended to the wall, drawing his sword.

"Get back, General," Marcus called to Justin as he drew his own gladius. As legate, he was expected to watch the siege unfold from afar, and only fight when things were dire.

However, Justin had never acted like most generals—and Marcus knew that.

The chill in his blood deepened, ice prickling his skin.

He had no intention of watching his men die while Toutorix and his warriors swarmed over them. Every soldier would have to fight tonight if they were to prevent Ardoch from being overrun.

And so Justin advanced to where a Picti had just leaped onto the wall. The warrior was young and lithe, his bare chest smeared with blue woad. Snarling curses, he cut down the camp prefect. Felix Magnus fell, his cry of agony ringing out across the fort.

The warrior whirled, and spying the general, he went for him, teeth bared. Justin ducked his strike and smashed his shield into the man's chest, driving him backward.

He then swung his gladius and drew blood.

XXIV. GO IF YOU MUST

STANDING IN THE courtyard, Fenella pulled her woolen shawl about her and peered into the sky. She couldn't see anything from here—a fact that frustrated her no end. The praetorium had no outward-facing windows, and she was leery of sticking her head out of the entrance just yet.

Justin would have men flanking it, and she didn't want to make them suspicious—not until she had to fight her way past them.

Sniffing, she marked the char in the pre-dawn air. Smoke was drifting down from the ramparts.

Her pulse quickened.

Had they set the fort alight?

Even here, at the heart of Ardoch, the thunder of battle reached her. And it was getting louder.

The attack had been going on for a while, but instead of rising to a crescendo, and then dying away, the roar intensified.

They've breached the walls.

Her people were inside Ardoch.

Justin.

No, she couldn't think of him—not now. Instead, she had to focus on making her escape.

Sucking in a deep breath, Fenella gripped her shawl around her tighter still. It wasn't cold this morning, yet goose pimples covered her skin. Curse her. She'd looked forward to this day, had thought her heart would rejoice to know her freedom was imminent, yet instead, her bowels had turned to ice, and she felt oddly light-headed.

She still had to get out of the praetorium, collect her rope, and make her way to the watchtower above the Porta Principalis Dextra, fighting any Roman who barred her way. Then she'd rope down the other side.

Timing would be everything.

Fenella clenched her jaw tight before spinning on her heel and heading for the kitchen. The others were in there, waiting out the siege.

As she'd expected, Aedan was pacing the length of the space, restless, while the others sat at the scrubbed wooden table, fingers wrapped around cups of hot broth.

They all looked Fenella's way as she entered.

"The air's heavy with smoke," she announced. "The sound of battle grows louder." Her gaze met Aedan's. "They're inside the fort."

"What?" Ava clutched at Caius. "They can't have breached the walls?"

"Of course they can … if there are enough of them," the steward muttered.

"We need weapons," Aedan spoke up.

"The general has some in his room," Kahina replied, rising to her feet. Her face was taut, although her voice remained steady. "I'll get them."

A search of Justin's quarters turned up two daggers and a spear. Caius took a pugio, Aedan helped himself to the other, and Kahina grasped the pilum. Fenella and Ava made do with weapons from the kitchen. Ava armed herself with a cleaver, while Fenella took a boning knife with a long thin blade—one she'd had her eye on for a while.

The steward and cook took refuge in the kitchen then, leaving the three slaves to hide elsewhere.

They lingered in the courtyard, while above them the sun was rising, staining the smoky sky crimson. It was an ominous color. But even more disconcerting were the shouts and screams now ringing through the fort. The fighting was close enough that they could hear the clash of blades.

"Minerva, defend us," Kahina whispered. Her brown eyes glittered. Her knuckles, which clenched the shaft of her spear, had gone white. "We should find somewhere to hide."

Fenella's heart started to pound.

This was her chance. She had to go now—before the attackers reached this house. She'd be trapped inside with the others once they did.

However, her feet wouldn't move.

Even if Kahina and Aedan attempted to hide in one of the rooms lining the portico, they'd be discovered if the praetorium was overrun. She couldn't leave them to the Wolves.

"There's no point hiding," she gasped, turning to her companions. "We need to go."

Aedan stared at her. "What?"

Horror shadowed Kahina's eyes. "But the general ordered us to remain within the praetorium."

"And the general has likely been skewered on a Cruthini blade by now," Fenella countered. Bile stung her throat then. Gods, she hoped not. Her gaze flicked from Kahina's face to Aedan's. They were both gawking at her as if a changeling stood before them.

"Listen to me," she said, her voice low and hard. "I know a way out ... but we have to leave now."

"I'm not going anywhere," Kahina shot back, her voice rising. "I'll not abandon Aquila."

"What?" Fenella viewed her friend with disbelief. "You owe him nothing, Kahina ... you're his *slave*."

However, Kahina took a step back, deliberately distancing herself from her. "Go if you must, Fen ... but I'm staying."

Muttering a curse, Fenella turned her focus to Aedan. "Don't tell me you're loyal to these people too?" she said, bitterness souring her mouth.

The Brigante stared back at her. A nerve jumped under one eye, but unlike Kahina, he appeared to be considering her offer. He was clearly torn.

"Make your choice, Aedan," Fenella growled, taking a step toward the portico. "We don't have much longer."

But no sooner had she spoken, when shouts and the clang of clashing blades drifted into the courtyard from the atrium. The guards Justin had left to defend his residence were fighting for their lives.

Fenella froze, her belly twisting. Curse them all, it was too late. The battle had come to them.

Swallowing, she glanced back at Aedan. "Maybe we can talk our way out of this."

He nodded before glancing at Kahina. "Best you hide at the back of the portico."

Kahina stared back at them, anger smoldering in her dark eyes. She looked as if she wanted to curse them both. However, instead, she did as bid, stalking over toward the far end of the portico. Kahina had just hidden behind the trailing veil of honeysuckle near the bathhouse when the crash of doors splintering echoed through the atrium.

"Here we go," Fenella whispered, taking off her shawl and tossing it away. Such a garment would only hinder her if she had to fight.

"You should speak first," Aedan murmured, his gaze trained upon the archway. "They'll notice my accent ... and wonder what a Brigante warrior is doing here."

It was a valid point, although Fenella didn't have time to answer, for an instant later, four blue-painted warriors, all of them male, barreled onto the portico.

One look at them, and Fenella's heart sank.

They had the crazed look of men in the thrall of battle fever. Blood-splattered, and dressed in nothing more than leather and plaid trews, the warriors came to an abrupt halt on the colonnaded walkway at the sight of Aedan and Fenella.

A heartbeat passed as their gazes raked over them—and Fenella chilled.

Of course, although their tribal markings were evident, and their look was clearly native, both she and Aedan were clad in sleeveless, knee-length slave tunics.

One of the warriors, a huge man with black hair and a blood-streaked face, took a step forward, his green eyes narrowing. "Who are you?"

Fenella moved toward him, careful to keep her boning knife low and relaxed at her side. "I'm of the Wolf," she replied, aware that the man was now staring at the tattoo upon her right arm. "This is my man."

One of the warriors behind the leader spat on the ground. "And what are you doing in here? We just smashed our way through the only entrance."

Fenella stared back at him, her mind suddenly going blank. She hadn't had the time to think any of this through.

"We got in through a tunnel under the floor," Aedan replied.

The raven-haired warrior scowled. "You're not one of the Cruthini."

Aedan raised his chin, his own gaze narrowing. "No, I'm a Brigante."

"We're wasting time here," another of the warriors growled. "Where are the servants?" The gleam in the man's eyes needed no explanation. He was hoping for a prize, a woman to rape.

"They're all gone," Fenella replied, surprised at just how steady her voice was. "We've already checked."

All four warriors scowled at this news, their faces hardening.

"You're dressed like one of them," the black-haired warrior noted. "Why is that?"

"We've been hiding in the village outside the walls," Fenella answered. "It's easier to blend in this way."

"She's lying," the one who'd spat earlier, growled. "I can smell it on her."

"Aye." The big warrior eyed her, hunger glinting in his mossy eyes. "She's mine, lads."

He then lunged.

Fenella danced out of his way, swiping low with her boning knife. The blade scored a deep cut across his arm, and the warrior snarled a curse.

Meanwhile, the other three closed in on Aedan.

The Brigante held his ground, his gaze narrowed. "Are you sure you want to do this?" Aedan murmured. "I've no wish to kill you."

One of the warriors snorted a laugh. "Listen to him."

"Aye," another sneered. "I'm going to cut his pretty face into ribbons."

They attacked, although Fenella didn't have a chance to see how Aedan was faring—she was too busy defending herself from their leader.

He wielded a long blade and moved with fluid grace. They circled each other, while Fenella went through all the tactics her father had taught her. She'd grown up sparring with Eogan, and although she hadn't chosen the warrior's path, Fenella was fast with a blade and quick on her feet.

Her opponent realized this now, and so he watched her with calculating intensity. "I like humping the wild ones," he said, grinning. "I'm going to enjoy this."

Fenella broke out in a cold sweat. He was trying to scare her, and succeeding. Nonetheless, she couldn't let him smell fear or this was over.

Grunts, followed by an agonized cry, filled the courtyard.

Either Aedan or one of the men he fought had just fallen.

Fenella was tempted to glance sideways, to see how the Brigante was faring, but she didn't dare.

The black-haired warrior lunged once more, his blade whistling past her, again and again, as he drove Fenella backward.

Heart in her throat, she ducked and twisted, cursing her small knife. She wasn't close enough to get under his guard and use it—and the bastard knew it.

Another scream echoed through the courtyard, yet her attacker paid it no mind. Instead, he plowed forward, jaw set in grim determination.

Moments later, Fenella found herself backed up against a pillar.

Panic tore at her throat, yet she clutched at all the tricks she'd learned over the years. The only way out of this was to fight dirty.

She dropped low, just as the warrior reached out with a hand to pin her to the pillar, and slashed him across the ankle. His howl of pain rent the air, yet she was already rolling away. Bouncing to her feet, Fenella came up behind him and sank her knife deep into his neck.

The warrior's knees buckled, his sword clattering to the pavers. Blood now pumped from his neck, but he wasn't yet dead. Gritting her teeth, Fenella stepped up behind him and drew her blade across his throat.

The warrior slumped to the ground.

Spinning around, Fenella's gaze alighted upon a surprising sight.

Two of the attackers were dead, although another three had entered the courtyard.

But they didn't just have Aedan to contend with. Kahina had left her hiding place and was holding her own. She stabbed her spear through the guts of a warrior, while Aedan finished him off with his dagger.

Fenella scooped up the sword of the man she'd just killed and joined the fray.

Her pulse beat hard in her throat now, despair sweeping over her. There would be no escaping now—but she might as well go down fighting.

The warriors kept coming. Another group burst into the courtyard. With a howl, they rushed at her.

Standing back-to-back with Aedan and Kahina, Fenella slashed and parried. The three of them had done a fine job of defending themselves, but there were too many warriors now.

They wouldn't be able to hold them off for much longer.

XXV. DON'T MOURN HIM YET

AEDAN RUSHED FORWARD, his blade clashing with the first of the warriors who lunged for them. Like Fenella, he too had taken the sword of one of the fallen men.

The Brigante slashed his way into the midst of the attackers.

Muttering an oath, Fenella dove after him. Although Aedan was clearly skilled with a blade and recklessly brave as well, he wouldn't survive long if he got himself surrounded.

They fought back-to-back once more, the pavers beneath their feet turning sticky with blood. Now that she wielded a proper sword, Fenella managed to bring down another two men. Nonetheless, the muscles in her arms and shoulders burned and her hands were slippery with sweat. Aedan appeared tireless, yet she wasn't. Physical toil had kept her strong during her time at Ardoch, but she wasn't sure how much longer she could wield this blade.

Shouting rang through the courtyard then, men's voices.

Not in her tongue, but in Latin.

Fenella's belly swooped when a familiar, broad-shouldered figure burst into the courtyard, a purple cloak billowing behind him.

He's alive!

The dawn sunlight gleamed off Justin Aquila's helmet as he cut down any warrior who crossed his path. He'd returned to the praetorium—and just in time too. Three of his men followed close behind, sword-blades dark with blood.

But Fenella couldn't take her gaze off Justin. Even at this distance, she spied the gore that splattered him; his fine purple cloak was filthy and rent.

The warrior Fenella had been fighting whirled away from her, flinging himself at the general. But moments later, he too fell under Aquila's blade. And shortly after, all the attackers lay dead or twitching on the courtyard pavers.

Breathing hard, Justin kicked his last opponent's body aside and moved forward. His gaze swept the faces of his slaves. Aedan was bent double, struggling to catch his breath after the furious fight. He'd suffered a shallow cut to one arm but appeared otherwise uninjured. Behind him, Kahina still held her bloody spear in a death grip, her face splattered with blood.

Justin's gaze came to rest upon Fenella. "Are you hurt?" he rasped.

She shook her head. Her heart was beating so hard that it felt as if it might burst from her chest.

"The siege?" Aedan panted.

"It's over. The fort is secure once more."

Fenella's gaze flew wide. *It is?*

Justin glanced around. "Where are Caius and Ava?"

"In the kitchen," Fenella replied. "They're safe."

Nodding, Justin stepped forward, searching Fenella's face as if making sure that she was indeed unhurt. "The attackers scaled the walls and tried to torch the buildings … but we drove them back in the end." He paused then. "Toutorix is dead."

Fenella's heart lurched against her ribs, weakness flooding through her limbs. She must have swayed upon her feet, for Justin reached out, his hand fastening around her arm, steadying her.

Her reaction had unsettled him; she saw it in his gaze. However, his jaw unclenched when she finally murmured, "Good."

Dizziness swept over her then, queasiness curdling her belly. It wasn't grief for her traitorous husband, she was glad Toutorix was dead, but fear for her kin.

Justin's news boded ill for her father and brother. *Have they fallen?*

She glanced then at Kahina. The slave's face was composed, although her eyes glinted. Fenella's breathing grew shallow. This was Kahina's chance to drop her in it—to tell Justin she'd planned to escape.

The two women's gazes fused for a long moment before Kahina's attention flicked to her master.

Holding her breath, Fenella braced herself.

"What of Centurion Camillus?" Kahina asked.

Exhaling sharply, Fenella raised a trembling hand to her breast.

Not noticing Fenella's reaction, Justin focused on Kahina instead. His face turned grave. "Marcus took a spear to the chest," he murmured. "He's been taken to hospital ... and is in the hands of a surgeon now."

Fenella found Kahina in their cubliculum, seated upon her sleeping pallet, head in her hands. The door was open, letting in daylight, for—like the other rooms in this building—the room was windowless. During the day, the light filtered in from the doors that ringed the portico.

Wordlessly, Fenella moved across to the pallet and lowered herself down upon it.

"Kahina," she murmured, placing a hand upon her friend's trembling shoulder. "Are you unwell?"

Kahina's shoulder went rigid, and when she lifted her tear-streaked face, her peat-brown eyes were bleak. "Why are you still here?" she croaked. "I thought you'd have fled by now."

"It's too late for that," Fenella replied, her voice still soft. "The opportunity has been lost."

Kahina stared back at her before her mouth twisted. "Have you been planning this then?"

Fenella nodded.

"But why? You're treated well here … and a bond has formed between you and the general."

"I'm still his slave," Fenella answered, her voice roughening. "In the end, he's just another man who wishes to control me. I want to be free, Kahina. Is that so wrong?"

Her friend stared back at her. "No," she murmured.

Silence fell between them. A groove formed between Kahina's eyebrows as she tried to understand her. They were women in a man's world. Kahina had accepted that long ago, yet Fenella didn't want to spend the rest of her life bowing to a man's will.

Daughter. Wife. Slave. She'd always been someone's property. She just wanted to belong to herself.

"Why didn't you say anything to Aquila?" Fenella asked finally.

"It wasn't for your benefit," Kahina murmured, looking away. "He's a good man, Fen … and I didn't want to hurt him."

Fenella's throat constricted. "Oh, Kahina," she said, a wobble in her own voice now. "You are too soft-hearted for your own good."

"I know," Kahina gasped before burying her head in her hands once more. A choked sob followed.

Watching her, Fenella knew her tears weren't for the man she served, or for the likes of her. Instead, she wept for Marcus.

Reaching out, Fenella wrapped an arm around Kahina's back and held her fast. The soft sound of Kahina's weeping filtered out into the portico, and anyone nearby would be able to hear. However, after the slaughter in the courtyard, the inhabitants of this household weren't likely in the mood for eavesdropping.

They'd cleared the courtyard of the bodies, before Fenella and Kahina had washed the blood-stained pavers down with soapy water, and scrubbed away the signs of the violent skirmish. Nonetheless, the siege had left all of them shaken.

"Marcus lives still," Fenella murmured after a while, rubbing her friend's back. "Don't mourn him yet."

Raising her face to Fenella's once more, Kahina's throat bobbed. "You're so strong, Fen," she whispered. "I've never seen a woman fight like you did today ... you were magnificent."

Fenella huffed a laugh before reaching out and wiping away Kahina's tears. "As were you with that pilum."

Kahina managed a weak smile. She then sniffed, scrubbing at her wet cheeks. "How were you actually planning to escape?"

Fenella pulled a face. "I had a rope hidden behind where Aedan keeps fuel for the furnace. I was going to climb up to the Porta Principalis Dextra, stab anyone who tried to get in my way, and then use the rope to lower myself down to the causeway."

Her face warmed as she recounted this. Revealing her plan out loud made it sound foolhardy. Would she have made it to safety, even with Aedan at her side?

Kahina's gleaming eyes widened. "Jupiter," she breathed. "You really are fearless."

"No," Fenella murmured, her cheeks growing hotter. "Just reckless."

Kahina's brow furrowed in confusion, but Fenella placed a hand over hers, squeezing gently. She didn't want to talk about herself; instead, she wished to make it up to her friend. Kahina had done her a great kindness in keeping her secret safe.

She wanted to make amends for disappointing her.

"I think we need to assure ourselves that Marcus will indeed rally," she said firmly. "Come on ... let's pay the hospital a visit."

Outdoors, buildings smoldered, dark smoke staining the morning sky. The char of burning and the metallic stench of blood filled the air, catching at the back of Fenella's throat. Dark patches stained the street, and although men had started to clear the bodies away, a few corpses still littered the ground.

Kahina murmured something under her breath and raised a hand to cover her mouth.

Next to her, Fenella frowned.

Perhaps venturing out of the praetorium at present wasn't the best idea, but she was determined that Kahina should see Marcus.

One of the guards had reluctantly agreed to accompany them after Fenella insisted that Aquila had given them permission to visit the hospital. The guard had been wary, but there was no way for him to confirm the order. The general was busy overseeing the men securing the fort's defenses.

And so, brow furrowed with disapproval, the legionary escorted the women through the smoking fort. Heaviness descended upon Fenella as she followed him.

She should be free now, running through the pines in search of shelter.

Instead, she was still inside Ardoch. Still a slave.

The valetudinarium, the hospital, sat at the southeastern corner of the fort. A long wooden building with a tiled roof, it crouched in the shadow of the walls.

The Roman dead lay in neat rows in the yard outside the hospital, as orderly in death as they'd been in life.

"Jupiter," Kahina breathed, her voice catching. "So many."

Fenella swallowed hard as she surveyed row upon row of corpses. Gods, it really had been a slaughter.

Their escort didn't linger outdoors. Instead, the guard pushed through the doors into the hospital. The women followed him into a huge rectangular hall, crammed with pallets. Medics moved from patient to patient, shouting to orderlies. The stench of blood was even stronger in here, and Fenella choked down a gag, resisting the urge to clamp a hand over her mouth.

This had been her idea, after all. Suddenly, she was regretting it.

Squaring her shoulders, she met her escort's eye. "We need to find Centurion Camillus."

The legionary's dark eyebrows crashed together, his jaw tightening at being ordered around by a slave. However, Fenella's imperious look had the desired effect, for, after a moment, he spun away from her and marched up to the nearest orderly.

After a brief exchange, the orderly pointed right. The legionary then motioned to the women and headed down the aisle between the pallets, dodging medics and orderlies as he went.

Fenella and Kahina hurried after him.

They found Marcus in a smaller chamber at the far end of the hospital building. He shared the space with four other high-ranking officers. Curtains hung between the pallets, giving the patients a modicum of privacy. Nonetheless, that didn't matter to Marcus, for he was insensible.

Face ashen, he lay propped up on a nest of pillows. Bandages swathed his naked chest, and although they appeared freshly applied, blood soaked through them.

Kahina emitted a choked sound at the sight of him, her slender body going rigid.

"What's this?"

The party turned to find the curtain had been drawn back, and a tall, angular man stood behind them. His hands were bloodstained. A lanky orderly grasping a basin of water, with clean bandages slung over one arm, cringed behind him.

Their escort bowed his head. "Surgeon Falco ... apologies for the intrusion."

The surgeon's craggy face twisted into a scowl as his narrowed gaze swept over the legionary and two female slaves. "Who are you, and why are you here?" he growled.

"We are here at General Aquila's request," the legionary replied. "To check on the status of Centurion Camillus."

Falco's mouth pursed. "Did the general really sanction this?"

"Sanction what?"

Breath catching, Fenella spun around to find the man himself standing in the doorway.

XXVI. THE SIREN

JUSTIN FOLDED HIS arms across his broad chest, amber gaze narrowing. "Answer me, soldier."

"Sir!" The legionary's spine snapped rigid, a fisted hand slamming against his heart. "I brought these women here upon your command."

Justin's frown deepened. "I commanded no such thing."

The soldier visibly blanched, but Justin's attention wasn't upon him—it was on Fenella. He then glanced to where Kahina stood, frozen like a hind in a hunter's sight.

Alarm clutched at Fenella's chest. She didn't want her friend to get in trouble because of her.

"This is my doing," she gasped. "Kahina was worried about Marcus ... and I decided we should visit him."

The legionary she'd duped was glowering at her now, yet she ignored him. Her focus was on Justin.

Heaving a sigh, the general removed his black-plumed helmet and tucked it under one arm. His dark hair was plastered to his scalp, his skin still smudged with dirt, soot, and dried blood.

Fenella's throat tightened. He looked exhausted.

Glancing at where Surgeon Falco stood watching them, Justin's features tightened. "And how is Centurion Camillus?"

"Still alive," Falco replied. "The spear missed his lung by the grace of the gods, although he bled heavily." The surgeon glanced over at where Marcus lay, unnervingly still. "I've given him something strong for the pain ...

he'll sleep for a while yet. We'll know more in the coming days."

Nodding, the general turned then to the soldier. "Escort Kahina back to the praetorium," he ordered, his tone clipped now. Justin then shifted his attention back to Fenella. "You're coming with me."

Outside the hospital, Fenella had to jog to keep up with Justin's long stride. They'd gone a few yards when she glanced at his stern profile and drew in a deep breath.

"That really was my doing back there," she admitted. "Don't punish Kahina ... or the guard."

Justin glanced her way, his expression softening. "Fear not, I won't. I knew the moment I saw the three of you who was behind it." He then gave a rueful shake of his head.

Fenella released her breath, relief fluttering through her. His expression had been so grim inside the hospital that she'd braced herself for his wrath. They made their way down the Via Praetoria now, but instead of turning for home, Justin led her across the parade ground to where the street continued to the fort's main entrance.

"Where are we going?"

Justin looked her way once more. "We've laid out the dead," he replied. "Most of the besiegers were Wolves ... but there are other Picti among them and quite a few Damnonii." He paused then. "We shall burn them upon a pyre this afternoon, but I wanted to give you the chance to search the dead first ... in case any of your kin are among them."

Fenella's throat thickened. "Thank you," she said, her voice catching slightly. "That's kind."

Their gazes fused. It was indeed a generous gesture. Her people had butchered those defending the vicus outside the fort, and slain a number of Justin's men. But he still allowed her to search for her family amongst the dead.

His act both surprised and discomforted her.

Uneasiness must have shown on her face, for Justin's expression softened. "Ready yourself, Fenella," he murmured, his voice lowering. They were passing under the Porta Praetoria. The great iron and oak gate bore score marks and dents, yet the attackers hadn't managed to breach it, or the iron portcullis that had been drawn up above it. "What lies beyond isn't for the faint of heart."

An instant later, Fenella's gaze alighted upon a head, jammed upon a pike to the left of the gates.

Toutorix the Wolf's gaping face stared back at her, his pale blue eyes sightless.

Fenella's step faltered, and she drew to a halt.

The man who'd once been her husband—the man who'd handed her over to the enemy so that he could live on to seek reckoning upon them—wore a surprised expression. Toutorix's reputation as a warrior to be feared had circulated the mountains and glens of this land for years, but no longer.

Long moments passed, and then Fenella glanced Justin's way.

She'd expected to see a hard expression on his face, as if bringing her here had been a test of some kind. However, his eyes weren't calculating but understanding.

"Did you kill him?" she asked.

He nodded.

Fenella glanced back at Toutorix's severed head.

"I hope you made him suffer," she murmured. It was a bloodthirsty thing to say but no less than this man deserved.

When Fenella swiveled back to him, she saw the glint in Justin's eyes.

A chill feathered over her skin.

That look told her all she needed to know.

They continued down the causeway, and Justin led her to the lazy bend in the river where the bodies of the fallen Cruthini lay.

Fenella went cold at the sight of them: rows and rows of corpses, their limbs streaked in blue woad and blood.

Justin waited at the edge of the dead, while Fenella walked amongst them, her gaze searching every face.

There were more women than she'd expected. Aye, female warriors fought in Toutorix's ranks, yet chieftains only sent them into battle when things were dire. Toutorix had clearly held nothing back for this battle.

Pulse beating in her ears, Fenella moved slowly up and down the rows. Part of her wanted to turn and run, for she wasn't sure she could bear seeing her father and brother laid out there. She wasn't close to her family these days, especially after her father had given her to Toutorix. However, blood was blood. She didn't wish harm on any member of her family.

She recognized many faces—warriors who'd lived at Loch Tatha mainly—but when she stopped at the end of the last line, relief swept over her, causing her knees to tremble under her.

She looked up then and turned to where Justin still waited silently by the riverbank. He approached her, his expression veiled.

"None of my kin are here," Fenella greeted him, her voice husky.

Aye, she was glad not to see her father and Eogan with cut throats, gashes to the belly, and gaping holes in their chests—yet the sight of the dead would haunt her for a long while to come.

This was a dark day for her people.

Dizziness swept over her, and Fenella closed her eyes, swaying on her feet. It was too much—the stress of the day finally caught up with her.

An instant later, Justin was at her side, his arm encircling her shoulders. "That's enough now, Fenella," he said, his voice both rough and gentle. Tears burning behind her closed eyelids, she leaned into his strength. "It's time to go inside."

Fenella sank deep into the water with a sigh.

The sweet scent of honeysuckle drifted into the bathhouse, mingling with the steam. The heat of the water and the heady perfume could almost drown out the horror of the day—almost.

In here, she could wash away the stench of blood, grime, and ash. Here, she could pretend that death didn't surround her.

But it did.

Ducking under the water, she allowed the warmth to sink into her bones before she resurfaced.

Her gaze alighted then upon the naked man who lounged in the water at the far end of the pool. She and Justin had brought clean clothes and drying cloths in here, before undressing and lowering themselves into the steaming water.

Around them, the house was silent, the atmosphere heavy. Outdoors, dusk had long settled. Supper had come and gone: a simple meal of bread and cheese, which was all Ava had been able to manage, for her nerves were frayed.

As were Fenella's. And whenever she recalled the fight in the courtyard, her belly twisted. She was fortunate indeed that Aedan had been with her and Kahina, and that Justin and his men arrived when they did—otherwise things would have ended badly.

Fenella met Justin's eye now, watching as his mouth lifted at the corners. However, his gaze was shadowed. Water glistened off his broad shoulders and muscular upper arms, running in rivulets down his chest, as he braced himself against the edge of the pool.

"Enjoying the water?" he asked, his voice rumbling through the humid air.

Fenella nodded, paddling over to him. "I could stay in here forever."

His smile widened, a little of the darkness lifting from his gaze. "You'd turn into a fish then ... or perhaps a siren."

She cocked an eyebrow. "A siren?"

"Half woman, half fish ... and wickedly beautiful. They sit upon rocks and sing to sailors, luring them to their death."

His words were said with a teasing edge, yet they made Fenella shiver despite the warm water she sat in.

How would he react, if he knew she'd planned to escape during the siege?

XXVII. ANIMA MEA

"YOU FOUGHT WELL today," Justin said, brushing a lock of damp hair off her forehead. "Although, my heart nearly stopped when I saw you in the midst of those warriors."

"I'm relieved you arrived when you did," she admitted. "I'm not sure how much longer I'd have lasted."

His gaze shadowed once more. "It was carnage out there," he murmured. "I've fought in a number of battles in my time, but none as savage as this."

"Then you did well to win," she replied, even as her pulse accelerated. Talking of the siege put her on edge. "Especially against such a large army."

"The attack was well-planned and carefully executed," he continued. "They brought down the watchtowers nearest the fort. This afternoon, I learned that they hit our two northern outposts as well. Dalginross has fallen again, while Bochastle hangs by a thread. I've sent men north to escort the survivors safely back to Ardoch."

Fenella swallowed. "What will happen now?"

Justin let out a long exhale, before reaching out, catching her by the wrist, and pulling her against him. He then placed a kiss on the crown of her head. "I don't know."

"Will you seek retribution?"

"No ... we don't have the men for it. And most of those who attacked Ardoch are dead now anyway."

Fenella marked the bleak edge to his voice. Reaching out, she slid her hand across his chest, her fingertips tracing the wet whorls of crisp dark hair there. "You're weary of this life, aren't you?"

He huffed a laugh, however, there was no humor in it. "Is it that obvious?"

"Only to me perhaps ... only tonight."

"I don't let my guard down easily," Justin admitted then, his voice lowering. "But I want to with you." His fingertips trailed a lazy path down her neck to her spine, traveling between her shoulder blades.

His touch made Fenella arch against him, even as her chest tightened.

She wished he wouldn't say things like that. It made tenderness well, made her want to lower her own defenses. Emotions bubbled close to the surface tonight, in the wake of so much killing.

Justin's fingers hooked under her chin then, raising her face to his.

The vulnerable look in his eyes robbed her of breath, but she had no time to dwell upon it before his mouth claimed hers.

With a groan, Fenella sank against him. She craved forgetfulness now—as if their passion could wash the blood from the ground, could erase the violence of the past day.

She entwined herself with him, their slick bodies sliding together as he cupped her backside and pulled her closer still. She felt his shaft hard and hot against her belly, and reached for him, stroking him until he growled into her mouth.

Their kisses drew out, growing increasingly feverish. The heat of his mouth, the slide of his tongue, made Fenella forget all else. She wanted him to take her here, in the warm water, to chase away the shadows.

But Justin had other plans. He pulled away, disentangled his limbs from hers, and hauled himself up onto the edge of the pool. Reaching down, he helped Fenella out, before gently pushing her onto her back upon the cool tiles. He spread her out beneath him and then crawled over her, his mouth capturing hers once more.

Fenella trembled under him, gasping his name when his mouth trailed down her jaw to her neck. He inched down her body, loving it, and whispering endearments as he did so.

"Carissima ... anima mea."

My darling ... my soul.

Fenella's eyes flickered shut, and she gave herself up to him. Tomorrow the harsh world they inhabited would intrude. But now, the heat of his mouth between her spread thighs, his murmured words, transported her to another realm. And when he spread her wider still, and sank deep into her, Fenella quivered.

"Look at me, Fen," Justin rasped. "I need you with me now."

She opened her eyes, gazing up at him as bid. Justin held himself up over her, his face taut. Fenella's breathing stilled; the intensity of the moment was too much. If she held his gaze now, he'd see into her heart and glimpse the war within her.

As if sensing her struggle, Justin reached up, cupping her face. "Stay with me ... don't hide from me, carissima."

His golden gaze snared hers, holding her fast. He then rolled his hips, dragging a gasp from her. A moment later, he began to move within her.

And all the while, their gazes remained fused.

Justin took her slow and then fast, shallow and then deep, alternating between circling his hips and driving hard.

It was so intense, so raw, that Fenella splintered, her back arching off the tiles. However, he held her fast, plowing her with the same intense determination that he showed in all areas of life.

And when he took hold of her hips, drawing them up so that he could take her deeper still, Fenella cried out. He touched her in a place that melted her, that made her writhe wildly against him.

Fenella did look away then, her head dropping back as pleasure drowned everything else and she shattered. Crying Justin's name, she let go.

Afterward, they clung together. It was quiet in the bathhouse save for the rasp of their breathing and the drip of water.

Fenella buried her face in Justin's neck, breathing him in as her pulse calmed and she became capable of forming rational thought once more. He'd shifted so as not to crush her under him, pulling her against his chest. The hammer of his heart against her cheek slowly calmed to a steady thud, as they lay entwined.

Eventually, Justin broke the silence. His voice, although quiet, was sure. "I'm giving you your freedom, Fenella."

Raising her head from his chest, she blinked, before his words sank in. She then gasped, "You are?"

Justin's mouth curved, even if his gaze remained serious. "I am."

She swallowed, in an effort to ease the sudden tightness in her throat. "Just like that?"

He nodded. "Usually the process of manumission requires I bring you before a magistrate and formally declare your freedom ... but out here on the edge of the empire, it's enough that I declare it with a witness." His cheek dimpled as his smile widened. "Caius can do us the honor now."

Blinking owl-like, the house steward gazed upon the general with bemusement. "Excuse me?"

Justin made an exasperated sound in the back of his throat. "I hereby give Fenella her freedom," he repeated. "Do you bear witness?"

Glancing from the man he served to his slave, Caius rubbed a hand over his face in an attempt to wake himself up. They'd roused him from sleep, and he now stood in the doorway to his cubiculum, holding a lantern aloft.

The steward looked as bemused as Fenella felt. She was still reeling from Justin's declaration. Afterward, they'd quickly dressed, and he'd taken her by the hand, leading her down the portico.

"Yes, General," Caius said after a pause. "I do." He cleared his throat then. "However, I must—"

"Good man." Justin slapped him on the shoulder, cutting him off. "Sorry for waking you. Go back to bed, and we'll see you in the morning."

The steward's mouth worked, and he took a step forward, "But, General—"

"Goodnight, Caius." Justin was already leading Fenella away, toward his own quarters.

And she followed him, her heart now thudding hard against her breastbone.

I'm free? This was all happening so fast that she was having difficulty taking it in.

Together, they entered the general's cubiculum. Golden lantern light illuminated the room and bathed Justin's face as he turned to her, his amber eyes warm.

Fenella stared up at him. "Why?" she whispered.

He reached out and cupped her cheek; the roughness of the callouses on his palm gently chafed her skin. "Because I know it's what you want," he replied softly. "And it's what I want too." He paused then, his features tensing. "I wish to make you my wife, Fenella. It might take a little longer to organize than freeing you ... for I will need to gain permission from a magistrate. But, if you will be patient, I will see it done."

The resolve in his voice left Fenella in no doubt of his sincerity. Once Justin Aquila set his mind on something, he wouldn't let go. And just for a moment, she let herself believe that they could have a future together. She imagined then a life where she would wake up at Justin's side every morning, a future where she'd bear his children. The image was so enthralling that her throat thickened, her vision misting.

But then her chest began to ache, a chill seeping through her limbs.

He was spinning a fantasy—one she had to destroy. If she didn't, she'd be shackled again.

"No, Justin," she whispered. Lifting her hand, she gently removed his from her cheek and stepped back from him. "I'm sorry, but I can't wed you."

XXVIII. THE BREAKING

JUSTIN'S EYES GUTTERED, his handsome face tensing. A long beat of silence followed before he whispered, "Why?"

"You gave me my freedom," Fenella replied, "and I wish to take it. I'm leaving."

"You wish to return to your people?"

Fenella nodded, even as nausea assailed her. The Hag curse her, this was what she'd wanted. Why wasn't she jubilant?

"I'm in love with you." His admission was gently uttered, yet the words fell heavily in the cubiculum. "I want to share my life with you, grow old with you." His throat bobbed then. "After what we've shared … I thought you felt the same way."

The knots in Fenella's gut twisted tighter. "We've tumbled a few times," she replied, her voice brittle now. Nonetheless, she forced herself on. "Just because we can't keep our hands off each other, doesn't mean we're fated to be mates. You're a Roman. I'm a Picti. We have no future."

A nerve jumped in his cheek. "I disagree."

"You don't know me," she snapped.

"Yes, I do." He moved forward, closing the gap between them once more. "You hate to be caged, but I wouldn't do that. I want you at my side … for us to build a life together."

Fenella shook her head, denying his words. They were beguiling, yet they'd trap her if she wasn't careful. "You're in love with the idea of me, not the reality." She sucked in a deep breath before plowing on. This would hurt him, yet he needed to understand the truth of things. "Ever since you brought me here, I've been biding my time, looking for a chance to flee. I only swore to obey you so you'd let me out of the pit. In truth, I planned to run the day I went shopping with Kahina in the vicus. But Eogan's arrival prevented me."

"Of course you did," he countered, not remotely shocked by her admission. "I take responsibility for that, carissima, for I took you as my slave."

Fenella's heart started to race, panic kindling under her ribs. Curse it, he wasn't listening to her. "I intended to escape yesterday too," she continued, "and I would have if those warriors hadn't entered this house."

Justin stiffened. Finally, she'd gotten his attention.

"I knew Toutorix's attack was coming," she admitted, holding his eye. "Eogan told me. I knew, and I said nothing ... *now* tell me you still want me."

Long moments passed, and when Justin spoke his voice was rough. "I understand what you're doing, but it changes nothing. I still want you as my wife." His gaze glittered then. "I *need* you."

He reached for her, but Fenella stepped away. Her lip curled. "You need a woman who'd stab you in the back without a second thought?"

He swallowed. "You wouldn't."

"Listen to me, man," she snarled. "I have lied to you, withheld valuable information. You should want to take your fists to me!"

"And how would that help?" he shot back. "Even if you'd told me about the coming attack, it wouldn't have prevented it. I knew trouble was brewing." Justin broke off then, his chest now rising and falling rapidly. "You still don't trust me, don't you?"

Fenella stared back at him.

Folding her arms across her breasts, she shook her head and tried to ignore the tearing pain in her chest. "No, Aquila ... I trust no man."

Long moments passed, and then Justin's face shuttered. Only the pain in his eyes betrayed him. "Very well." His voice was hollow now. "You are a freewoman

... I can no longer hold you here against your will. If independence is what you want, you must take it." He moved then, heading toward the door. "Stay in here tonight ... I will sleep elsewhere. If you wait to depart at dawn, I'll organize a pony and provisions for you."

Fenella watched him go, cold stealing over her.

She'd won the fight, had successfully pushed him away. Yet it didn't feel like a victory. Instead, it felt as if she'd taken his pugio and stabbed herself in the chest with it. "Justin," she croaked. "Wait."

He'd reached the door, his hand upon the handle, yet he turned, glancing back over his shoulder. His expression was bleak.

The urge to break down, to rush to him and fall at his feet, was overwhelming, but Fenella fought it. Freedom had its price, and this was it. Inhaling sharply, she dug deep for strength. "I never wanted to hurt you ... I'm sorry."

Justin held her gaze, the tight muscle in his jaw feathering. "So am I."

And with that, he left the cubiculum, shutting the door firmly behind him.

One of Justin's men knocked on Fenella's door early, before dawn.

Handing her a pile of clothing, the legionary took a smart step back. "Here ... I'll be back soon."

Numbly, Fenella nodded, closing the door.

Placing the clothing down on the bed, she examined it. A leather vest and skirt: these were her old garments, the ones she'd been captured in. She'd thought Kahina had burned them, but she'd washed, folded, and put them away.

A lump rose in Fenella's throat.

Kahina ... I should bid her farewell.

It was too early; she didn't want to wake her, or Aedan. No, it was best she stole away. Justin would tell them what had happened.

Coward.

Aye, she was about some things.

Undoing the belt about her waist, she stripped off her tunic. She then pulled on her old clothing. The leather felt oddly restrictive and uncomfortable after the soft folds of her tunic, but she pushed the comparison aside. Such reflections wouldn't aid her this morning.

Soon the life she'd had here would be but a memory.

Jaw clenched, she picked up the woolen cloak the legionary had brought with her clothes. The weather could be fickle this time of year. Justin didn't want her to catch a chill.

Fenella's fingers tightened around the mantle.

The man should hate her now, yet he still managed to show her consideration.

Stop it, she told herself firmly. *Don't think about how noble he is.*

Fenella swung the cloak around her shoulders, wrapping it about her. It wasn't an overly cold morning, yet she felt chilled to the marrow all the same.

Justin waited for her in front of the stables. A sturdy fen pony stood at his side.

Walking alongside the guard, Fenella's gaze alighted upon the general's tall, broad-shouldered figure. The sky above was a deep, dark purple. Fires still burned upon the walls, and lanterns glowed under the eaves of the surrounding buildings. Crisp air feathered across Fenella's bare arms. She'd entered this fort barefoot, yet she was leaving it wearing a sturdy pair of Roman sandals.

"General," the guard greeted Justin, stopping and saluting. "Shall I escort the woman out?"

"No, soldier. I shall do it. You may return to your post now."

With a nod, the legionary turned and marched away, leaving the two of them alone.

Fenella's gaze returned to Justin.

The gods strike her down, she couldn't help but take in every detail for the last time. He wore his lorica, gold and black gleaming in the lantern light, and his purple cloak hung from his shoulders, although his head was bare. And without that ornate helmet, and its black fan, he seemed a man rather than the godlike general who'd taken her from Loch Tatha all those months ago.

Of course, she'd stopped seeing him as the hated 'an Iolaire', the Eagle, a long while back.

Fenella waited for him to speak. During her sleepless night, she'd feared he wouldn't want to see her this morning. But at least he'd given her the chance to say goodbye.

Justin handed her the reins. "Here ... the gelding is faster than he looks and should carry you swiftly wherever you wish to go." As she took the reins, their fingers brushed. The warmth of his hand made her chest constrict. Suddenly, it was difficult to breathe.

She noted then that a bow and quiver of arrows had been strapped behind the saddle, as had a leather satchel. Seeing the direction of her gaze, Justin spoke. "You shouldn't travel unarmed ... there's food too."

Fenella reached up, rubbing at her aching breastbone with her knuckles. A parting gift. Even now, he was still looking out for her.

"You might want to head into the Cairngorms," Justin said then. "My scouts discovered Toutorix rebuilt his crannog over one of the lochans there."

Fenella stilled. "You knew where he was hiding?"

He nodded.

"And you didn't attack him?"

Justin's mouth lifted at the corners, although his gaze was somber. "I was waiting for him to come to me ... and he did."

Facing him, Fenella struggled to keep her composure. There was so much she wanted to say—so much she wouldn't.

"I will never forget you," Justin said softly.

The rawness in his voice, the pain in those amber eyes, nearly undid her. "Goodbye, Justin," she whispered. Then, throat aching, she vaulted up onto the pony's back.

"Keep off the roads." Justin's voice had a strangled edge to it now. "There will be a lot of soldiers traveling south ... you don't want to meet them." Their gazes met then. "Safe journeying, Fenella."

Not trusting herself to speak, she nodded. She gathered the reins then and dug her heels into the pony's furry sides. It sprang forward into a jolting trot. They headed off down the street toward the main entrance to the fort.

Dawn was breaking fully now, the first rays of sun peeking over the eastern ramparts, but Fenella focused on the looming gate ahead, the outline of the jagged iron teeth of the raised portcullis.

True freedom beckoned—and yet no excitement beat in her breast at the prospect. Instead, despair sat in her gut like a great stone.

She needed to get out of here, to put all of this behind her.

Fenella swallowed convulsively now. It felt as if someone was grasping her throat—a reminder that no matter how far or fast she rode, she wouldn't be able to forget Justinian Aquila.

Standing upon the wooden tower above the Porta Praetoria, Justin watched the woman atop a shaggy bay fen pony trot down the causeway. He'd followed her along the street, and then taken the steps up to the wooden tower above the main entrance.

There were four sentries up here, and upon seeing the general step up onto the wall, they all snapped to rigid attention, saluting.

"At ease," Justin greeted them, moving closer to the edge of the ramparts, his gaze never leaving Fenella. "This isn't an inspection."

From this height, his lover looked tiny seated upon the stocky, feather-footed pony.

But when he'd seen her walking toward him earlier, dressed as she'd been that day at Lake Taus, his heart had started beating so hard it felt as if it would tear itself free from his chest.

As long as he lived, he'd remember her that way: the huntress he'd met in the pinewood, a bow slung over her back and fire in her eyes.

He'd taken her into his household, forced her into a life that wasn't hers.

Was it any surprise things had ended this way?

He'd retrieved Fenella's old clothing from Kahina the eve before. The slave had been curious, but he'd assured her he'd explain all the following morning—and he would. Once he could breathe again, once he didn't feel as if he were being buried alive.

He watched as Fenella urged the pony into a canter, her hair flying behind her now. A thin mist curled in from the river this morning, drifting across the wet grass—and moments later, it swallowed pony and rider whole.

Reaching out, Justin gripped the palings closest, anchoring himself there. It was either that or turn, race down from the wall, and pursue his lover into the mist. Sweat slicked his skin, his heart pounding so loudly it deafened him. His life was unraveling, and the urge to try and yank back control was overwhelming.

Stultissime.

Yes, he'd been a complete idiot—and now he was paying the price.

In his arrogance, he'd assumed that once he freed Fenella, she'd readily agree to be his wife. It had been a punch to the gut when she'd refused him. He could give her so much—love, companionship, and security—but instead, she'd chosen freedom.

Justin clenched his jaw hard, his teeth aching under the strain.

He didn't want to lose the woman he loved, and yet he'd let her go.

Too late, he'd realized she wasn't his to keep.

XXIX. ASHES

FENELLA DREW UP her mount on the shore of Loch Tatha, her gaze sweeping over the ruin of what had once been a thriving crannog. Now, only the burned-out shells of dwellings and walkways remained, their blackened outline reflected against the glistening water of the loch.

She'd ridden north, heading for the Cairngorms as Justin had suggested. However, along the way, she'd made a slight detour. As she'd suspected, no one had rebuilt Toutorix's crannog.

Heaving a sigh, Fenella leaned forward and stroked her pony's sweat-damp neck. They'd ridden hard all day to reach their destination by mid-afternoon. She could have pressed on, yet she was weary.

Tonight she'd camp on the shore of the loch, and tomorrow she'd make for the Cairngorms. She could see the mountains rising to the north. The tallest of them, Ben Macdui, was still frosted with snow.

Fenella swung down from the pony and led it along the shore, away from the skeleton of the crannog.

The chieftain of the Wolves of the North was dead now, his people leaderless. Fenella should have felt relieved that she wouldn't have to face him, but today she found it difficult to feel anything at all.

After leaving Ardoch, numbness had descended upon her.

She'd taken Justin's advice and stayed off the roads the Caesars had built, straight lines that tore through the landscape. And it was just as well, for when she'd crested one of the heather-strewn hills and glanced east, she'd seen a company of soldiers, marching south, crimson and steel gleaming in the sunlight.

Fenella knew she should have ridden on, should have ensured she stayed out of sight, yet she'd watched them all the same.

Even though they were abandoning the north, there was nothing chaotic about these men. They marched in neat rows, flanked by the cavalry that had been sent to escort them to safety. Banners fluttered in the breeze.

They were returning to Ardoch.

Turning away, Fenella had ridden on, urging her pony into a fast canter so that the wind whipped against her face and tore through her hair. She had been glad the journey was long today. She needed to keep moving.

But now she had to stop. The day was gradually fading, and as she gathered wood for a fire, memories of all she'd left behind crept in.

The numbness started to thaw, and her throat constricted.

"Stop it," she muttered aloud. "Don't think of him."

But the emotions she'd denied all day had no wish to be silenced. And when Fenella finally sat down before her fire and retrieved the satchel Justin had provided for the journey, they gripped her by the throat once more.

Her belly had been in knots all day. Indeed, she hadn't eaten since supper of the day before. She still wasn't hungry, yet she now felt light-headed from lack of food. And so, jaw clenched, she opened the satchel and withdrew the bread, boiled eggs, and cheese.

Looking down at the meal, Fenella's vision swam. Moments later, tears were running down her face and splashing onto the bread.

"Idiot," she gasped. "Why are you weeping?"

This was what she wanted. She was a free woman now. Finally, her future was her own. She should be rejoicing, not crying.

But that didn't stop her from grieving for what she'd lost.

Aye, she was free, yet never again would she look up from her work to see Justin Aquila striding toward her, his helmet under his arm, his golden gaze seeking hers out. Never again would she hear the low timbre of his voice, feel his touch—or relax into the safety of his arms.

All of it was gone, blown away like oat husks in the wind.

She had deliberately let it go.

A sob clawed its way up Fenella's throat, yet she choked it back. She couldn't let herself weep over Justin, not while everything was so raw.

"Fen?"

Sucking in a sharp breath, she snapped upright, blinking away tears, even as she reached for the knife she'd found with her food. She'd thought she was alone here on the edge of the loch, but it seemed she wasn't.

A lanky figure approached.

Coming to her feet, Fenella saw a familiar face. "Eogan?"

Joy exploded in her breast, eclipsing her grief for a few instants. Although she hadn't found her brother amongst the dead at Ardoch, it was a relief to see he hadn't been badly injured either.

They hugged, the embrace brief and hard, although Eogan's brow furrowed when he drew back. "You look upset, sister." His gaze scanned her face. "Fear not, we are all safe and well."

Fenella's breathing caught, guilt crushing her chest.

Her sorrow hadn't been for her kin, but for herself.

Knuckling away her tears, she glanced behind her brother, to where a band of warriors looked on. They'd emerged from the trees behind her with such stealth that she hadn't heard them.

She'd been too distracted by thoughts of the man she'd left behind.

Eogan stepped closer. "I looked for you during the attack ... but I never got inside the fort." He smiled. "You managed to escape then?"

She nodded.

"How?"

"I stole a dagger and some rope and crept up onto the walls after the siege ended," she replied, surprised at how easily she lied. "Everyone was too busy tending the injured and clearing the dead ... they didn't see me go."

Eogan's gaze glinted. "Well done. I don't suppose you slit the Eagle's throat before you went?"

Fenella swallowed before shaking her head. Gods, she needed to change the subject, or she'd break down.

"I see no one has returned to Loch Tatha," she said huskily.

Eogan shook his head. "No, we've made a new crannog north of here ... at the foot of Ben Madui," he replied, confirming what Justin had told her. His gaze then flicked to the fire she'd lit a few feet away. "Tomorrow, I'll take you there ... but tonight my men and I will camp here. Can we share your hearth?"

"Hadrian wants a full evacuation of the north." Tribune Sebastian Flavius Lucius leaned back in his chair and regarded Justin under veiled lids. "How soon can you manage it, General?"

Seated opposite the tribune in the principia, Justin resisted the urge to growl a curse and rake a hand through his hair. However, the young tribune—blond, fresh-faced, and supremely arrogant—was watching him keenly, as if looking out for signs of strain.

This unexpected visit was the last thing he needed right now.

And Tribune Lucius was even cockier than he remembered.

"A week at most," Justin replied after a pause.

Eight days had passed since the attack, since Fenella had ridden from his life. In that time, Justin had sent a report to Hadrian, and the response had been swift indeed.

The news the tribune had brought wasn't that unexpected—but all the same, it rankled. Ardoch was his. The thought of abandoning it tore at his guts.

Flavius continued to watch him, his gaze narrowing. "The emperor is disappointed, General ... you assured him you could hold the north."

Justin stared back at the younger man. Flavius was beneath him in rank, although you wouldn't have thought so from the tribune's supercilious manner. As the emperor's emissary, he was full of himself today.

"We have ... Ardoch still stands, does it not?" Justin replied, refusing to be baited.

"So, you didn't realize the Picti were gathering against you?"

"Of course I did ... and I was ready," Justin replied. "That's why we prevailed ... however, the northern tribes united this time."

The tribune scratched his chin. "I suppose that's rare."

"It is."

Flavius cocked a dark-blond eyebrow. "Of course, if you'd killed Toutorix the Wolf when you had the chance, you'd have prevented this attack."

Justin drew in a deep, steadying breath, fighting not to show any reaction. He'd been transparent in his reports to Hadrian; the emperor knew what had happened the previous autumn. With a sinking sensation, Justin realized he was being punished for his lapse in judgment.

"I did what I thought was right at the time," he said after a pause. "I was wary of causing Toutorix's allies to rally against us."

Flavius's mouth pursed. "And yet they did anyway."

"And we repelled them." Justin's tone flattened then. "Hundreds of Picti warriors died during the siege ... we killed a number of their chieftains. They won't be causing us any more problems for a while."

"No, but you won't be taking back Dalginross or Bochastle ... or Pinnata Castra," the tribune reminded him. "Admit it, Aquila ... despite that you successfully held Ardoch, your control on the rest of this territory has unraveled."

Justin's gaze narrowed. "I assume the emperor has decided the north is more trouble than it's worth?" He wasn't a fool; he knew there was more to Hadrian's decision to withdraw than the problems they'd been having with the Picti.

"He has," Flavius replied.

Silence fell in the office. The doors were open, letting in a soft breeze, and beyond the principia, they could hear the shouts of troops on the parade ground. Even after the losses of late, order still reigned at Ardoch. And it always would while he commanded here.

A dull sensation pulled at his chest then. Regret. He'd defended himself to the tribune, yet they both knew the truth of it. He was well aware that he should have driven his pugio into Toutorix's throat when the bastard had stood before him in that roundhouse.

Nonetheless, talking about it wouldn't change what he'd done. It was time to turn talk away from his failure. His mood was bleak this afternoon as it was, and the smug tribune wasn't helping.

"So, Hadrian is at the Wall?" Justin asked finally.

Flavius nodded. "He'll be there for the next few months ... overseeing work." He flashed Justin a grin. "You should see it, General ... the Wall will be magnificent when done, eight feet wide and twelve feet high ... with milecastles along its length."

"I'm sure it will be," Justin murmured.

Once, he too would have been as excited as the tribune at the prospect of this great feat of engineering: a high fortified wall that stretched from one coast to another. But ever since Fenella's departure, he felt jaded and old beyond his years.

These days, he could barely dredge up the will to show any enthusiasm at all for the glory of the empire. The ambition that had once driven him had burned away, leaving only ashes at his feet.

"Mithras, you're looking rough these days," Marcus greeted Justin as he approached his bed. "As bad as I feel."

Justin decided to ignore his friend's candid observation. He was aware the strain was starting to show and didn't need reminding of it. He slept poorly these days, ate sporadically, and drank more than usual. However, he didn't wish to discuss himself. After his meeting with the tribune, his patience was thin indeed.

Halting, he folded his arms across his chest. "Surgeon Falco tells me you're on the mend. No early retirement for you."

The primus pilus snorted. "Of course not ... there are plenty of good fighting years left in me yet." Marcus was propped up against a nest of pillows, and was indeed looking the healthiest Justin had seen him since the attack. His face, which had been taut with pain at first, had relaxed, and there was color in his cheeks. He flashed Justin a grin. "Fear not, we'll stand together in battle again."

"Not at Ardoch, we won't."

Marcus's grin faded.

"Tribune Lucius is here," Justin informed his friend without preamble. "He brings orders from Hadrian ... we are to abandon the north."

The centurion's mouth pursed, his dark eyes narrowing. "What?"

"The emperor wants Valeria Victrix at the Wall ... to help build and defend it. He has decided to leave Caledonia to its people for the time being."

Marcus scowled. "So all our work ... the last five years at Ardoch, and all the men we've lost defending it, will be for nothing?"

"It would seem so."

Justin's words were measured, controlled, even if his gut clenched. It wasn't up to him to question the will of the emperor, only to follow orders. His wishes were immaterial, as were Marcus's. They would do as they were told—as they always had.

The two men's gazes locked. The centurion's expression altered then, concern shadowing his eyes.

Justin tensed. Despite that he and Marcus had known each other for years, he hadn't confided in him about

Fenella. The centurion knew Justin had given the woman her freedom, and that she'd chosen to leave—but nothing else.

Nonetheless, the look on Marcus's face now warned Justin that his friend had guessed the reason for his bloodshot eyes and haggard face.

"When are we going?" Marcus asked finally.

"Within days."

Marcus took in this news, his jaw tightening. "So soon?" Then with a sigh, he sank back against the pillows before running a hand down his face. "Cacat," he murmured.

Shit.

XXX. NOT IN THIS LIFETIME

Lochan Uaine
Cairngorm Mountains, Caledonia

One month later ...

"YOU CAN'T LIVE with us forever, daughter. It's time you found yourself another husband."

Stiffening, Fenella straightened up from where she'd been flipping oatcakes over the griddle. Her gaze then settled on where her father sat upon a stool on the opposite side of the fire pit. "I don't want another husband. I'm happy alone."

Bricius snorted. "Nonsense, woman. You can't remain unwed, and I don't want to be responsible for you either."

"Bricius," Fenella's mother, Mona, spoke up, a rare note of chagrin to her usually soft voice. "Fen's our daughter ... she's always welcome under our roof."

Bricius muttered an oath under his breath and reached for the pot of honey before slathering it on his oatcake. "We've already got three mouths to feed." He cast a hard look across the fire at where Fenella's younger siblings—Ena, Maddoc, and Fife—sat. All three of them were under fourteen winters of age—not old enough to yet wed or fly the nest, yet that didn't stop him from resenting them. "At least Eogan has moved out."

Glaring across at her father, Fenella clenched her jaw. Her brother now shared a hut with three other unwed warriors, and Bricius never wasted the opportunity to boast about his son—or to lament how his eldest daughter was his greatest disappointment.

It had started the day after her return, although he'd never been as blunt as he was this morning about his desire for her to move out.

"I repeat, I'll not wed," Fenella said, her gaze never leaving her father's face. "You forced me into marrying once ... you'll not do so twice." She broke off there, her breathing quickening as her ire rose. "But if my presence here galls you so, I shall leave."

Indeed, she was only here because she'd yet to decide what to do with the freedom she'd been given. If she was to strike out on her own, she needed time to prepare. She'd thought her family would welcome her back for a moon or two in the meantime, but it seemed she'd overstayed already.

"Fen." Mona leaned forward, placing a hand on her daughter's arm. "Of course you don't have to go."

"Aye, she does," Bricius muttered.

"I want my alcove back, Ma," Ena, her sister, piped up. The eldest of the three still at home, Ena hadn't hidden her resentment when Fenella returned to live with them. "There's no room for Fen here."

Fenella scowled at her sister, her temper simmering, while her younger brothers both grinned.

Her mother was her only ally under this roof.

She hadn't expected living with her kin again to be easy, but with the passing of the days, she discovered that her time at Ardoch had tainted her in their eyes. She'd barely seen Eogan since her return. Was he embarrassed by her?

"That's right, daughter," Bricius replied with a nod. "Fenella needs to go." His brow furrowed then, his gaze fixing upon the elder of his two daughters. "I'll not have a Roman *whore* residing under my roof."

Heat swept over Fenella as she stared back at him.

There it was—finally. Aye, she was tainted all right. Whispers had followed her of late. She hadn't missed the looks the villagers gave her, although she'd hoped her kin would remain loyal. After all, she'd been taken away by force.

That hadn't prevented Bricius from making plenty of insinuations since her return. But this morning, he was out of patience.

Drawing in a sharp breath, she silently prayed to The Mother for the will to control her temper.

When her father had handed her over to Toutorix, resentment had boiled within her for a long while afterward. During her time at Ardoch, she'd almost forgotten how ill-tempered he could be, how unjust—but now all the old memories came back. Her mother was as cowed as ever, Bricius even more outspoken. And her siblings were strangers.

Fenella's gaze swept over the faces around the fire pit. Her sister and brothers were all watching her, their glazes gleaming in the firelight. Meanwhile, her mother wore a downcast expression as she stared at her untouched oatcakes. Poor Mona had spent too many years in Bricius's company. The bully had worn her down, like sand on stone.

"I'm going out to milk the goat," Fenella announced coldly, stepping back from the fire. She usually enjoyed her morning meal of oatcakes, but her father's insult had robbed her of appetite.

"Good," Bricius grumbled. "Make yourself useful before you find yourself a man ... there's a market on this morning. You might meet someone desperate enough there."

Fenella stared at her father for a long moment. The urge to rage at him spiraled up within her. But instead of giving in to violence, she spun on her heel, grabbed a wooden pail, and left the roundhouse.

Ducking out from under the low lintel, she strode along the wooden walkway toward shore.

Sucking in a deep breath, and then another, she tried to forget her father's words. However, they dogged each step.

Roman whore.

Aye, that's how everyone here saw her.

Teeth clenched, Fenella strode down the walkway toward the lakeshore. A cluster of tightly packed dwellings stretched out over the waters of Lochan Uaine—a small loch that nestled in a valley amongst the mighty Cairngorm range. Above the mountains, the vast domed peak, Ben Macdui, rose high against the pale morning sky. It no longer glistened white, for spring was upon them and Bealtunn approached.

Lochan Uaine was a sheltered, safe spot, a place for her people to rally and build their strength once more. Fenella had hoped to heal here, yet with each passing day, her discontent and restlessness grew. It didn't help that she was now an outsider among her own people.

Leaving the walkway, she crossed to an enclosure where her family's goat waited. On the way, she looked to where a crowd gathered on the shore of the loch this morning. Folk were bartering over livestock and produce, their voices traveling across the still water.

Fenella viewed them with a jaundiced eye, noting that there were indeed many men among the throng. However, the Reaper would claim her before she took a husband at her father's behest.

And what will you do instead?

Fenella's chest tightened.

That was the problem. These days, she was wracked by indecision. All her life, her future had been decided for her by men. It was both exhilarating and frightening to be able to choose her own path—and it had paralyzed her.

She spotted Eogan amongst the crowd then. Her brother swaggered through the milling men and women, flanked by two friends. As she looked on, he stopped to flirt with a girl selling live fowl.

Feeling someone's gaze upon him, Eogan glanced up, meeting Fenella's eye.

She smiled and raised a hand in greeting, hoping that her brother would abandon his flirting and friends and come over to talk to her.

However, he merely flashed her a distracted smile and focused once more on the young woman. Eogan appeared to murmur something to her, and the girl laughed, the merry sound drifting across the crowd.

A sigh gusted out of Fenella. Turning from the crowd, she ducked into the enclosure. The goat bleated in greeting, and she let it nibble her hand as she pulled up a stool to begin milking.

No one besides her mother had any time for her these days. Sometimes she caught Mona watching her, an unusually probing expression upon her face. She was obviously curious about her daughter and her time at Ardoch, yet she was too timid to question her.

Sighing, Fenella rested her forehead against the goat's warm belly, closing her eyes.

After leaving Ardoch, she'd thought the ache in her chest would eventually ease.

But it hadn't.

Thoughts of the man she'd left behind plagued her whenever she had a moment alone. She wondered how he was faring. Such thoughts were a knife to the belly, yet she couldn't prevent them.

They followed her everywhere.

How would Bricius react if he knew the truth—that his daughter actually cared for the Roman who'd taken her as his slave—and that he'd let her go?

Heaving another sigh, Fenella opened her eyes. She then started to milk the goat, the rhythmic squirts of milk into the pail easing her tension a little. She enjoyed this chore, for it got her out of the dark, smoky roundhouse, and away from her father's censure.

However, the task was over all too soon.

It was the full flush of spring, and the goat had yielded half a bucket of milk, most of which she would turn into curd cheese to go with tomorrow's noon meal.

Letting herself out of the enclosure, Fenella headed back toward the walkway. She walked slower this time, dreading her return home.

Aye, she had to leave—and it would have to be soon. Otherwise, she'd blacken her father's eye, and there would be consequences.

She moved through the edge of the crowd, and had almost reached the loch's shore, when a man's voice hailed her. "Fenella!"

Surprised that one of the villagers was actually calling to her, she turned.

But when her gaze alighted upon the tall man with long red-brown hair and moss-green eyes striding toward her, Fenella went rigid.

Years had passed since she'd seen her former lover, yet he hadn't changed. The warrior still walked with long-limbed grace. His sleeveless vest showed off finely muscled arms and tribal markings. The last time she'd seen him, he'd been angry, for she'd just struck him across the face. However, this morning his handsome face was creased into a wide smile.

"I heard you'd escaped." He opened his arms as if to embrace her.

Fenella took a rapid step back, the milk sloshing in the pail. "Aye," she replied stiffly, not returning his smile. "Good morning, Lorcan."

Lorcan halted, his expression sobering. "I'm relieved you managed it, for you must have suffered much, Fen," he murmured. "I still can't believe Toutorix handed you over to the enemy."

"Well, he did."

Lorcan's gaze roamed her face, his green eyes shadowing. "I'm so sorry."

"What about exactly?" she asked coolly.

Even after Lorcan had hurt her, there had been a part of her that had hoped to see him again. Her skin crawled whenever Toutorix touched her, but she'd desired Lorcan. But that want had died within her years ago. And now, despite that he was as handsome as ever, she felt nothing as she looked upon him.

Her former lover stepped closer, his voice lowering when he replied, "All of it, Fen. I should have run away with you, as you wanted. I could have spared you Toutorix ... and what came afterward. The man stripped you of all honor."

Fenella scowled. "You'd have abandoned your wife?"

A muscle flexed in his jaw. "She died ... giving birth to our second child." He paused there, his gaze dropping to the ground between them. "I'm now raising our son on my own."

"So, you'd have abandoned a woman who would shortly perish in childbirth?" Fenella asked, incredulous.

"She was going to die anyway," Lorcan replied softly, raising his gaze to hers once more. His moss-green eyes were pain-filled. "I made a mistake in not being honest with you from the beginning. I loved you, Fen. I love you still."

Fenella stared back at him. Had she heard right? Had he just told her that if he'd realized his wife—a woman he was supposed to care for—was going to die, he'd have left her?

Surely, even he couldn't be so callous?

If she cared for him, she'd have been aghast. But now she merely looked at him with gathering pity. The man was an opportunist, always looking out for himself. Someone this selfish would never find happiness.

"You didn't love me, Lorcan," she said after a pause. "And I didn't love you either. I thought I did at the time ... but I never looked beneath the surface, never knew you properly."

"You don't mean that." He stepped closer still, reaching for her. "You're just bitter things went awry."

Fenella shifted back, avoiding his touch. "I *was* bitter," she admitted, her mouth lifting at the edges. "But no longer."

"We can start again." His expression was desperate now.

Gods, this man didn't know when to stop talking. "No, we can't."

"Aye, you're alone now ... and ruined. You need a husband, and I need a wife."

Ruined. Fenella's belly twisted, a red tide sweeping over her. She'd had enough of being insulted.

However, Lorcan wasn't finished. "I don't care that the Roman whoreson humped you." His expression softened then, his green eyes changing from imploring to sultry. "You know how good it was between us ... it will be like that again. I promise."

"Lorcan." Fenella did step forward then, raising her chin to ensure she held his gaze. "I'm going to say this only once, so listen well. I will not become your wife ... not in this lifetime or any other ... and if you come near me ever again, I shall geld you." She paused, watching as shock rippled across his handsome face.

Finally, he understood.

And then, without awaiting his response, Fenella turned and walked back to her father's roundhouse.

XXXI. AN INTRICATE WEB

JUSTIN DUG HIS shovel into the damp earth, blinking as sweat ran into his eyes.

Around him, the air vibrated with the clang of iron against stone and wood, the thud of earth being turned, and the dull roar of men's voices, rising and falling in the damp air.

Although he'd been at Vindolanda nearly a month now, Justin was yet to get used to the noise here. Engineers, masons, carpenters, turf cutters, and laborers had descended upon Vindolanda, working tirelessly from dawn until dusk.

Wiping his forehead with the back of his arm, Justin resumed his toil. He stood at the bottom of a deep trench, shoulder-to-shoulder with his men. It was back-breaking work, yet he welcomed it—and welcomed the mind-fogging exhaustion that would follow.

"Commander!" Justin glanced up to see Tribune Lucius standing above him. The man was scowling. "Jupiter's balls, what are you doing down there?"

"Working," Justin bit out, turning from him. His shovel bit hard into the earth, and he silently prayed the tribune would move on and let him be.

However, the gods weren't listening to him this morning.

"Get out of there, Aquila," Sebastian Lucius ordered brusquely. "Now."

Justin halted once more, his jaw clenching. Of course, the shit-weasel could order him about these days. Justin had been demoted. He no longer led the Twentieth legion. Instead, he was commander of Vindolanda fort.

Tribune Lucius was now his superior.

Climbing the rickety ladder out of the deep ditch, Justin took a drying cloth from one of his men and wiped the sweat and mud from his face, neck, and arms. As he did so, his gaze swept behind him, at where Hadrian's glory was steadily taking shape.

Vindolanda was one of the many forts and milecastles stretched out along the length of the Wall. Hadrian had ordered the garrisons to be built first; the Wall itself would then rise between them.

Men crawled like ants over the fortification. In the past, such a sign of industry—proof of his people's skill and hard work—would have made Justin smile.

But not this morning.

He hadn't smiled for weeks now.

Instead, his face felt frozen into a stern expression. His men were wary of him these days, as was his household. Previously, Justin had entertained his fellow officers in the evenings, but since arriving at Vindolanda, he'd thrown himself into physical toil. Come nightfall, he was too exhausted to host anyone.

Sometimes, even the physical fatigue wasn't enough to keep thoughts of Fenella at bay, and so he'd empty a ewer of wine after supper. Anything to numb himself.

But the numbness never lasted.

The tribune cleared his throat then, and Justin tore his attention from the wall. Resplendent in his crimson cloak, his silver helmet glinting in the spring sun, Lucius eyed him.

Justin stiffened under his scrutiny. Infernus, this smug bastard was the last person he wished to see this morning.

"The Vallum is coming along nicely, is it not?" Sebastian Lucius swept an arm toward the ten-foot ditch

that Justin had just clambered out of—the ditch that
Hadrian had ordered to be dug along the length of the
Wall. Pride shone from the tribune's handsome face, as if
he were personally responsible for it, and not the team of
sweaty men below who lined the ditch, hard at work
digging.

"It is," Justin replied tersely.

"I must say though, it seems a lot of trouble to go to."

"The emperor wants a buffer between the Wall and
the lands to the south."

The tribune's brow furrowed. "I suppose we shouldn't
trust the Brigantes not to stir up trouble. Our emperor is
wise indeed."

Justin grunted, wishing the tribune would go away.
Every time he saw Sebastian Lucius, he was reminded of
his failures. Lucius was favored by Hadrian and destined
for a sparkling political career.

Unlike Justin.

Upon arriving at Vindolanda, he'd appeared before
the emperor. Their meeting hadn't gone well. He'd spent
the afternoon with Hadrian, providing answers to every
question the emperor asked him. However, few
responses had appeased him. In their lengthy interview,
the emperor had made his disappointment in him clear.
He shouldn't have been surprised when Hadrian ended
the encounter by stripping him of his rank, yet he had
been. If Justin had hoped to move into politics, he'd find
doors closed to him. Sebastian Lucius's career might be
soaring, yet his had ended.

He'd walked out of the emperor's tent in a daze.

Justin was now grateful that Hadrian was off visiting
one of the other forts along the wall. He'd return to
Vindolanda in a few days, but for the moment, Justin
had been left alone—except for Tribune Lucius, who had
taken to following him about like a bad smell.

It was clear the tribune wouldn't permit him to return
to the ditch, so Justin turned and set off back toward the
fort. Ahead, the grey stone walls caught the morning sun.
The day was young, yet it wasn't too early to take his

men through drills. Hopefully, Lucius would remain to admire the Vallum.

No such luck. To his ire, the tribune fell into step with him.

"This wall will be the greatest feat of engineering the empire has ever seen," the man continued, gesturing to where men were heaving heavy stones onto pulleys. "A fine legacy for Hadrian."

"Indeed."

All Rome's emperors liked to leave something behind, for history to remember them by, but Hadrian had outdone himself.

Justin's mouth thinned. These days, he could barely bring himself to care about the things that had once mattered to him.

The east gate to the fort loomed before him, and Justin lengthened his stride.

Ever since Fenella had left, there seemed little point in anything.

"Your move."

Justin glanced up from where he'd been staring at the Latrunculi board. "What?"

Aedan frowned. "The pieces won't move themselves, Commander."

Justin blinked, coming out of his reverie. He then shifted his gaze back to the game. He'd had a strategy earlier, yet he couldn't recall it now. His thoughts had been miles away.

Picking up a piece, he moved it diagonally. He then reached for his calix of wine and took a deep draft. "Your turn."

When he looked Aedan's way once more, the Brigante was still frowning. "You didn't think that one over, did you?"

Justin snorted. "What?"

Leaning forward, Aedan shifted one of his counters, boxing Justin's second-last one in. He then turned that counter over. "Can you get out of 'alligatus'?"

Justin's gaze narrowed as he surveyed the board. Mithras, he was half asleep. How had Aedan managed to beat him so quickly?

Muttering a curse, he leaned back in his chair. "You win."

Aedan nodded, although he hardly looked victorious. Instead, his expression was enigmatic as he plucked Justin's last counter from the board. "You never give me such an easy win."

Justin pulled a face. "I'm just tired," he muttered.

That wasn't a lie. With the tribune popping up at inopportune moments, he'd been unable to rejoin the men working on the Vallum. Instead, he'd exhausted himself by taking his men through drills for the rest of the day. It was now late afternoon, and he regretted attempting a game of Latrunculi with his sharp-witted slave.

Aedan picked up his own calix and took a sip. They sat at a table in the tablinum of the praetorium—Justin's new residence inside Vindolanda. It was a huge room, twice the size of the one he'd had at Ardoch, with colorful murals on the walls, but Justin preferred his old tablinum and the memories it held.

"I didn't realize you were in love with her," the Brigante said after a pause.

Justin's fingers clenched around the stem of his calix. He was surprised that his slave had the balls to bring up Fenella. This was his fault; he'd treated Aedan like an equal too often over the years. The relationship between slave and master had merged into a friendship of sorts.

But no one, not even Marcus, would have dared talk about Fenella so plainly with him.

Sensing Justin's anger, Aedan's jaw tightened. "A woman like that can never be happy caged. You did the right thing letting her go."

Justin scowled, wishing his slave would shut his mouth. He wasn't sure how much longer his fraying patience would endure. He now wished he hadn't told his household that he'd freed Fenella and then proposed to her. However, he'd informed them just after she'd ridden out, while things were still raw. "I didn't want to cage her," he replied tightly. "I wanted her to be my wife."

"You took a risk," Aedan agreed. He leaned back in his chair and scratched his jaw. "Although, I think you underestimated how much freedom is worth to a slave."

Anger spiked through Justin's gut. "I knew how much it mattered to her."

Aedan met his eye, his own sea-blue gaze hardening. "How could you?" There was an edge of bitterness to his voice then. "You have spent your life ruling over others. You have no idea what it's like to have your liberty stripped from you ... to become someone's property."

Justin's breath gusted out of him. "You forget yourself, Aedan," he growled. "Don't mistake my leniency for weakness."

But the Brigante didn't heed him. "I'm the eldest son of a chieftain," he shot back. "When you took me as your slave, I was days away from wedding the woman I loved. I was destined to lead my tribe, to have sons to carry my bloodline. You stole all of that from me."

Justin sucked in a deep, steadying breath, and then another, fighting the urge to lunge across the table and grab his slave by the throat. What was wrong with Aedan tonight? All the same, he hadn't realized the Brigante was a chieftain's son, or that he'd been about to wed.

He'd never asked his slave about his past, hadn't cared to know.

A brittle silence fell over the tablinum. Aedan swallowed now, as if realizing that he'd earned himself a whipping.

Muttering a curse, Justin dragged a hand down his face. "Don't pretend you don't know how the world works," he replied heavily. "There are slaves, and there are masters."

"Aye, depending on whom the gods favor," Aedan replied, his tone sharpening once more.

Justin huffed out a sigh. He didn't want to punish the slave, yet his iron self-control was on the verge of shattering. All the emotion he'd swallowed since Fenella had gone threatened to break free in a boiling tide. "I think we're done here," he said, his voice low and hard. "Leave me."

Nodding stiffly, the slave got to his feet and made for the door.

Justin let him go without another word.

Alone in the tablinum, he let the moments slide by.

Aedan's words tormented him, driving into his flesh like iron spikes. Was he really so oblivious, so arrogant? Had the fact he'd taken Fenella as his slave doomed their relationship from the very beginning?

Nona, Decuma, and Morta—the three Fates—spun an intricate web. Aedan was right, the gods had shone upon him for most of his life—yet they didn't any longer.

With a snarled curse, he swept the Latrunculi board off the table and sent it crashing to the floor.

XXXII. FIGHT FOR HIM

Lochan Uaine
Cairngorm Mountains—Caledonia

FENELLA DUG HER needle into the tunic she was mending, before raising her face to the sun. It was growing late in the afternoon, yet the day was still warm. She and Mona had taken their mending outdoors. The interior of their roundhouse was dark and smoky, and it was a relief to escape it.

Seated on stools near the entrance, mother and daughter worked in silence for a while.

After the morning she'd endured, Fenella welcomed the peace. Bricius had gone hunting and taken Maddoc with him. Meanwhile, Ena and Fife had gone off to gather raspberries for supper.

It was a rare moment of quiet, and both women enjoyed it.

However, Mona eventually shattered the silence between them.

"I'm sorry your father nags you so, Fen," she murmured. "I tried to speak to him about it after you left this morning ... but he's stubborn."

Fenella sighed, casting her mother a sidelong look. Mona's face, careworn beyond her years, was creased in concern, her blue eyes clouded. Something tugged deep within Fenella's chest then. When she'd been younger, she'd dismissed her mother as weak, but she saw things differently now. Mona was a kind soul, a woman who'd married a dominant man. She loved her children, and the rift between Bricius and Fenella upset her.

Reaching out, she placed a hand on her mother's arm. "I know, Ma. He's right about one thing though ... I can't remain living with you all." She favored her with a sad smile. "Too much time has passed since I last resided under Da's roof. I'm a different person now."

Mona's expression sagged. "Where will you go?"

"I don't know ... but fear not, I'll survive." Fenella's smile turned rueful. "I always do."

Her mother shook her head. "You're so resilient, Fen. I've always wondered how I bore such a daughter."

Fenella gave a soft laugh. "Ena's a feisty one too," she pointed out. She sobered then, squeezing her mother's arm. "You have a different kind of strength, Ma ... one I haven't appreciated until now."

Mona favored her with a wry smile. "Your father isn't *that* hard to live with. He only does what he thinks is right for his family."

Fenella snorted in reply.

"I'll admit, he can be bullish at times," her mother continued, still smiling, "but when we're alone, Bricius shows a softer side."

Fenella cocked her head. "He has one?"

Mona's smile widened. "Aye."

Shaking her head, Fenella turned back to her sewing, nipped off the thread with her teeth, and reached for the next item to be mended.

Silence fell between them once more. The late afternoon sun glittered off the still waters of the lochan. Squeals of laughter from children playing on the shore reached them.

"You never talk of him," Mona said then, drawing Fenella's attention once more.

Fenella cocked an eyebrow. "Who? Toutorix?" She gave a dramatic shiver. "I'd rather not. I'm glad the bastard's dead."

"No ... *an Iolaire*."

The Eagle.

"There's little to say," Fenella replied, forcing a lightness into her tone she didn't feel.

The Mother forgive her, she wished that were the truth.

"I don't believe you."

Fenella glanced Mona's way once more to see her mother watching her intently, a gleam in her eye. "If you hated him, you'd have told tales of his cruelty, of how you prayed to the gods to punish him for eternity. But instead, you haven't said a word."

Shifting uncomfortably on her stool, Fenella glanced away. "Perhaps, I don't wish to dwell on my time at Ardoch." Bitterness filled her mouth then. "You can hardly blame me ... when Da calls me a Roman whore."

Her mother flinched. "Perhaps," Mona replied softly, "but I've observed how you stare off into the distance sometimes, when you think no one is watching you ... and the sadness that shadows your eyes at times. You grieve someone ... and I think it's him."

Fenella's throat constricted. Gods, since when had her mother become so adept at reading folk?

Murmuring an oath, she put down her sewing and knuckled her stinging eyes.

"So, it *is* him?" Mona's hand, thin and cool, closed over Fenella's forearm. "Why haven't you told me?"

"And say what exactly?" Fenella met her mother's gaze once more.

Mona held her stare. "That you love him."

Fenella's heart jolted. What was her mother saying?

Moments passed, and then she cleared her throat. "I miss him," she whispered as her chest started to ache. "Does that mean that I'm in love?"

Mona favored her with a soft smile. "I'd say so, Fen."

Fenella's throat thickened. She blinked rapidly as her vision blurred. However, a tear still escaped, trickling down her cheek. She then murmured a soft oath under her breath.

Mona continued to watch her before a groove etched between her brows. "Does he feel the same way?"

Fenella heaved in a shuddering breath and then nodded. "He asked me to wed him, although I'm sure he's regretting that now."

Her mother took this in, still frowning, her gaze roving her daughter's face. "A proud one, eh … like you."

Fenella hiccoughed as tears flowed freely down her cheeks. The Hag give her strength, she was on the verge of crumbling completely. She'd held herself together since leaving Ardoch, and hadn't even been able to weep at night, for she shared a cramped alcove with blade-tongued Ena. But just a few words from her mother, and she risked dissolving into a sobbing heap.

"When you were taken, I feared the worst," her mother admitted. "I thought the Eagle would have treated you cruelly … as Toutorix did. He is one of the Caesars, after all."

"As did I," Fenella replied, wiping at her cheeks. "But instead, he was kind."

Mona's eyes glittered with tears now. She took Fenella's hands, squeezing tightly. "You trusted him then?"

Fenella swallowed hard, as her throat thickened once more. "Aye," she rasped, admitting the truth fully to herself now. "With my life."

Night lay over Lochan Uaine, a full moon sailing high above. Silver reflected over still waters while the crannog slumbered.

But Fenella didn't sleep.

Instead, she sat behind her family's dwelling, on the edge of the walkway, legs dangling over the water. A satchel sat next to her, filled with a bladder of water, oatcakes, and some hard cheese. She was leaving the crannog with the dawn and didn't want to disturb her family.

Craning her neck up, Fenella gazed upon the moon. It shone so brightly tonight that she could be traveling now.

But where would she go?

She sighed then, rubbing her hand over her face. Her conversation with her mother earlier had been like the lancing of a festering wound. All the things she'd been nursing had poured out of her. Finally, she'd been honest with herself. And in the end, Mona had held her while she wept.

Her mother hadn't questioned her further; she'd merely listened while Fenella recounted her life at Ardoch. And when Fenella had finished her tale, Mona had favored her with a wistful smile. "At least you have memories you can cherish."

Her mother's words returned to her now, churning over in her mind as she swung her legs back and forth over the water.

Memories.

She didn't want the best of her life to be behind her.

She didn't want to live with regret for the remainder of her days.

He doesn't know I love him.

Justin had proved that not all men would hurt her. He alone was worthy of her trust.

Glancing back at the moon, Fenella inhaled the cool night air deep into her lungs. "What should I do?" she whispered to its friendly face.

Go to him. The whisper echoed to her, soft yet sure. *Fight for him.*

Fenella's breathing quickened, her skin tingling.

Her gaze narrowed as she continued to stare up at the moon. Was her mind playing tricks on her?

Perhaps, but she had an answer nonetheless.

This is madness. To return to Ardoch and face Justin again terrified her. And yet as the plan formed in her mind, the ache under her breastbone eased.

Aye, such a move could end badly for her, but at least she wouldn't spend her days wondering what might have been. His feelings could have changed. But if Justin spurned her, he'd do so knowing that she loved him.

Aye, she had her freedom back. She could choose her path forward—and she chose him.

Clambering to her feet, Fenella picked up her satchel and slung it across her front. The road back to Ardoch was long; she might as well get a head start. She still had the fen pony Justin had gifted her, which would make the journey quicker.

She could wait till morning, but she wouldn't.

Now she'd made her choice, she wished to act on it.

Fenella drew her pony up before the blackened shell of Ardoch.

Disbelieving, she gazed upon the ruin of the once-mighty fort, before she urged her pony up the causeway and through the charred frame of the Porta Praetoria.

The pony snorted, tossing its head. Urging it on, Fenella scanned what was left of Ardoch. Heaps of ash lay where the barracks had once stood on either side of the Via Praetoria, the sharp scent of burned matter stinging the back of her throat.

Fenella tried to calm the rapid rise and fall of her breathing, but when she reached the parade ground before the principia, her heart started to hammer in her ears. Both the fort headquarters and the commander's residence beside it were ruins.

Drawing up before the praetorium, Fenella swung down from the saddle.

"Gods," she gasped, her voice catching. "What happened here?"

But more importantly, what had happened to those who'd once lived here?

Reaching up, Fenella clutched at her heart, which now pounded fiercely. She then moved forward, up the ash-covered steps to the praetorium.

"I wouldn't go in there," a gravelly voice intruded.

Grasping the knife at her waist, Fenella whipped it free from its sheath and spun around. Her gaze alighted upon a thin man with wispy black hair streaked with grey. He'd spoken in her tongue, and one glance told her he was one of the local Damnonii tribe. He was barefoot and wore a tunic belted at the waist and frayed leather trews. The tunic was sleeveless, revealing faded tattoos upon his upper arms. Across his front, he wore a bulging leather bag.

"I've already been inside," he rasped, eyeing her with interest. "A pillar nearly fell on me when I started poking around." He then patted the bag he carried. "Those miserly bastards didn't leave much behind them, but I've managed to scavenge a few things."

Fenella stared at him, cold washing over her. The man was a vulture. Nausea rose, and she swallowed bile. "What happened?" she croaked. "Was there another attack?"

The man shook his head, grey-blue eyes gleaming. "No, they just packed up one day and marched away."

Relief hit Fenella so hard that she gasped. Rubbing her breastbone, she glanced around her at the devastation. She still didn't understand what had happened here. "But why is everything burned?"

"That's what the Caesars do, woman," the man muttered. He was losing interest in her now, moving toward the blackened shell of the principia building. "They torch their forts when they abandon them so they're no use to anyone else." He spat on the ground then. "Good riddance to them."

Taking this in, Fenella resheathed her knife. Her pulse slowed now that she knew Justin and his household hadn't all been burned in their beds. "Do you know where they went?"

"South, of course," the man replied, glancing back over his shoulder. "There are whispers that they're building a great wall that will stretch from the east coast to the west." His face screwed up then. "Typical ... only the Caesars would be so arrogant."

XXXIII. BEFORE THE WALL

Vindolanda fort, the Wall,
The Caledonia-Britannia border

"I'M GIVING YOU both your freedom."

Justin repeated the words he'd uttered upon entering the kitchen, yet Kahina and Aedan just stared at him, poleaxed, as if he'd turned into a satyr before their very eyes.

Sighing, Justin glanced down the table to where his cook and house steward sat. They'd both been buttering slices of bread, but now gaped at him as well. "Ava, Caius … do you bear witness to this?"

Caius recovered first, closing his mouth and nodding mutely.

"Of course," Ava murmured a moment later.

Satisfied, Justin shifted his attention back to Kahina and Aedan. "That's it then … you're both free now."

Kahina's eyes went wide, her expression stricken. Likewise, Aedan's face had gone taut. Justin frowned. He didn't understand. This wasn't the reaction he'd expected from either of them. He'd imagined they'd be overjoyed.

He'd thought long and hard after his argument with Aedan a few days earlier. He'd seethed at first, and had kept his distance from the Brigante lest he lashed out at him. But, eventually, when his anger calmed, a gnawing disquiet had set in.

The night before, he'd lain awake for a long while wrestling with his conscience, but as the first fingers of light filtered into his cubiculum through the shuttered window, he made his decision.

"Are you sending us away, Commander?" Kahina gasped. "Have we angered you in some way?"

"That's a 'no' to both questions," Justin replied, his irritation rising. He glanced back at Aedan, noting the man's shocked expression. "If either of you wishes to stay on, as servants, you may. However, you will receive a wage, as Ava and Caius do."

He halted once more, his gaze searching their faces. And as the moments passed, realization dawned in both their eyes.

Aedan then murmured an oath in his own tongue, his eyes gleaming. "Thank you, Aquila," he said, his voice rough with emotion.

"I still don't understand." Kahina's voice was barely above a whisper. "Why now?"

It struck Justin then what a shock this would be for her. Aedan had been taken as a slave six years earlier, and still remembered well what it was like to live as a freeman—but Kahina had been sold by her father when she was all but a child.

She'd spent most of her life in slavery.

Justin met her gaze, marking the confusion he spied in her brown eyes. "We've been through much over the years, Kahina ... and you've always been loyal." He broke off, glancing at Aedan. The Brigante was watching him keenly. The two men locked gazes. "As have you, Aedan. I gave Fenella her freedom but overlooked you both. It's time to correct that oversight."

Stepping back, Justin motioned to the bread and fruit they'd been eating before he'd interrupted them. "Go on ... finish your meal. If you have any further questions, I shall answer them later."

He turned then and left the kitchen, skirting the portico and leaving the praetorium. On the street outside, he stopped, turning his head to the sky. They'd been having a spell of fine weather, and the sun warmed his face. Closing his eyes, Justin's mouth curved into the barest hint of a smile.

A weight had lifted off his shoulders this morning.

He was a broken man without Fenella, yet he couldn't let sorrow stop him from living. He had people who relied on him, and he wouldn't let them down.

"Enjoying the sun, Commander?"

A familiar voice intruded, and Justin opened his eyes, swiveling to see Marcus walking gingerly toward him.

Justin frowned. "What are you doing outside?" he asked, taking in the officer's gleaming lorica and the plumed helmet he carried under one arm. Marcus had gained permission to remain posted at Vindolanda, and was clearly keen to start his duties. "You're not expected back at work for another fortnight."

Marcus snorted. "I was going mad, cooped up in my quarters." He grinned then. "Fear not, Falco has declared me fit enough for light duties."

"Well, make sure you heed him," Justin replied. He then glanced toward the principia. He had a pile of administrative tasks to get through, although it was a shame to bury himself under paperwork on such a lovely morning. "Where are you off to?"

"I'm going to climb the northern palisade," Marcus replied, "and take a look at how the Wall is progressing."

Justin favored his friend with a smile. "Well, before you do, you might want to stop by my house and bid Kahina good morning."

Marcus cocked an eyebrow. "Why would I do that?"

Justin's smile widened. "I'm not blind, Marcus ... I've seen the way you two look at each other. The poor woman was distraught after you took a spear to the chest." He paused then, noting how Marcus's gaze widened, his lips parting in surprise. He'd succeeded in rendering his friend speechless. "It might interest you to know I've given Kahina her freedom."

Still smiling, Justin turned on his heel and walked off.

As Fenella neared the fort, she slowed her pony to a walk.

It probably wasn't wise to rush to the Wall. Even at a distance, she could see the outlines of men moving about, their pilums bristling against a cornflower-blue sky. They would have seen her by now, and some would have bows at the ready.

Best that she approached cautiously.

The pony's feathered feet clip-clopped up the dirt track leading to the fort. She'd followed the Twentieth legion south, using her hunting skills to track their path. An army that size couldn't hide its passing. Instead of following the coast, the path had veered west, bringing her here.

To the Wall that divided Britannia from Caledonia.

Fenella observed the great stone barrier rising against the sky before her, some of which was covered in scaffolding. The clatter of industry rang high into the morning air.

It was indeed formidable, although her mouth thinned at their hubris—to draw such a crude line across the landscape. She may have gotten used to some of the Romans' ways, even given her heart to one of their generals, but there were some things she'd never accept.

They might be building their great wall, but these were still Brigante lands.

Her lips quirked then. Aedan was home.

"Ho, woman ... what's your business here!" One of the helmed soldiers shouted down. His tone wasn't friendly—although Fenella hadn't expected a warm welcome.

Raising her chin, she drew up her pony and peered up at him. "My name is Fenella," she called back in Latin. "I'm here to see General Aquila. Is he in residence?"

She hoped he was.

Snorts drifted down from the ramparts.

"What do you want with him?"

"It's private."

Coarse male laughter followed. "I'm sure it is."

"*Lupa*," someone else called out. *Slut.*

Fenella ground her teeth, her temper flaring.

"Enough!" Another voice cut through the jeering. "The next man who hurls an insult at this woman will get a beating!"

Silence fell upon the walls. Even the masons who'd been busy laying stones nearby halted, their gazes sweeping down to the north gate.

A dark-haired man stepped up next to the ramparts—and even at a distance, Fenella recognized him.

"Marcus!" she cried out. "You're alive!"

"It's Centurion Camillus to you, woman," one of the soldiers muttered.

Marcus cut the legionary a warning glance. He then leaned forward, gripping the edge of the stone battlement, a smile stretching his face. "Fenella ... this is a surprise."

She gazed up at him. "Is Aquila here?"

"He is."

Silence fell then. Fenella could feel the weight of many stares bearing down upon her, yet she didn't look away from Marcus. She sucked in a deep breath. "I've ridden a long way ... please, can I see him?"

They didn't make her wait long. However, to Fenella, it seemed like an eternity.

Marcus disappeared from the ramparts, no doubt going down to inform Justin he had a visitor. While he was gone, Fenella expected the insults from the guards still on the wall to resume—yet they didn't.

Instead, the men merely watched her.

Anxiety churned in her gut, but she remained where she was, seated astride her pony. Unconcerned by the wait, the beast flicked its tail to dislodge flies.

Nerves stretched tight, Fenella jumped when the grind and thud of locks releasing echoed toward her.

Her breathing quickened as she watched the gate draw open.

Fenella gathered her reins, preparing to ride in. However, she stilled when her gaze alighted upon a tall figure who strode through the swirling dust.

Justin Aquila was walking out to meet her.

Fenella forgot to breathe. All the words she'd rehearsed on the way here fled. Her mind turned blank. All she could do was stare at the man she'd ridden days to find. She hadn't expected to discover Ardoch abandoned, but that hadn't stopped her.

Nothing would.

If she had to travel the length of Britannia, she'd track him down.

But now that he was actually before her, her courage momentarily fled and her wits scattered.

The Mother save her, he was a sight. His head was bare, and he hadn't donned his lorica this morning, although he wore the leather harness and pleated leather skirt over his tunic. Her gaze traveled from his sandaled feet, up his muscular legs and arms—tanned from the warm spring—to his face.

His chiseled features were set in stern lines, his golden gaze narrowed.

Heart galloping, Fenella swung down from her pony and looped the reins over the pommel of the saddle. Her legs wobbled under her as fear momentarily threatened to overtake her. Yet she mastered it, her gaze never leaving Justin.

She then stepped toward him.

XXXIV. NOTHING TO FORGIVE

"MORNING, JUSTIN."

THEY weren't the words she'd intended to greet him with, yet Fenella's composure was on the verge of unraveling as it was. It was a miracle she'd been able to croak anything at all.

"Fenella," he replied softly. "This is a surprise."

"Aye." She cleared her throat. "I went looking for you in Ardoch first ... but found it burned."

He nodded. "The emperor ordered us to abandon Caledonia."

Their gazes held, and Fenella's throat started to ache. Gods, there were so many things she wanted to say to him, but she didn't know where to start—and nor did she want to utter the wrong thing.

Courage, Fen, she counseled herself. *You've made it this far, don't crumble now.*

Curious stares stabbed down upon her from above. She imagined the soldiers all craning their necks over the ramparts, ears straining to catch their words. But she didn't care. Her attention never wavered from Justin.

He stepped closer to her so that no more than four feet stretched between them, his throat bobbing. "Fenella," he began. "I—"

"I love you, Justin," she cut him off. "And I *do* trust you ... more than I have anyone." There was only one way to do this. Enough with hesitation. "I thought freedom was what I wanted ... and it is ... but leaving you ripped my heart out. All I can think about is you." She broke off, wetting her lips as fear threatened to choke her. "I don't know if you still want me, or if you can forgive me for hurting you ... but *nothing* would make me happier than becoming your wife."

His lips parted, his eyes darkening, and suddenly all Fenella could hear was the thudding of her own heart in her ears.

Justin moved closer still. "Two things," he said, his voice still low, yet husky now. His gaze seared hers. "Firstly, I do still want you ... and, secondly, there's nothing to forgive."

Fenella stared back at him, her breathing shallow now. "I've missed you so much," she whispered.

Justin stepped forward and bridged the final gap between them. Reaching up, he cupped her face with both hands. "My arrogance was my undoing." He looked down at her, his eyes glittering. "You taught me a valuable lesson, Fenella. I can't believe you're actually here, but I thank the gods you are."

And with that, he pulled her into his arms, his mouth capturing hers. Standing on tip-toe, Fenella wound her arms around his neck, hanging onto him. Tears streamed down her cheeks, but she barely noticed them—her heart was too full.

Meanwhile, Justin kissed her passionately, wildly, uncaring that all his men were still watching from the walls.

"Kahina ... Aedan!"

Fenella hurried under the shady portico and into the courtyard beyond. The space she stepped into was vast—at least thrice the size of the one at Ardoch. A squat well sat in the heart of it, while urns of herbs dotted the pavers. Stone benches lined the edges, and a man and woman sat upon one on the opposite side. A brown and black striped cat lay curled upon the woman's lap.

They'd been talking, but, at hearing their names called, both Kahina and Aedan glanced up.

The surprise on their faces made Fenella skid to a halt.

It occurred to her then that they might not be pleased to see her. After all, she'd departed without saying goodbye to either of them.

Resuming her path toward the pair, although more cautiously now, Fenella gave a hesitant smile. "Justin tells me you're both free."

"Fen!" Kahina croaked. "What are you doing here?" She clutched Electri so hard that the cat gave a loud meow of protest and started to struggle in her arms. Kahina put her down so the cat didn't scratch her arms to ribbons.

Fenella's smile turned rueful. "I had a few things to say to Aquila."

"And have you said them?" Aedan's expression was no less surprised than Kahina's, although his eyes gleamed.

"Aye," she murmured, "we are to be wed."

Silence fell in the courtyard, while Electri stalked over to Fenella and wound herself around her ankles, purring loudly. The uncomplicated affection made Fenella's throat thicken. Her attention flicked back to Kahina. "I hear congratulations are also in order for you and Marcus."

Kahina smiled, her long eyelashes lowering in sudden shyness.

"And with any luck, you will be wed soon, too." Fenella continued. "Marcus and Justin have gone to pay the magistrates a visit."

Kahina's chin jerked up, her dark eyes flying wide. "What … now?"

Aedan laughed. "Those two don't waste time." He rose to his feet and stepped forward then, before reaching out a hand. Wordlessly, Fenella moved closer and took it. "It's good to have you back, Fen."

"We've missed you," Kahina blurted out, her eyes sparkling with tears. She leaped up and rushed forward then, knocking Aedan aside and flinging herself into Fenella's arms.

Justin stormed out of the magistrates' office, Marcus at his side.

"Bull-headed bastards," Justin snarled. "Curse them and their petty rules."

Face grim, Marcus stopped in the street, turning to Justin. "I agree, but that doesn't change things. What are we going to do?"

The two men stood in the midst of the vicus, the bustling village that sprawled beyond the western wall of Vindolanda. The settlement was a sizeable and prosperous one. It housed a tavern, a popular bathhouse, and a temple to Jupiter. However, the four magistrates who presided here were pedants.

Initially, they'd fawned when the garrison commander and one of his officers had paid them a visit. However, their obsequious behavior ceased when the pair asked for marriage licenses to wed former slaves. The magistrates had flatly refused them.

"I'd feared they might oppose us," Marcus muttered, stepping aside as a turnip-filled cart, pulled by an ox, rumbled by. "On the northern frontier, things were lax ... but things will be different here."

"This *is* the northern frontier," Justin reminded him with a scowl.

"Yes, but two of those magistrates have just moved up from Londinium. I've never met more pompous asses." Marcus's expression was bleak as it met Justin's. "What now?"

Justin held his friend's gaze, fury churning in his gut.

It couldn't end here. He and Marcus could take their women as servants in their households, but both Fenella and Kahina deserved better than that. They would be wedded; he'd make sure of it.

However, in order to see it done, he'd have to swallow what little pride he had left. He'd hoped it wouldn't come to this, but he was left with no choice.

Heaving in a deep breath, Justin pulled a face. "It looks like I'm going before the emperor ... again."

XXXV. AN AUDIENCE WITH HADRIAN

"THE EMPEROR WILL see you now."

Stepping forward, from where he'd been waiting outside the vast peaked tent in which the emperor of Rome currently resided, Justin nodded to the toga-wearing attendant.

He wasn't looking forward to seeing Hadrian again—not after his last encounter with the man.

But it couldn't be helped.

The emperor wasn't expected back at Vindolanda for a few days at least, but Justin couldn't wait for his return. Instead, he'd ridden west along the Wall to Carvoran—a small wooden fort nestled against gently rolling, lush green hills. Building work was a little behind Vindolanda, hence why the emperor had stopped here a few days.

Justin entered the imperial tent through a wide opening, where heavy damask curtains had been drawn apart and tied with tasseled cords. Wooden flooring decorated with Persian rugs covered the ground, and intricately wrought lanterns dangled from the poles holding up the roof, sending delicate shadows across the tapestries that hung on the walls of the tent.

The faint scent of jasmine incense wafted through the air, and slaves—beautiful youths in fine tunics edged in gold—moved around the space. It wasn't yet noon, but the slaves were already placing platters of dried fruit upon a long table before a raised dais, and bringing in ewers of wine.

And upon the dais perched a high wooden chair—painstakingly carved, the 'curule seat' was foldable, transportable, and had the appearance of a chariot. However, Justin's gaze wasn't drawn to the imperial chair but to the man seated upon it.

Flanked by two of the Praetorian Guard, Hadrian reclined against the back of the seat. A purple toga swathed his muscular form, and his long legs were stretched out before him, crossed at the ankle. The emperor was around ten years Justin's elder—a tall man with curly brown hair and dark eyes. He had a long, straight nose and a strong bearded jaw. His gaze narrowed as it settled upon Justin.

Likewise, Hadrian's two guards—big men dressed in red tunics, scorpions engraved upon the breastplates of their black armor—eyed him coldly.

"*Commander* Aquila," Hadrian greeted Justin, emphasizing his new title. It was a reminder of what he'd done the last time they'd met—and that he was capable of much worse if angered. And during their last meeting, Justin had noted that the emperor was a complicated man, capable of generosity, but also of spite.

Justin took the warning, bowing his head, and lowered himself onto one knee. "Ave, Imperator."

Hadrian made a dismissive sound in the back of his throat. "And what brings you back to see me so soon?"

"A request, Imperator."

The emperor snorted. "I'm not sure you're in a position to request anything from me these days."

Justin bowed his head farther, even if doing so galled him. This was the emperor of Rome, yet he wasn't a man used to kneeling. Nonetheless, he had the good sense to hide his irritation. "You speak justly," he replied, keeping his voice low, humble. "But a matter of great personal importance brings me here ... I wish to ask a favor of you."

Hadrian laughed. It was a rich sound that carried through the tent, but the emperor's mirth merely made Justin clench his jaw. Hadrian was intent on making this as unpleasant for him as possible.

"This gets better and better, Commander," the emperor said, still chuckling. "Get to your feet, man. Groveling doesn't suit you."

Gritting his teeth, Justin did as bid.

Hadrian was grinning now, revealing straight white teeth. He then gestured to one of the slave boys waiting nearby. "Fill two cups with wine."

The slave hurried to do his bidding, before carrying a calix to the emperor and one to his guest.

Taking a sip of wine, Hadrian viewed Justin long and hard. "You intrigue me, Aquila ... go on ... out with it."

"I wish to wed, Imperator."

Hadrian cocked a dark brow. "You don't need my permission for that ... find yourself a magistrate."

"They have refused me." Justin heaved in a deep breath, his fingers tightening around the stem of the calix he'd yet to take a sip from. "For the woman I wish to wed was once my slave ... and she is one of the Picti."

The emperor took another sip of wine before idly scratching his bearded jaw. "She isn't the woman you took from that chieftain, is she?" His gaze narrowed then. "The man you let live so he could lay siege to Ardoch?"

Justin cleared his throat. "Yes, she is."

Hadrian's frown deepened. "Well, that's irregular, indeed."

"I know, Imperator. But I would not take up your valuable time if this wasn't important to me."

"And you love this savage, I take it?"

"I do." Hearing the emperor insult Fenella made Justin's belly clench. All the same, he hid his reaction under an inscrutable mask he'd perfected over the years. This was all a game to Hadrian, even if it meant much more to him.

The emperor's gaze raked over him then, his mouth lifting at the corners while his dark eyes remained shrewd. "Justinian Valerius Aquila," he murmured. "You do surprise me."

"Imperator?"

"When I met you years ago, you were Trajan's favorite … young, ambitious, and destined for great things. But now you stand before me, your once-promising career ruined, asking for permission to wed a Picti woman—a former slave. What happened to you?"

Justin straightened his spine, lifting his chin.

And for the first time since entering the tent, he met Hadrian's eye squarely. It was a bold move, and one he might soon regret, but ire now burned under his ribcage, and he could feel his self-restraint slipping.

Hadrian was deliberately goading him.

"Living on the fringes of the empire changes a man," Justin replied after a pause. He wanted to choose his words carefully, yet it was hard to. "Five years I held the north … kept the chieftains under control. All I ever wanted was to serve Rome, to see the glory of the empire shine in every corner of the world. But then I took the wife of a Picti chieftain as my slave … and something in me changed. I am still as loyal as ever to Rome, but I no longer serve with single-minded determination, willing to sacrifice everything for my career."

"Lust is a distraction indeed," Hadrian murmured, his eyes glinting.

"It was more than lust," Justin corrected him. "Fenella has made me face the dark corners of myself I'd rather not see. She is the part of me that has always been missing. She is worth fighting for … worth even risking your anger for."

Silence fell after these words.

Justin was aware of the slaves lining the space, shifting uncomfortably. Upon the dais, the two praetorian guards traded looks. He imagined they were wondering how Hadrian would respond to such an admission. An emperor could order a man's death with one word.

Hadrian took another contemplative sip of wine. It was a lazy gesture, as if he had all the time in the world.

When the emperor eventually spoke, his voice was a drawl. "You certainly have balls, Aquila … I always liked that about you." He paused then, his gaze spearing

Justin's. "I'm swayed, I must admit, but if I agree to this, it might set a precedent. I don't wish to encourage others to take savages as wives."

Justin sucked in a deep breath. "You might, Imperator, for I have a second favor to ask of you. One of my officers, Marcus Camillus, also wishes to wed a former slave … a woman of Numidia. Like me, Camillus has given his life to serving Rome." He continued to hold Hadrian's eye. "We *both* ask for your blessing."

Biting her bottom lip, Fenella attempted, for the fourth time, to adjust the palla—a long rectangular shawl—about her head and shoulders.

"Why can't I get the hang of this?" she muttered as it slipped off her head.

"Here." Kahina stepped up, her mouth curving in amusement. "Let me help."

The two women stood in the commander's cubiculum—the room Fenella would share with Justin once they were wed. She'd only been at Vindolanda a day, but before traveling west in search of the emperor, Justin had gone into the vicus and bought her new clothing.

It was early evening, and Fenella wore a long, ankle-length tunic and a stola—a lovely sleeveless, high-waisted dress fastened to her shoulders with clasps.

Kahina had been trying to show her how to wear the voluminous shawl for outdoors, but Fenella was struggling. She wasn't used to so many layers of clothing.

Wrapping the palla about Fenella in deft movements, Kahina then stepped back, smiling as she viewed her work. "There," she murmured. "You look beautiful, Fen."

Fenella's cheeks warmed under the praise. "Thank you," she replied, returning her friend's smile. "As do you."

She wasn't exaggerating either. Like her, Kahina wore a stola. It was the color of amber, a hue that complemented Kahina's coppery skin. Her dark, curly hair was loose, falling over her bare shoulders. Her face shone with happiness this afternoon.

With a sigh, Fenella unwrapped the palla and glanced down at her own dress. It was a deep blue, the color of the sky after sunset before the moon rose.

Kahina had told her it matched her eyes.

It was a bit premature to don the garments, for neither of them was yet a wedded woman. But soon they wouldn't go about wearing tunics any longer—for they would be Roman ladies.

Unease prickled Fenella's skin then, drawing her attention from their new garments.

Only if Justin can convince the emperor.

The magistrates had denied them, and although Justin had vowed he'd do whatever was necessary to gain permission for the weddings to take place, Fenella worried nonetheless. Nothing had been easy for her and Justin—and she didn't expect the gods to shine on them now either.

"What's wrong?" Kahina asked, her smile fading. "Don't you like your new clothes?"

Fenella huffed. "I like them well enough," she replied, draping the shawl over a stand, "although I'm likely to trip with all this fabric around my legs."

"So, why the furrowed brow?"

"Justin will have met with Hadrian by now," Fenella replied, smoothing the fabric around her hips. "I worry about how things have gone."

Kahina's hand fastened around her arm, and Fenella glanced up to see her friend watching her. "You need to have faith in him, Fen," she replied, her lips curving once more. "Justin Aquila isn't a man to give up easily."

"Well said, Kahina."

A man's voice intruded, and both women spun around to see Justin standing in the doorway. Dust covered his clothing, and his tanned skin glowed with sweat. However, he was smiling as he leaned against the doorframe and folded his arms across his chest.

Fenella's belly swooped. "Justin!"

"How did it go?" Kahina gasped, her hand tightening around Fenella's arm. It seemed that her friend was more nervous than she'd let on.

"The emperor has given us permission to wed," he replied. "*All* of us."

Kahina squealed with delight. "Does Marcus know?"

Justin's smile widened. "Not yet … I thought you'd like to be the one to tell him."

Kahina nodded, let go of Fenella's arm, and made for the door. Justin stepped aside to let her go. But she paused, reached out, and grabbed his hand. "Thank you so much, Aquila. I will never forget this."

Justin smiled down at her. Eyes shining, Kahina then hurried off, her sandals whispering on stone.

And when they were alone, Justin turned to Fenella.

His gaze raked over her; it was a dominant, male, look that turned her breathless. That look made her want to launch herself at him and tear off his clothes. The evening before, they'd barely gotten inside the cubiculum when they'd attacked each other. They hadn't made it to the bed either; Justin had taken her, hard, against the door.

As if sensing the direction of Fenella's thoughts, Justin favored her with a slow, sensual smile. "I like that stola," he said, pushing off the doorframe. "Very pretty."

"You chose well then."

"I did." He moved toward her.

An instant later, Fenella closed the remaining distance between them, giving in to the urge to throw herself into his arms. Hands splayed across the breastplate of his lorica, she raised her face to his, her lips parting hungrily as he slid his hands through her hair and claimed her mouth.

When they broke apart from the kiss, they were both breathless.

"You did it," Fenella whispered, gazing up at him. She reached up then, her fingers tracing the strong line of his jaw.

Justin's mouth quirked. "Hadrian's not an easy man to convince, but eventually, he came around."

"What did you say to him?"

"The truth ... it's the only thing that works in the end," he replied, his voice turning husky. He raised his hand to where hers cupped his cheek. "I told him what you mean to me. It was a gamble, but I discovered that our emperor is a man who understands love."

Fenella's breathing constricted. Gods, he was reckless. How she adored that about him. There were so many things she loved about him—and she'd gasped out each one the night before as he'd taken her against the door.

"You are quite a man, Justin Aquila," she murmured. "When will you make me your wife?"

He smiled, his eyes crinkling at the corners. "Impatient?"

She nodded.

His smile widened. "Well then, how about tomorrow?"

EPILOGUE.
HOMECOMING

Vindolanda fort, the Wall,
The Caledonia-Britannia border

Four years later ...

"OVA!" A CHILD'S delighted voice cut through the crowd.

Glancing down, Fenella saw that her son, Leo, who'd been clinging to her skirt just a moment earlier, was now barreling toward a man selling eggs. They were in the busy market in the vicus, just outside Vindolanda's west gate.

The vendor watched the child's approach, eyes flying wide in panic.

Chubby hands outstretched, Leo made a grab for the eggs, giving a wail when Fenella scooped him up.

"No, love," she told him sternly, carrying his wriggling form back to where Kahina waited. "They're not yours."

At three winters of age, Leo didn't like being thwarted.

The boy started to wail then, causing shoppers in the crowded marketplace to turn and favor Fenella with baleful looks. Ignoring them, she gripped Leo tightly, while his temper cooled.

"Jupiter, the boy has a pair of lungs on him," Kahina muttered, next to Fenella. "It feels as if someone's just stabbed me through the ears."

Fenella cast her friend an apologetic look. "Hush now, Leo," she murmured, still struggling with her bawling son.

A faint cry issued from the sling Kahina carried across her front then. Leo had woken Dahlia. Murmuring soothing words, Kahina reached down and stroked her infant daughter's face. Dahlia was barely ten days old. It was the babe's first time outside the walls of the fort since the birth. She was Kahina and Marcus's second daughter. The infant's elder sister, Ines, stood at her mother's side, clutching hard to Kahina's hand.

Fenella turned to where Ava stood patiently behind them, heavy shopping bags in hand. "What else do we need to buy?" she asked the cook. These trips to market weren't so enjoyable when Leo threw tantrums.

"Just some cheese," Ava assured her, "although, Leo has just reminded me now that we are getting low on eggs."

"Very well," Fenella replied through gritted teeth. "Let's—"

She'd been about to tell them that she'd head back inside the fort and leave them to the rest of their shopping, when a horn's blast echoed off the surrounding walls. The deep, haunting sound carried to all corners of the fort and the settlement beyond.

"They're back!" Kahina gasped, a grin splitting her face.

Leo abruptly halted his wailing. "Pater?"

"Aye," Fenella replied with a smile. The boy was quick, and already associated the goings-on inside the fort with his father. "Shall we go and see him?"

The boy's face lit up, the eggs he'd so badly wanted to crush forgotten.

"We'll see you back home later," Fenella told Ava. She then followed Kahina and her daughters through the jostling crowd, back to Vindolanda's west gate. Entering the fort, they hurried down the Via Praetoria, skirting around the hospital and the garrison headquarters, to emerge at the east gate.

The horn blasted once more, the sound rippling through the warm early summer air.

And there in the distance, Fenella spied dust rising against the horizon.

Justin had led his men out on a patrol eight days earlier, and had been away longer than usual. She'd begun to worry, just a little, while Kahina had openly fretted. Marcus had only spent two days with her and their newborn daughter before riding out, and she'd missed him terribly.

Gaze trained on the eastern horizon, Fenella waited. The earth started to vibrate then, and her skin prickled. A moment later, pilums and standards appeared through the dust, piercing the pale sky. And then red plumed helmets, polished silver and bronze gleaming in the sun, hove into view.

"Pater!" Leo wriggled in Fenella's arms, pointing at the soldiers.

"Aye, he's there, love," Fenella assured her son. "Behind the standard-bearer ... look."

Commander Aquila was impossible to miss as he led his men back to the fort. He rode a spirited black horse, with Marcus close behind him. The rest of his men marched on foot, the thud of their feet, the rattle of shields and armor, forming a dull rumble.

Fenella didn't take her gaze off her husband.

The man appeared invincible in his gleaming lorica and helmet, sitting upright in the saddle, his gaze trained upon the fort. He hadn't yet seen her.

Watching him, Fenella was transported back to that day, many years earlier, in which she'd set eyes on him for the first time—in that pinewood near Ardoch, when she'd been racing to see her lover. Justin and his men had emerged from the trees, their cloaks billowing in the wind. Even then, she hadn't been able to look away from him.

The Eagle.

Kahina had once teased her that she'd tamed him, but he'd also gentled her. Loving Justin Aquila had changed everything about how she saw the world and her place in it.

Her husband spied her then, a wide smile stretching across his tanned face. Urging his horse forward, he passed the standard-bearer and cantered up to where Fenella and Kahina stood before a gathering crowd lining the way into the fort.

Drawing up, he grinned down at his wife and son. "Well, this is a homecoming."

Fenella smiled back. "Leo has missed his father."

"And what about you, wife?"

"I was getting worried," she replied, her gaze never leaving his. "You were gone longer than we expected."

"We had to oversee some repairs to the Wall at Haltonchesters ... they suffered a raid a month ago." He paused then, his gaze fusing with hers. "I saw Aedan while we were there."

"Really?" Kahina drew closer. "How is he?"

"The man's wedded now and lives in the vicus outside Haltonchesters." Justin's mouth quirked then. "He's taken a Roman woman as his wife."

"Really?" Kahina grew wide-eyed at this news. "Who is she?"

"How did he meet her?" Fenella added, also curious to hear more.

Justin's gaze twinkled at their nosiness. "I don't know ... but he's done well for himself. He apprenticed to a carpenter after leaving us, and now runs his own business."

Fenella's smile widened at this news; she was relieved to know Aedan was well. They'd all wondered what had happened to him over the past few years. After he'd been given his freedom, the Brigante had decided to leave Vindolanda. His decision hadn't surprised Fenella. She'd thought he might return to his people though, but it appeared he had not.

The pounding of hoofbeats made her look up then. Marcus had seen his wife and daughter, and ridden up to join them. Drawing up his horse, he swung down from the saddle and went to Kahina.

Fenella watched the family, noting how Marcus's eyes shone when he gazed down at the face of his newborn daughter, and the tender way he stroked Kahina's cheek before he scooped Ines into his arms.

"Have you been behaving yourself, Leo?" The rumble of her husband's voice drew Fenella's attention back to her own family.

Justin had dismounted and lowered himself down to his son's level.

Leo clutched at him. "Yes, pater ... I'm always good!"

Justin glanced up and caught Fenella's eye. "Is that so?"

"He can be willful," she admitted with another smile, "although, that's not surprising ... with the two of us as his parents."

Justin laughed. Reaching out, he ruffled his son's dark hair. Even at the age of three, it was clear Leo had inherited his father's looks and his golden eyes.

Fenella watched her husband and son, her chest constricting with love for them both. After losing two babes during her marriage to Toutorix, she'd worried she'd never be able to carry one the full nine moons. When her womb had quickened with Leo, she'd feared another disappointment, but the pregnancy had been healthy. She hoped to bear Justin another child, but that hadn't yet come to pass. Perhaps it never would. But it mattered not. The three of them were a family.

Justin and Leo were all she needed.

Scooping his son up, Justin rose to his feet.

Fenella went to him, nestling against his chest as he slung an arm around her shoulders. She then raised her face to him. "Welcome home, anima mea," she murmured.

Aye, he was her soul, and she had no doubt she was his—for he told her so regularly.

Their gazes met once more, and then Justin lowered his head and kissed her. And, as it always did when they embraced, the rest of the world receded.

Fenella swayed into the kiss, breathing in the scent of his skin.

When they eventually broke apart, Justin's sensual mouth curved. "So you did miss me, wife?"

Fenella smiled up at her husband. Gods, he was breathlessly arrogant. But there was so much more to Justinian Aquila: he was honorable, strong, and big-hearted.

And in a world of selfish, cruel men, he'd proved that good ones did exist.

Reaching up, Fenella stroked his cheek, rough with stubble. "I *always* miss you when you're gone," she whispered.

The End

FROM THE AUTHOR

TAMING THE EAGLE was a story that had been brewing in my mind for a few years before I sat down to write it—a story that I just had to tell! It also marks a return to the Dark Ages, the era I started my writing career in.

When I wrote BARBARIAN SLAVE a few years back, it was about a Pict warrior and a Roman woman. I knew that I wanted to turn the tables and write about a Pict woman and a Roman soldier, but in the meantime, other projects took over.

But all the while, Justin and Fenella's story started to build. And it wouldn't let me go.

This novel is a blend of enemies to lovers and the slave/captor tropes. There was already a huge power imbalance between men and women in ancient times—but if the hero takes the heroine as his slave, that difference is going to be huge. That's why you need a really strong heroine! Cue, Fenella! She's wild, proud, and independent, and has spent her whole life fighting against male dominance. So when her husband gives her to a Roman general, she responds by secretly vowing that she will never submit.

One of the difficulties of writing a slave/captor relationship is that their roles and the restrictive environment limit the range of scenes the author can put them in. But from Day One, Fenella plans her escape! However, when the arrogant general falls hard for her ... the lines between captor and captive become blurred indeed.

Although all my romances are standalones, I usually write them as part of a series that has an overarching storyline. Not so with this book. TAMING THE EAGLE stands completely alone, so I had to tie everything up by the end!

If you loved Justin and Fenella's story, please let me know. If enough of you want it, I may write another Pict-Roman romance!

Jayne x

ACKNOWLEDGEMENTS

A big thank you to Karlene Clark, who graciously provided me with the name of the heroine for this novel!

HISTORICAL NOTES

As you may have already guessed, I did A LOT of research for this book. Diving into research rabbit holes is my happy place. I love learning as I write, and I discovered many things while researching TAMING THE EAGLE!

To make things a little easier to reference, I've provided a glossary (in the next section), which covers some of the terms you encountered during the novel. However, in this section, I wanted to do some historical 'scene setting' for you.

TAMING THE EAGLE deals with slavery—something that was commonplace in the 2nd Century. As such, it's not surprising that freedom is a major theme I explore in the story! Both the Picts and the Romans had slaves, and how they were treated depended on the owner. Although the idea of owning a slave seems alien and repellent to us now, it was part of life in ancient times. That doesn't mean that slaves were happy with their lot, or that some didn't try to escape the bonds of servitude.

In the novel, I refer to the process of 'manumission'. This was the process whereby a master gave his slave their freedom. There were various ways in which this occurred, ranging from an informal declaration in front of witnesses to a formal ceremony before a magistrate. There were plenty of laws regarding the status of former slaves and marriage. Roman soldiers weren't technically permitted to marry during their service to the empire. Even as high-ranking officers, Justin and Marcus would have had to request permission to take wives. However, marrying former slaves would have been seriously frowned upon, hence Justin having to take his request to the emperor!

This story kicks off around the time that the Ninth legion of the Roman army famously disappeared (if you've read my IMMORTAL HIGHLAND CENTURIONS series, you'll know all about this!). Basically, around five thousand men marched into the mists of northern Caledonia in the winter of 118 AD, never to be seen again.

Most of TAMING THE EAGLE takes place in the aftermath of this event. The Twentieth legion, Valeria Victrix, was one of the legions stationed in the north in the years following, and it was involved in the construction of Hadrian's Wall.

Four years after the annihilation of the Ninth legion, Emperor Hadrian decided to build a great wall that would divide Britannia and Caledonia. There are several documented reasons for his building of the wall, but it couldn't have been a coincidence that it was erected shortly after the Ninth disappeared. Hadrian began work on his wall in 122 AD, completing it in 128 AD. Today, the wall stretches 73 miles (117.5 kilometers) across northern England.

There would have still been a Roman presence in Caledonia after the disappearance of the Ninth, and so I created the character of General Aquila and his garrison at Ardoch. Once he started work on the wall, Hadrian called back his troops and the northern forts were eventually abandoned. However, there would have been a period of gradual withdrawal. The Romans would go on to launch new campaigns in Caledonia, rebuild their old forts and start work on the Antonine Wall farther north, but this wouldn't occur until around twenty years later.

My telling of the events in 121/22 AD, and the attack on Ardoch are purely fictional accounts, and all characters that appear in the novel (except Emperor Hadrian) were also fictitious. Nonetheless, Ardoch itself was a real

Roman fort, and I have tried to be as accurate as possible in my descriptions of it.

Ardoch is one of the best-preserved earthworks in the Roman Empire. Today, you can see a rectangular area of around two hectares, surrounded by a rampart and five ditches. The Roman army occupied the fort on several occasions and built onto it. The fort is part of what is now known as the Gask Ridge series of Roman fortifications, built close to the Highland Line.

Like all Roman forts and marching camps, Ardoch would have been intersected by two streets: Via Praetoria and Via Principalis. At the point where these streets crossed sat the commander's residence (the praetorium) and the headquarters (the principia). The fort would have had barracks, storehouses, granaries, and a hospital. A civilian settlement, a vicus, would likely have existed outside the walls.

Vindolanda was a thriving Roman fort along Hadrian's Wall. Today, it's one of Europe's most important Roman archaeological sites. The site itself is actually made up of nine forts built on top of each other. Soldiers from all over the Roman Empire were garrisoned here. The stone fort dates to the third century, and the remains include the fort walls, the headquarters building, the Commanding Officer's house, granaries, and barracks. Extensive remains of the vicus lie just west of the fort, with buildings lining the main street. The ruins here include houses, shops, a tavern, and a bathhouse.

If you wish to learn more about Vindolanda, I highly recommend this site: www.vindolanda.com/roman-vindolanda-fort-museum

In the 2nd Century, Picts and Celts of Scotland and Ireland often lived in crannogs—artificially created islands built out upon a loch. A bridge, or causeway, usually connected the dwellings to the shore. The houses themselves were squat wooden (alder, oak, and willow) structures with high, cone-shaped roofs thatched with reed and bracken. Hazel was woven into panels for interior walls and partitions.

In TAMING THE EAGLE, I take you to Loch Tay (called Loch Tatha by the locals, and Lake Taus by the Romans) in Perthshire, where there was an actual crannog settlement.

Find out more about these fascinating structures at the Scottish Crannog Centre here: https://crannog.co.uk/what-is-a-crannog/

In my story, I refer to Fenella's people as the 'Wolves of the North'. This is an entirely fictional Pict tribe that I placed on the border between what we know today as the Highlands and the Lowlands. The Cruthini (or Picti as they were known by the Romans) inhabited northern Caledonia, and they were a people the Romans never managed to fully subdue. The local tribe that resided around Ardoch was the Damnonii.

The poem that appears in Chapter 21 is a variation of an ancient lullaby, one that refers both to ravens and magpies.

I hope you found my notes helpful and insightful. I write Historical Romance, but I adore history and like my novels to be rich in detail. I want to truly take you back to another time and place!

GLOSSARY

Pict and Latin words (alphabetical order)
atrium: entrance hall
Caesars: the Ancient Romans
Caledonia: the Roman name for what is today Scotland
cena: midday meal (Latin)
crannog: an ancient fortified island constructed upon a lake or marsh in Scotland or Ireland.
Cruithentúath: the name the Picts gave their land
Cruthini: the name the Picts gave themselves
cubiculum: bedroom
fava: broad bean
Futuo!: Fuck! (Latin)
infernus: hell (Latin)
Latrunculi: Roman chess
legate: rank of general in a Roman army
lorica: plate armor worn by Roman soldiers
lupa: 'she-wolf' in Latin—used as a sexual slur to mean 'slut'
Madaidhean-allaidh a tuath: Wolves of the North (the name of Fenella's tribe)
Picti: the name the Romans gave the Picts (literally: 'the painted ones')
praetorium: fort commander's residence
primus pilus: the senior centurion of the first cohort in a Roman legion
principia: fort headquarters
Saturnalia: Roman mid-winter festival
stultissime: a complete idiot (Latin)
tablinum: living room
tribune: an elected official in ancient Rome
valetudinarium – hospital
vesperna: supper (Latin)
vicus: a civilian village outside a Roman fort

Place names (in alphabetical order)
Ardoch: a Roman fort in what is now Perth, Scotland
Ardunie: a Roman signal station

Ben Macdui: mountain in the Cairngorm range
Dalginross, Bochastle and Fendoch: Roman outpost forts (now known as 'Glen Blocker' forts)
Eboracum: York
Loch Tatha: Loch Tay (known as Lake Taus in Latin)
Lochan Uaine: small lake in the Cairngorm mountain range
Londinium: London

Cruthini Gods and Goddesses of Caledonia*
The Mother: Goddess of enlightenment and feminine energy—the bringer of change
The Warrior: God of battle, life, and growth, of summer
The Maiden: Young goddess of nature and fertility
The Hag: Goddess of the dark—sleep, dreams, death, winter, and the earth
The Reaper: God of death

Cruthini festivities*
Earth Fire: Salute to new life and the first signs of spring (February 1)
Bealtunn: Spring Equinox
Mid-Summer Fire: Summer Equinox
Harvest Fire: Festival to salute the harvest (Aug 1)
Gateway: Passage from summer to winter (October 31/November 1)
Mid-Winter Fire: Winter Equinox

* Author's note: I have taken 'artistic license' when it comes to the names of Pictish tribes, festivities, and gods and goddesses. The historical evidence is very scant, making it a challenge for me to get an accurate picture of gods and festivities in 2nd Century Caledonia. The Picts were an enigmatic people, and we only have their ruins and symbols to cast light on how they lived and whom they worshipped. To make my setting as authentic as possible, I have studied the rituals and religions of the Celtic peoples of Scotland, Ireland, and Wales of a similar period and have created a culture I feel could have existed.

ABOUT THE AUTHOR

Award-winning author Jayne Castel writes epic Historical and Fantasy Romance. Her vibrant characters, richly researched historical settings, and action-packed adventure romance transport readers to forgotten times and imaginary worlds.

Jayne is the author of a number of best-selling series. In love with all things Scottish, she writes romances set in both Dark Ages and Medieval Scotland.

When she's not writing, Jayne is reading (and re-reading) her favorite authors, cooking Italian feasts, and going on long walks with her husband. She lives in New Zealand's beautiful South Island.

Connect with Jayne online:
www.jaynecastel.com
www.facebook.com/JayneCastelRomance
https://www.instagram.com/jaynecastelauthor/
Email: contact@jaynecastel.com

www.ingramcontent.com/pod-product-compliance
Lightning Source LLC
Chambersburg PA
CBHW021108110726
47900CB00007B/2079